LA BELLE FAMILLE

AMELIA MARIA VERGARA

DAMOCLES' BLADE PRESS

LA BELLE FAMILLE

By A.M. Vergara

Published by Damocles' Blade Press.

First Edition, USA

Library of Congress Control Number: 2024901991

ISBNs: Paperback 978-1-962246-07-1, Ebook 978-1-962246-06-4

The cover was designed by A.M. Vergara, using photos that were licensed for the purpose of this cover by the original photographer, Cosmo Condina and altered using Canva Pro. No part of this cover was generated by artificial intelligence. Typography provided by Casey White.

CONTENTS

For Kathy, James, Reggie, Frank, and Harvey.
"And for those who follow the gleam there is always light sufficient to show them their way . . ."

AUTHOR'S NOTE

This is a work of fiction. Adam, Lidia, Sofie, Will, and Kanęhsawéhte did not exist, at least as far as historical records can prove. Nor is there any documentation of how exactly word reached the British at Fort Niagara of the oncoming French reinforcements. Doubtless the true story is much more heroic than the scenario I've imagined. Though the main characters of *La Belle Famille* did not exist, many supporting characters were real, including Captain Lignery, Captain Aubry, Doctor Boiford, Lieutenant Colonel Massey, and Captain De Lancey. However, this book should not be considered biographical, and extensive creative license was taken in the portrayal of these individuals.

The events leading up to the battle of La Belle Famille, and the battle itself, were also real. I have attempted to recreate these occurrences as closely as possible to all the actual events as detailed in historical records. Additionally, the attack described at German Flatts did, in fact, take place, and the close association and friendship of the German Palatine people that lived in Mohawk Valley with the

Oneida, Mohawk, and other Native American nations is well-documented.

Though the main characters depicted in this story are not real, I suspect that the pain, growth, and revelations experienced by these fictional individuals are true to the pain, growth, and revelations experienced by many real people that lived during the harsh and brutal days of the United States' colonial period.

ADDITIONAL NOTE ON CONTENT

Some scenes in this book may be upsetting for some readers. A non-exhaustive list of potentially upsetting content may be reviewed at my website for those so inclined:

https://amvergara.com/la-belle-famille-content-warning

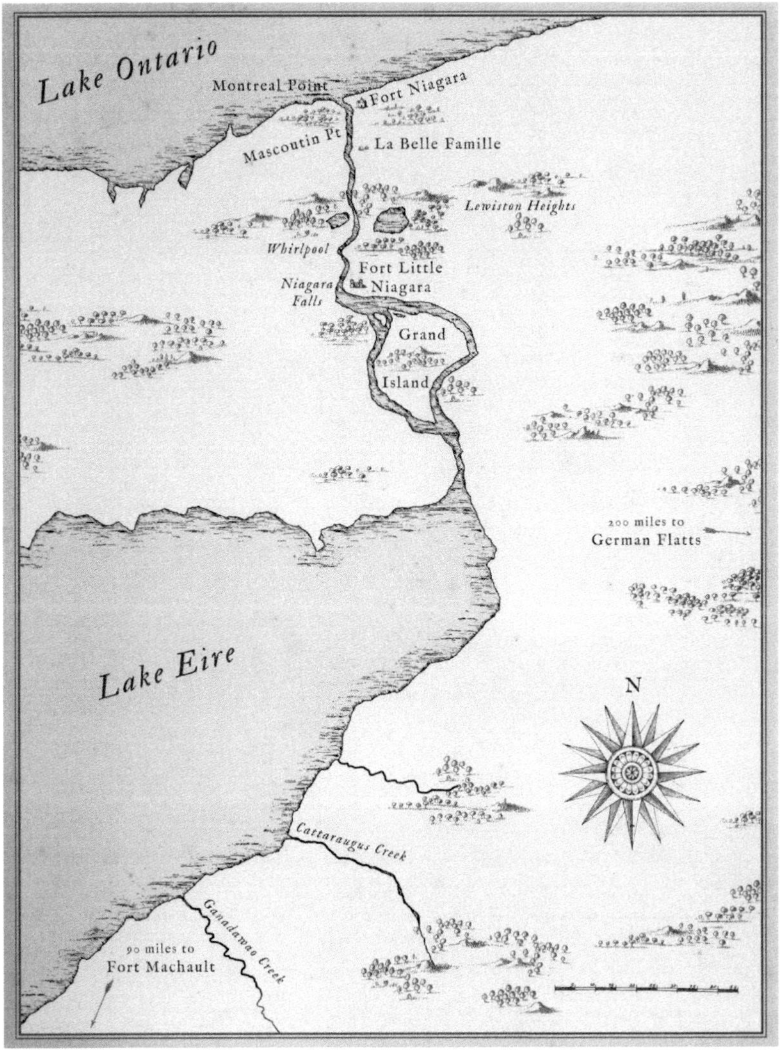

Lake Ontario
Montreal Point
Fort Niagara
Mascoutin Pt
La Belle Famille
Lewiston Heights
Whirlpool
Fort Little Niagara
Niagara Falls
Grand Island
200 miles to German Flatts
Lake Eire
N
Cattaraugus Creek
Ganadawao Creek
90 miles to Fort Machault

1

ADAM

~

July 14, 1759
Forty miles north of Fort Machault

It was nearly midday and the corporal still hadn't realized that Adam had swiped his flask during the night. Or perhaps, Adam mused, he did know, but didn't care because the whiskey in it tasted like sweat and horse manure. This Adam knew because he had taken advantage of the few times the corporal disappeared ahead of him in the dense deciduous forest to sample the beverage. After the first taste he almost wanted to give it back. Almost. Despite the flavor, it warmed his mouth and gave him that proper heady, joyful feeling, his fingers tingling, a burst of liveliness animating him. Alcohol was the only thing that gave him that feeling anymore.

Adam studied the corporal's broad back. Renaud, that was his name, or something like it, born and raised in Old France. He was a loud, gruff man, some years older than

Adam, and enormous, like a grenadier should be. Adam suspected Renaud had come to New France to fight as a way out of some scandal or, more likely, debtor's prison. Still, he had that swaggering, cocky quality about him that all the men that came over from Old France had. As if being born there somehow made them better than the French born in the wilderness of this untamed new world. As Adam watched, Renaud dug in his ear with one grimy finger, smearing his findings on the shoulder of his once-white uniform.

The air was sweltering in the thick wool justaucorps of a soldier of France's *troupes de la marine*. Despite the presence of his superior officer, Adam had left his coat, waistcoat, and even his shirt partially unbuttoned. But the open shirt allowed the relentless mosquitoes and gnats ample flesh to nibble. It seemed that for every one mosquito Adam swatted a hundred more sprang up to take its place. Adam pulled his horse up for a moment to pick a few plump thimbleberries from a heavy-laden bush, and, ignoring the waving green caterpillar on one of the berries, he smashed them into his mouth, insects and all.

"Why do you stop? At this rate *le capitaine* may as well bring word of the reinforcements to Pouchot himself," snapped the corporal, glaring back at his young subordinate. It seemed to rankle the man to no end to have been paired with such a useless slob as Adam to take Captain Lignery's message to Fort Niagara. He never missed a chance to berate the younger man. "We'll arrive only in time to warn the British after they've already surrendered."

"Need to keep my strength up," replied Adam around the mouthful of juicy berries, grinning purple and feigning the usual insouciant attitude that all the men in his company knew him for. "Besides, the Indians *le capitaine* sent will reach there long before us. I don't know why you want to rush."

"Impossible! You are impossible," Renaud ranted. "Pah, like a dog you are. No ambition. No cares. This is what becomes of men born of high blood. All worthless. All scoundrels. Everything handed to them on a silver platter. That's why they don't care. Nothing matters to them. Give me a common Marseillais blacksmith any day before a dandy from Montreal. *Le capitaine* doesn't trust his Indian messengers, that's why he sent us. But Lignery is a fool, entrusting such a lazy pig to take such an important message."

"Lazy pig? You oughtn't be so hard on yourself, Renaud. You do the best you can with the soap His Majesty Louis XV sees fit to ration us," quipped Adam.

That did it. Renaud flew into a rage, speaking so rapidly with that thick Marseille accent that Adam could make nothing of it. The man was turning red and sweating. Adam thought with bitter amusement that he did look a little like a pig. Adam told himself he wouldn't do it—that he absolutely shouldn't do it—but he was enjoying himself and wanted to see how far he could take things. It didn't matter what Renaud did to him in the wilderness, after all. On any given day, nothing really mattered to Adam, the corporal had been right about that, and it had been three days since the young soldier had a proper brawl. Reaching down, he slid the flask out of his pocket and took a slow, measured draft of the foul whiskey, never taking his eyes off the corporal as he gulped the burning liquid down.

Renaud spurred his horse back through the nettles, snatched the flask from Adam with a curse and struck the younger man so hard across the face that he unhorsed him. Seeing colored lights bursting in his vision, Adam toppled into a bed of stinging woodland nettles. As he hit the ground, the image of the girl burst unbidden into his mind. The girl that haunted him, the blue-eyed young woman with the straight brown hair, the round, honest German face, and those flushed rosy cheeks. She had been so fierce, standing before him with her musket raised. That damn girl. A piercing jolt of guilt stabbed into Adam's heart, taking his breath away. He hated it. That terrible feeling he had known every day for almost two years. The terrible guilt for what he had done. The feeling that only alcohol kept at bay.

Adam was torn from his reverie when Renaud, who had dismounted, slammed a foot into his gut. Somehow the pain of the blow was less than the pain of Adam's guilt. He opened his eyes as Renaud spat on him. Then the corporal turned away, casting about for the flask he had accidentally dropped into the weeds in his rush to visit vengeance upon his subordinate.

Even with his eyes open, Adam could still see her, not standing up to him any longer, but lying still in the grass. Had she breathed? He had seen that moment play out more than a thousand times since that day in German Flatts, two years before, but he still was not sure if the girl was breathing when he fled from her insensate form. She shouldn't have been visiting him when he was awake. He was too sober, dangerously sober. He stared up at the corporal as the man stowed the flask in his coat and went to mount his horse again.

"Why do you start fights if you're not going to retaliate?" asked the corporal. "Useless coward. I will have you flogged when we reach Fort Niagara, flogged within an inch of your life."

Adam managed to affect his usual careless smile, climbing back to his feet unsteadily and hoisting himself into the saddle of his bay gelding. The animal danced nervously beneath him after Renaud's display of human ferocity.

"If it weren't for your father, you'd have been drummed out of the service entirely by Picoté, in disgrace, as you should have been. Worthless lout," Renaud grumbled, setting off through the forest.

Adam didn't reply. He didn't engage with the older man for the rest of the day. He was too busy thinking about the girl. He hadn't seen her in a few days, because he had been maintaining that drunken state that usually kept her away. But here she was again, back, and every time he closed his eyes—hell, every time he blinked, he could see her. He should have died to pay for that girl's life. Yet here he was, still too cowardly to kill himself, to atone for his crimes, even after two years of shame, shame for himself, his company, his regiment, his God, his country, and his family.

That night he lay awake, staring up through the overhanging tree branches at the wondrous stars beyond, fields of stars, so much brighter than they were from the bustling streets of Montreal. Gazing into the clusters of brilliant white, the milky fields in the jet-black sky, he was afraid to close his eyes. He wished that he hadn't flaunted the flask; then at least he might still have it. He needed the alcohol it contained, foul as it had been. He could already feel his hands trembling and he was drenched in sweat beneath his thin blanket roll, but worst of all he could not make her leave him alone. He glared at the girl floating in the corners of his vision. In desperation he thrust his fumbling fingers inside the pocket hidden in his coat's blue cuff, searching for a small, folded piece of parchment. Perhaps staring at something else, intently, as if reading—though it was too dark to actually read—perhaps that would drive the girl away. He drew the roll of paper out and opened it. It crinkled as his hands shook. He didn't need the light; he knew the words as well as he knew the rosary.

Capitaine Pouchot,

Take courage. As you have requested, I have delayed my move to attack Fort Pitt. I am leading close to a thousand French and Canadian militia as well as Indian forces to your relief, along with Captain Aubry of the Illinois contingent, and will recruit more as we travel north with all haste.

Be ready to open your gates to us on the 25th.

Capitaine François-Marie Le Marchand de Lignery.

Adam folded the paper and stowed it back in his cuff. He let his eyes drift closed and saw again the girl, the cursed, angry girl. At the same instant, he heard the voice of the corporal in his head: *We'll arrive only in time to warn the British after they've already surrendered.* His eyes snapped open. The glade where they had camped echoed with Renaud's snores. The stars stared down at him, softer, less accusing than they were before, less headache-inducing. Perhaps there was a way to redeem himself, a way to make the ghost of the girl leave him alone. He hadn't thought of it before, but when it came to him at that moment it seemed obvious. The settlers in German Flatts had no warning, or if they did, they had not heeded it. That was why they had been so easily defeated, so easily slaughtered. If he warned the British outside Fort Niagara, if he did what he thought no one had done for the girl and her family, perhaps she would leave him alone. He could save a thousand lives for her, then perhaps she would let his soul be at peace. Or, better yet, in the attempt to get word to the British, perhaps, at last, he would suffer the final and most just consequence for his crime, the thing he still hadn't dared to do himself all these months later.

He wrestled with the idea for hours. He could not sleep anyway, not with the girl there, flickering in and out of his vision, and he was too shaky and too sweaty. He needed alcohol. The images of all the horrors of the last four years flashed through his mind. The weight of every atrocity he had seen pressing like an anvil on his chest, as if to suffocate him. Finally, as the first calls of doves heralded the coming of dawn, Adam decided. He would do it. What did he have to lose? His father's regard? His honor? All long gone. But how to disable Renaud? He considered cutting the man's throat as he slept, but this was a step too far in his treason. He had lost his taste for killing the day German Flatts burned. He had lost his taste for a lot of things that day—though not for alcohol, he reflected with the flash of a grin.

He slipped over to the horses and undid the hobbles on the corporal's mount, giving her a gentle tap on the bottom. The mare began to wander, grazing the dry summer grass and foliage further from their little camp. The air was so full of the noise of cicadas and frogs that Renaud did not stir. Nor did he stir as Adam saddled his own mount, taking care to avoid jingling the harness. In a few minutes the bay stood ready, still half-asleep, chewing idly on his bit. Adam fixed the saddlebags to the horse, secured his own pack on his back, placed his musket in the sheath along the horse's side, and then he was suddenly ready, sooner than he felt he should be. The cicadas seemed to crescendo into a frenzied, deafening chorus. He glanced back at Renaud and froze. The gleam of the whiskey flask was just visible, protruding from within the man's justaucorps. It had been so easy to obtain the night before. He licked his lips and glanced at his horse, then back again at the enticing metal object.

Taking his horse's reins, Adam moved quietly toward Renaud, then crouched, gripping the reins with one hand, ready for flight at a moment's notice. He reached out, stretching until his fingertips barely grazed the smooth metal. The flask shifted in Renaud's jacket when he brushed it. He froze and drew in a slow breath, eyeing the other man. The corporal let out a loud snore but showed no sign of awakening. Biting his lip, Adam extended his hand still further, and then the cold metal was in his grasp. He tumbled backward, a triumphant grin splitting his face even as he fell onto his back. But then the grin faded as he saw Renaud's bleary eyes, red-rimmed and wide awake, staring at him.

The corporal wore a confused expression, and then a deepening frown, his gaze scanning over Adam with his pack, his horse saddled, clutching the precious whiskey flask to his chest. Then his eyes flitted to look across the glade toward where his own mare had been. That was all Adam had time to see before he scrambled to his feet, lunging toward the bay gelding. But Renaud was on him before he could rise into the saddle, yanking him free of the harness and tossing him bodily to the ground. The bigger man was cursing in his thick Marseille accent, and Adam saw the gleam of a knife in Renaud's hand. They tussled in the grass, Adam trying desperately to free himself from the enormous, smelly grenadier, noting, even as he fought, that his gelding was edging away from the tumult. Renaud rolled on top of him, raising his knife above his head, and Adam tried desperately to hold the weapon at bay.

"Would you desert, you scum? And leave me stranded here?" asked Renaud, gritting his teeth as he wrestled the younger, smaller man. "Where is my horse? You bastard, I'll put your bloody eyes out!"

Adam slammed his knee into Renaud's crotch, noting with satisfaction how the man's face crumpled into a mask of pain. However, he did not have much time to enjoy the spectacle. Taking advantage of the second he had, Adam rolled, tossing Renaud off him, and then ran, tripping and stumbling clumsily toward his horse. He didn't pause to use the stirrup, vaulting straight onto the obedient animal's back and spurring the horse away through the crowding maple and chestnut trees. Glancing over his shoulder, he saw Renaud kneeling, raising his musket. Corporal Renaud always kept his musket loaded, and he had a deadly aim. Adam had seen his work in wilderness skirmishes before. But, Adam thought with a bemused grin, what did he care? He had no desire to live anymore, and he had achieved his aim: he was free, and he had the whiskey.

He raised the flask to the sky in what he thought might be his final, triumphant toast, then took a quick, mind-numbing, tremor-halting swig. He swallowed the putrid liquid as the horse broke into a canter beneath him. For a few seconds Adam thought he was truly free, a successful deserter, for all his bumbling oafishness in the process. Then a bolt of lightning pierced through his torso, followed by the echoing crack of a gunshot. The pain vanished for a second and he thought that he was dead at last. But then the piercing, tearing agony through his middle returned. Every jolt of the horse's movements as it darted around trees and boulders was like being torn in half.

He was alive. God would not have mercy on him and let him die quickly. God wanted him to suffer more for what he'd done.

~

November 12, 1757
North German Flatts, New York

When Adam jerked awake it was so dark that for a moment he thought his eyes were still closed. He blinked, but it changed nothing. Despite the early hour, he could hear whispers all around him. The memory of what day it was set his heart thumping and twisting madly in his chest and his stomach tying itself into intricate knots. He had joined the *troupes de la marine* at fifteen, a year older than his father had before him, and for four years he had marched and drilled and practiced and dreamed of this day. Now, at last, there was going to be action. He was going into battle.

"*T'es prêt, mon ami?*" whispered the cheerful voice of Pierre near his ear.

Adam nodded, realizing as he did so that his friend couldn't see him. He grabbed his pack and the musket that lay beside him, floundering in the blackness for his saber. Few of the marines carried them, but the shining old weapon had been an impressive gift from his father on the day he enlisted, and he knew it made the older men jealous. He strapped it on, steam blowing around him each time he exhaled a shaky, excited breath. The frozen ground was layered with a thin crust of snow, enough for their white justaucorps to give them an advantage, for once.

They had a mile to push through the darkness, and then they would be upon their target. Adam knew little of what they were attacking. A settlement with blockhouses, he had heard, and a fort of some sort. This was to be a surprise attack, that much he knew, and he took care to move as silently as he could across the blanket of white that covered the earth, keeping in step with Pierre. All around in the night their allies among the Iroquois moved soundlessly, putting the king's frontier marines to shame. Adam fancied the shadowy warriors laughed at the French soldiers every time one of them clinked their sword against their canteen or broke a stick underfoot with a resounding snap.

Those cracking twigs did not matter; as it turned out, the settlers were deeply asleep. The only warning those settlers had was the barking of their dogs, but the Iroquois silenced the animals quickly. Then came a shrill scream in the night as Adam and the men in his company, crouching low on the approach, attained the first barnyard between them and the blockhouses. There were more screams around them, as other companies entered other residences, and then there were gunshots, and an ember glow growing swiftly from a neighboring house, set to light. Adam was trembling like a leaf, unable to point his gun as he saw the door of the farmhouse open. There was a flash of movement in the doorway and the dull gleam of a gun barrel.

A blast sounded by his ear. Pierre had fired at the house, and the figure within the doorframe crumpled. There were cries and he saw others—a woman, perhaps, it was hard to tell, and maybe children as well. The woman was bending to pick up the gun while the children were screaming, and Adam heard his sergeant order them to fire. He dropped to his knees, shaking, and heard another loud blast, but this time it was not one of his comrades that had fired. This time Pierre fell to the ground beside him. Adam dropped his gun. He could hear the other soldiers firing wantonly at the residence, and piercing shrieks of pain filling the night, but he had eyes only for Pierre. His friend was looking at him, reaching for him, blood bubbling up from a wound in his neck. He was gasping, desperate, gurgling incoherently, and then he was still, a film coming over the brightness of his eyes.

"*Pierre, non! Non! Mon ami, réveille-toi! S'il te plaît, Pierre!*" But his words fell on dead ears. Pierre was gone. A sob catching in his throat, Adam leaped to his feet, dashing to follow the other men into the farmyard, where they were setting fire to the curtains inside the residence. He tripped over the bodies of a man, a woman, a girl not much bigger than his own little sisters back home, and a boy still in skirts.

In a daze, Adam realized he had forgotten his musket, leaving it beside the fallen Pierre. There were more shots in the dark, proper volleys, with scattered answering rounds, and more whoops and war cries from the Iroquois—shrill, haunting sounds that sent terror through anyone listening.

Adam stumbled back through the melee to where Pierre lay. He tripped over his friend's body and lay still for a few seconds, tears welling up in his eyes. Then he searched with his hands, finding the weapon he sought. He rose again and turned back, but his comrades had vanished into the night. He stood for a moment, lost, and for a second there flashed in his head the image of his father watching him parading in Montreal. He had been dressed like a shiny doll, his uniform yet starched and stiff, as he marched beneath the fleur-de-lis of his regimental banner. The pride in his father's eyes—that unspeakable pride in his father's eyes that had made his heart soar.

He spun from Pierre's body and ran as fast as he could back toward the settlers' blockhouses, where he was sure his fellow marines must have gone. He raced mindlessly to join his comrades in battle. Battle? What battle was this? Just the killing of surprised families in their homes. He tripped over every log as he ran, stumbling over vines and branches even though his way was half-lighted by the multiple houses and barns burning around him. His foot caught on a thick vine and he fell for what felt like the thousandth time, thanking God above that his father wasn't there then, to see his bumbling coward of a son. This last fall knocked the wind out of him, and as he struggled to regain his breath, he heard a voice above him exclaim, "*Verdammtes Schwein!*", and he looked up and saw her.

She was a short girl, around his age, curved, strong, with straight brown hair and eyes the color of cornflowers, eyes that blazed with impossible hatred. She was dressed in her night shift, but in her hands she clutched a musket as long as she was tall. She clamped the butt of it against her shoulder, the barrel aimed at his head as he peered up at her. He saw her finger poised over the trigger and he leaped up, knocking the barrel aside, driving his head directly into her middle, bringing her to the ground and sending the musket flying.

He felt a terrible pain in his neck and realized that when he had knocked her to the ground, pinning her down, she had bitten him, and was still latched on, her teeth tearing through skin and muscle. He fell back and she released her grip, cursing gutturally in German as she grabbed the musket she had dropped, spinning to face him, raising that absurdly large weapon toward him again, the barrel wavering from the awkward weight. With a cry of anger, Adam swung his own gun, striking her head with the butt of it. She discharged her weapon into the forest, missing him widely as she collapsed.

He started forward instinctively to check the senseless girl for signs of life, but then he heard loud voices and stomping in the brush and trees beyond, voices speaking not French, not English, nor any of the Indian languages he had become familiar with, but German. He glanced at the girl, unsure if she was breathing, unsure if he saw the faintest movement—perhaps just the flicker of her eyelashes, perhaps nothing. Then he spun about and fled back the way he had come, dripping sweat, trembling, his heart beating so hard he thought it would come bursting out of his chest.

~

July 16, 1759
Ninety miles north of Fort Machault

SOMETIMES ADAM FANCIED THAT THE GIRL HAD RISEN, A PALE specter, and followed him back in his panicked retreat through the trees. She must have, really, for she had been with him ever since that night, following him with her eyes full of rage and accusation. The only time she left him alone was when he was stupid drunk. Because of her he had hardly been sober since that night, almost two years before. Sometimes he could hear her voice, cursing at him in German, and feel the sharpness of her teeth, and the trickle of blood down his neck and into his white shirt. He shook himself awake at the sensation. The girl was not there. There was no voice shouting in German. There were no teeth digging into his neck, but the blood . . . the blood was real, though it came from a wound along his right flank. He peered down blearily at the wetness of his justaucorps, the rust-brown stain becoming moist and scarlet red again in the center.

He dug into his waistcoat for the flask. He had no regrets about that particular risk. But he did regret that he had drunk it all over the past two days. He shook it and was not rewarded with the satisfying slosh of liquid. Nevertheless, his fingers thick, numb, and clumsy, he undid the cap and peered into the little vessel. It was, depressingly, decidedly empty, as it had been the last few dozen times he had checked it. If only they made a flask that spontaneously generated alcohol. Or, he reflected with a wry grin, if only he had Jesus as a traveling companion, to turn water into wine for him.

He sighed and patted the neck of the indefatigable horse. "Well, I suppose that's it; may as well lie down and die. The whiskey's gone. That is, of course, unless you have some secret stash of alcohol you haven't been telling me about, *camarade*?"

The gelding let out a long blowing breath, as if annoyed with his master, but did not reply to Adam's query. It was foolishness. Utter, useless foolishness. He was playing while he waited for his body to die. Adam had tried to staunch the bleeding, but he had lost a great deal of blood, and the constant jostling movements of the horse kept the steady ooze from fully clotting. Adam was getting more and more lightheaded, his weakness confounded by the symptoms of delirium from want of spirits, and he knew he couldn't make it much further. But he comforted himself with the thought that he had been brave, for once. He had so courageously attempted to betray his own people. He would die the distant cousin of a hero, thrice, perhaps four times removed, and that was something. The only witness to his one act of bravery would be the horse he was riding on, and it would tell no one.

Adam groaned, reaching over to grasp hold of his wounded right side and press against it, willing the pain to dull. The gelding threaded through a dense grove of hemlock and then halted, nervously shifting backward, eyes wide, ears turning back and forth between the forest ahead and his rider. Adam, still reeling from pain, stroked the animal's neck in a vain attempt to soothe him. He glanced up to see a shadowy gray form crouched on the ground, its lips drawn back in a menacing snarl.

Once he saw one, he realized the wolves were all around them, a pack on the hunt. They had probably been following him for miles, drawn by the smell of fresh blood from a wounded, weakened quarry. Adam pulled his musket from its sheath, but the horse, not waiting for its master to load the weapon, spun about and broke into a swift canter that nearly unseated his rider. Adam struggled to maintain his balance, clinging with his legs, stiff and spent from days of riding. He gripped the animal's thick brown mane with one hand while holding the musket awkwardly with the other. Glancing over his shoulder, he could see the wolves racing after him, trying to encircle his horse.

He let the gelding have his head, drawing in a deep breath, and despite the peril of their situation, a grin spread across his pale countenance. One last gallop, and then rest, sleep, forever—the perfect sleep of death. Eaten by wolves in the wilds around Lake Erie; it wasn't really the end he had anticipated, but it would serve as well as any other demise. Adam urged his horse still faster, kicking madly at the bay's flanks, while awkwardly, and uselessly clutching the musket. He could not aim a long gun from the back of a loping horse. Adam felt like he was flying, the horse's rapid strides eating up the woodland beneath them, and then, quite suddenly, the horse jerked to a stop and Adam no longer simply felt like he was flying; he was, in fact, soaring through the air.

He tumbled along a sheer sandstone wall that was slick with water, grabbing vainly at protruding rocks and branches, crashing through shrubs and saplings growing from the rock face. His wounded right flank struck hard against a branch, and he heard and felt the terrible crunch of his ribs. Then, at last, he landed prone in a shallow creekbed and lay still, listening to the sound of his musket clattering to the ground beside him. Turning his head, Adam tried to take in the world around him as it spun. He had fallen down a steep gorge that widened out near the bottom, where a nearly dry creek trickled over rocks made smooth by hundreds of years of flowing water. He lay still, waiting for things to steady, but they remained wavering and immaterial. He wondered if he might finally be dead.

"*Verdammtes Schwein!*" he heard a familiar voice cry, a strangely familiar voice.

Adam rolled over and stared up into the blazing blue eyes of the angry German girl, the same girl he had seen every day for almost two years. She was gripping his musket, pressed into her shoulder, the barrel inches from his head. He was dead, then, finally, and joined with the girl whose blood stained his hands. This, then, must be his purgatory —he would spend eternity having his brain repeatedly blown to bits by the girl he had killed in German Flatts. It was fitting, it was just, he reflected, as he saw her finger squeeze the trigger and everything went black.

2

LIDIA

~

July 16, 1759
Ganadawao Creek, New York

Lidia would have known him anywhere. She would have been able to pick that single face out of a thousand men, perhaps ten thousand; the one face she remembered from the day her parents died. Certainly he looked older, shockingly aged considering the brief amount of time that had passed, and he was thinner, and horribly pale, and diaphoretic, and there was stubble on his chin that had not been there that fateful, life-altering night two years ago, but still, it was the same boy. She knew it was the same boy, and she knew that she hated him, and she knew that God, in His mercy, must have given her this opportunity to avenge her parents.

The moment she heard the boy tumbling down the steep embankment, she ran to pick up his gun as it clattered on the shale stone of the creekbed. For a moment she thought him dead, lying prone on the ground, his body twisted into a contorted jumble of limbs. He had struck every stone and obstacle possible on his way down. She swore at the missed opportunity and then noticed with relief the water that eddied around his abdomen swirled with fresh, pulsing jets of scarlet, and she knew he was not dead. Corpses did not bleed. Whispering a prayer of gratitude that God had not stolen her chance at vengeance, she pointed the gun at his head as he rolled over. A strange expression spread across his face, almost a smile, a very contented smile. Then, staring unflinchingly into his warm hazel eyes, Lidia pulled the trigger.

There was no blast, no jolt of force in her shoulder, and no satisfying explosion of the young man's head. There was nothing but a click. So sure had she been that she was going to kill him in that instant that she froze, bewildered by her inability to complete her purpose. She stared at the gun, thinking at first that it was wet, but then she realized the musket was not loaded. She dropped to her knees in the water, trying to dig the now-unconscious trooper's cartridge pouch out from behind his back, yanking and tugging on his insensate form. The scarlet streams increased with every movement, swirling around her skirt and staining it red. She tossed the pouch open, and the contents spilled into the puddles of murky water. With a cry of exasperation, she dropped the gun and grabbed for the trooper's saber. An old-fashioned weapon for such a young man, she thought briefly, but she shook the thought away, shook away any curiosity about who the boy in the water was. He was a murderer and a brute, and in a moment he would be a dead brute, and that was all he would ever be to her. Standing over the unmoving young man, she raised the weapon over her head.

"Lidia?" came the deep, commanding voice of her sister.

Lidia spun around, letting the saber tip drop into the creek. Then she tucked the blade behind her back, an instinct born of hiding a thousand things from her older sister all her life. She did not want Sofie to find out what she was doing. She would be scolded. Sofie was always scolding.

The other woman slid down from the steep ledge into the creekbed, landing with a splash in a puddle a few yards from Lidia. Sofie was the opposite of Lidia; she was tall, broad-shouldered, buxom, with softer eyes, gray and pensive where Lidia's were piercing and bright blue, and Sofie had proper German hair, the color of summer marigolds.

Her older sister brushed a wisp of her yellow locks behind her ear and placed her hands on her hips, frowning at Lidia. "What are you doing? Who is this?"

"The boy! He's the boy from the attack!" cried Lidia. "I was going to—"

"You were going to commit murder. That's an unforgivable sin," accused Sofie.

"He murdered first. I'm only punishing an evildoer."

"And who gave you the right to pass judgment and sentence?" snapped Sofie, lunging forward and wrenching the saber from Lidia's hand.

Lidia crossed her arms over her chest, her face twisted in rage. "Who gave him the right to kill my parents?"

"*Our* parents, Lidia, and you don't know that he was the one. There were many soldiers involved in that attack. Besides . . . he looks like he's going to die any moment, no need for you to become a killer."

"He was there! He tried to murder me, or have you forgotten? Or perhaps you don't believe your little sister's tales." Lidia's voice became shrill with accusation and outrage.

"I believe you. But in the heat of battle, a man may do things he did not intend."

Lidia hated Sofie at times like this. The always wise, thoughtful, forgiving, long-suffering woman. She was a bloody saint, and Lidia felt strongly that Sofie believed herself better than everyone else. It was easy to believe yourself better than others from the high throne of pure, perfect morality that Sofie always sat on. As Lidia watched, Sofie set the saber aside and knelt, checking the boy's neck for a pulse, noting his breathing and then turning her eyes toward the bloody justaucorps, the once-white wool, now stained shades of rust, scarlet, and maroon with old and new blood.

Lidia reached down and grabbed her sister's arm, stopping her as Sofie began to undo the buttons of the young man's coat. "Don't do it. He tried to kill me, Sofie. Whether or not he killed our parents, he definitely meant to kill me that night."

"How do you know that he is the one? It was dark that night, and you were dazed and sick for days afterward from that blow to the head. How can you be sure?"

"You think I wouldn't remember the man who almost killed me? If a thousand years had passed I would know his face, Sofie. But, if my word isn't good enough for you . . ." Lidia released Sofie's arm and reached to the trooper's neck, deftly untying his black kerchief. When she pulled the fabric back, the scar of a deep laceration made by human teeth was unmistakable.

Then Lidia leaped backward as the young man reached up and caught her wrist, opening his eyes. He stared at her with an uncomprehending gaze and spoke through dry lips.

"*C'étaient des loups. . . loups voraces . . . ils ont senti le sang . . .*" Then his hand dropped and his lids closed again.

"What did he say?" asked Lidia as she pulled her hand back, rubbing it as if his grasp had sullied her.

"My French is poor. But I think he said something about blood and he's hungry, I think, and something about the sounds of boats? No, wait—"

A growl above the sisters' heads interrupted Sofie's fumbling translation. Both young women looked up to find a dark gray body leaping through the air toward them, while three more shapes descended along the steep face of the ledge. Seeing the wolf flying toward them, its teeth bared, Lidia shoved Sofie hard to one side and threw herself the other way. The wolf landed and started toward Lidia with a snarl, snapping at her legs. Lidia kicked out repeatedly, advancing as she did so and pushing the wolf back toward Sofie, who had snatched up the saber again and raised it above her head.

Sofie swung, and the wolf let out a yelp of pain, darting sideways, blood streaming from its haunch where the saber had grazed it. By then there were four more wolves in the ravine, two menacing Sofie from behind, the others circling Lidia.

Lidia snatched up a large stick, laying into the wolves circling her. The second one slipped away as she chased the other, whacking it repeatedly with her stick. Then she heard Sofie cry out from behind her and whirled around. Her sister had managed to fend off two of the wolves, but while she attacked them, a third had thrown itself at her, knocking her to the ground. The saber had fallen from her hands and lay a few yards away in the water. Sofie had both hands pressed into the wolf's neck, pushing it hopelessly back as it lunged at her face, snarling and slavering. Lidia began to run toward her sister, brandishing her stick. If Sofie could hold on, keep the animal's teeth off her face for only a few more seconds, Lidia would reach her in time. Then Lidia's foot caught in a crevice of the sandstone creekbed and she fell, horror and panic rising up as she hit the ground with a cry, her right ankle twisting unnaturally. But there was only a second of shooting pain, and then nothing but the need to get to her sister, the need to not be too late, like she had been the day her parents died.

Scrambling to stand on an ankle that would not bear her, Lidia looked up toward Sofie, fear rising like choking bile in her throat. But Sofie was neither dead nor mauled. She lay on her back, half-risen on her elbows, looking with shock and surprise at the spot where she had struggled with the wolf a moment before. The French marine, like a ghoul risen from the grave, was wrestling with the animal as it scrabbled and scratched at him. With one hand he held the wolf to the ground, pinning its neck down; with the other he hefted a large rock. Then he began repeatedly slamming the rock into the wolf's face. The wolf fought against him, clawing and flailing, but still the youth held on, battering the animal with all his strength. A resounding crack split the air and then the wolf sprinted off down the creekbed, its lower jaw hanging awkward and deformed. Behind it the other wolves fled, some following the injured animal along the ravine, others climbing the steep banks. The French trooper, sitting on his knees, stared after the retreating gray forms for a long moment, wearing a strange look of regret on his face; then he slumped to the ground in a senseless heap, and the ravine was silent.

Sofie reached the young man's side first, rolling him over, checking him again for a pulse, for breath, both of which she must have found, for Lidia saw her shoulders relax a little and her older sister let out a faint sigh.

"Are you all right?" asked Lidia, limping painfully toward her sister and the French trooper.

"I'm all right," whispered Sofie. "Thanks to this soldier."

"Don't soften to him now. You said yourself that in the heat of battle a man may do things he didn't intend to."

"He saved my life, Lidia."

"And tried to take mine from me, not two years ago. Does one act of goodness outweigh the other?"

"Perhaps," said Sofie, seeming lost in thought for a moment. "We have to take him home, Lidia, and let him die in peace there if he is indeed wounded unto death. It's . . . it's what Mother would have done, and Father would have supported her. It's the Christian thing to do."

"And look where all that goodness got Mother and Father!" returned Lidia, the anger welling up again. "We bring a Frenchman into our home? Show him where we live? What would Will say?"

"Will would understand. And if he is indeed dying, then what do we lose by caring for him? Lidia, please, for once, don't fight me. Just let me help this boy. He saved my life. I owe him this much."

Lidia glared, but she relented. The trooper had saved Sofie's life, and he did appear to be dying. She would let her sister's charitable urges win this time. She hadn't quite abandoned the idea of killing the boy, though—perhaps when Sofie was asleep, a quilt pressed to his face would do the trick.

"I'll take his feet," Lidia said. "Taller person should take the head."

Before they could lift him, a loud crashing noise interrupted them. Lidia lunged toward the soldier's saber, convinced it would be the wolves again, or more French troopers looking for this boy. A flash of dark fur moved in the trees above, and then, at the top of the narrow trail into the ravine, a bay horse appeared, cautiously easing its way along the tight, steep path to the creekbed. They could see from its tack that it was the French marine's horse.

Lidia approached the animal slowly, struggling to hide her limp as she walked. The horse shied from her at first but then allowed her to catch its tangled reins and lead it back toward her sister and the fallen trooper.

"Must've been scared by the wolves," she said. "This beautiful animal will make lugging the murderer back much easier."

Sofie frowned at the last jibe but did not scold Lidia this time.

The horse sniffed at the trooper, almost sadly, Lidia thought, nudging his unheeding form with its nose. Lifting the young man was not as hard as Lidia had anticipated. He was thin beneath his layers of uniform, like a man whittled away by consumption. In fact, so fragile did he seem that she wondered how he had had the strength to break the wolf's jaw. A strength born of desperation, perhaps. She angrily suppressed her curiosity again, hating that she continued having little flickering thoughts about this boy's motivations and past.

The sisters laid him across the horse's saddle, Sofie fussing with things to make him more comfortable. They used the reins to bind him in place and led the horse by its headstall as they set off upstream, clattering along the stony creekbed.

Lidia gritted her teeth as she marched behind Sofie,

trying to step normally. Her right ankle was twice the size it should be, red and puffy. Every time she put weight on her right foot, she felt as if someone were driving a spear through her heel and all the way up into her pelvis. Several times she fell behind and noticed, with irritation, Sofie glancing back at her, concern evident on her face. Lidia scowled in return. Sofie should have hated this French boy; she should have joined Lidia in ending him, this boy who had struck her across the face with his musket almost two years before, knocking her unconscious. This boy, who was part of that mob of killers that descended on German Flatts and slaughtered more than forty peaceful settlers, including their own parents. This boy was the reason Lidia now lived with Sofie and her husband, Will, before he went away. This boy was why she lived here, which was nowhere, a hundred miles from any civilization. Even the Haudenosaunee people that lived nearby rarely passed through these parts. They were in the harshest, loneliest part of the wilderness, surviving on trapping, foraging, hunting, and a paltry garden in a cleared patch of forest. Filled with these bitter reflections, Lidia let the memory of the boy's good deed fade, hating him more and more as they marched back along the creekbed, deeper and deeper into the forest.

The home Lidia resented so much was a cave in the ledges of another ravine, about a mile upstream from where they had found the wounded trooper. Here Lidia had lived since her parents died, working with Sofie to feed them both and make the cave as hospitable as possible. William Light, Sofie's husband, had built a wall on the outside, with a smooth pine door that creaked on rusty hinges when they entered. The dank, dark walls were covered by quilts that Lidia had brought from German Flatts. The sparse furnishings were illuminated by the daylight that streamed in when they opened the door, chairs, a bed, and stools, all constructed by Will. A central fireplace made the cave smoky and toxic. Beyond the fireplace sat a cradle, and when the two women entered, hefting the young man's limp body between them, a wailing cry greeted them.

"All right, into the bed with him. Let me get the baby," Sofie grunted, sweating from their endeavors.

"The bed?" returned Lidia, incredulous. "You're giving him our bed?"

"Have a heart, Lidia, he's dying. We can wash the sheets after."

Lidia halted, glaring. She was holding the trooper's legs, while Sofie had wrapped her arms under his armpits and around his chest.

"Lidia!" hissed Sofie. "Let's give him a death of some comfort. Lord knows it looks like he's seen enough trouble and war. Please. I have to nurse."

The infant's wailing had become louder, more desperate, maddened by the sound of his mother's voice so near. Lidia sighed and shuffled forward begrudgingly, and together the sisters hefted the young man into the bed, atop the blankets. Sofie, after inspecting the situation for a moment as if to satisfy herself that he was not going to fall out, turned to the cradle. Lidia slipped outside to care for the soldier's horse, limping more dramatically once away from Sofie's studying gaze.

The animal looked as if it had been ridden hard, and as soon as she removed his saddle he began sniffing the ground for a place to roll. Setting the saddle aside, she led the gelding up out of the ravine. Above the ledge in which the Light family's cave home sat was a wide, grassy knoll with a ramshackle pasture fenced with saplings and slim logs. Lidia watched with joy as the bay rolled in the spare woodland grass, kicking his black-socked legs high in the air. Once he had turned his whole body over a few times, he rose and began grazing as if he had never eaten before. With a sigh, Lidia hobbled back to the cave, biting her cheek from pain as she walked.

Sofie had finished nursing her child, who now rested half-awake in his cradle. She was setting up a fire, but when Lidia entered, she rose, wiping the soot off her hands and onto her apron. "All done? Good. Can you get the fire going and prepare some cornmeal for dinner? We could eat some of these berries you picked yesterday with it. I'll see to the boy while you do that."

"See to him?" Lidia's brow wrinkled, her eyes narrowing.

"I just . . . want to take a look at that wound, Lidia. Clean it, and dress it. It's the right thing to do. The Christian thing to do."

Lidia let out a disgruntled "humph" and took over the business of preparing a meal for them. She struck the flint with violent, perhaps excessive force, until a spark leaped into the small teepee of tinder and sticks that Sofie had built. While she worked, mashing the dried ground corn into their one pot, she couldn't help but steal glances at the young man Sofie was undressing on their bed. It didn't appear easy for her sister, taking clothes off a limp, unconscious full-grown man, but she removed his garments, one by one, the thick, blood-crusted justaucorps, waistcoat, neck stock, gaiters, shoes, and stockings. Each layer of cloth closer to his body was more saturated with blood than the one before it. He was thin, but sinewy, lean muscles stood out across his arms and chest. At last Sofie peeled back the last layer of cotton shirt, drenched around the right side with fresh wet blood. Lidia craned her neck to catch sight of the wound and then yelped in pain as heat scorched her index finger. Putting her scalded digit in her mouth to cool it, she turned her attention back to the cornmeal she was burning over the fire.

3

SOFIE

~

July 16, 1759
The Light Home

In that bloody, insensate young soldier, Sofie Light saw echoes of her own husband, and she hated it. Will had known she didn't want him to go, and still he had left, and she hadn't even said goodbye because she had been so angry. She had watched him ride away on his little buckskin mare, his long legs stretching down past the horse's protuberant barrel, his gun sheathed beside him. He had left with that easy, confident air that he always bore. His red hair, with only a few grays mixed in, had gleamed in the rising sun, his beard had been so thick and full, and his eyes had glinted with excitement, though behind his joy had loomed resentment and even anger at his wife's disapproval.

He had abandoned his wife to serve as a scout and translator for the British Army, and she was sure that he would die, that perhaps he already had died. She hadn't told him then about the child growing within her. Why give him the news that he was going to have a child if he wasn't going to live to see the baby? She had been bullheaded, angry, and unforgivably stubborn, and she regretted it. It had been nearly six months since she heard of him, and that had only been from a passing Oneida hunter, who claimed to have seen him working with the forces of a Captain De Lancey. There had been nothing else specifically about her husband, but another passing band of Seneca had told her a few days ago that De Lancey was part of a large force besieging the French fort at Niagara.

A faint moan from the young man snapped Sofie's attention back to her ministrations. It was not Will under her probing fingers, but this young French trooper, pale as a ghost. He was younger than Will, and smaller, only a little taller than Lidia. But, while Lidia was stout and strong, a proper German girl, this boy was rail thin. Asleep on the bed, he looked younger than he had in the creekbed, around Lidia's age.

Sofie had brought a pail of water inside when Lidia went to tend the trooper's horse. She dipped a rag in the cool water and began gently clearing away the caked blood on the trooper's abdomen, looking for his wound. She drew in a sharp breath when she found it: a gunshot had sawed through his right flank. The bullet had cut clean through him, breaking the lower ribs in his back and leaving a gaping crater in the front. She gently washed it, but he moaned and became agitated at her touch, and every time she wiped the blood away, more sprang up. Finally she pressed the cloth into him and held it while he pulled feebly away, dripping sweat. At last he lay still, and Sofie took some of the scarlet elf cups she kept as a precaution. She crumbled the dried fungus into the bandage as a styptic, the way the Oneida people had taught her, and packed the wound hard, wrapping loops of cloth tight around his abdomen. Finally, she covered him with blankets. She sighed as she surveyed her work, not liking the young man's chances of survival, and then she turned to find Lidia already seated on a rough-hewn stool, nibbling at a steaming bowl of corn-meal porridge.

"I made you some," said Lidia, nodding toward the wooden bowl by the fireplace.

"Thank you," whispered Sofie, feeling dull and drained. She sat down on another stool with the porridge in hand and lifted the spoon to her lips, blowing on it.

"Well?"

"It hasn't become infected yet—it's a fresh wound. The danger in it, I think, is how much blood he has lost," replied Sofie, carefully measuring her words, not wanting to set her sister off again.

"Let's hope he's lost enough, then," retorted Lidia.

"How can you? He's barely more than a boy. Just caught up in a war that he didn't cause and probably doesn't understand. Fighting for his country the way he was taught. Have some mercy, Lidia."

"He didn't have mercy on me when he hit me in the face with his gun."

"I don't believe the good book says 'do unto others as they have done unto you.' I think the verse goes quite differently, actually."

Lidia was pouting, her lip protruding as she glowered at the young man on the bed.

"Your face will stick like that if you keep making that expression."

"Where are we supposed to sleep tonight?" asked Lidia. "I still can't believe you would bring a French soldier into our home, *your* home, where your defenseless child lives, and then give him our bed, like it's nothing."

"Lidia, stop," commanded Sofie, tired and irritated with her sister's vicious, untamable rage.

"What are we going to do with him if he recovers?"

"I don't know, send him on his way?"

"Turn him over to a Seneca war party, that's what we should do. They'd make short work of him, or rather . . . long work."

There was a note of glee in Lidia's voice at the prospect of the trooper's torture and death that made her older sister shudder. Her patience exhausted, Sofie set her half-finished bowl of porridge down on her stool and moved to the darker recesses deeper in the cave, beside her child's cradle. There she removed her outer garments and, sitting in her light chemise and stays, began sewing the rents in her skirt from the battle with the wolves, ignoring Lidia as her younger sister hobbled about their home, cleaning up their dinner and putting out the fire.

It was hot and oppressive in the cave that summer night. There was a dense humidity in the air outside, and inside it was worse, as if the atmosphere had thickened into a syrupy blanket, making it hard to breathe, hard to think, and hard to move. Lidia was trying to hide her limp from Sofie, like she always tried to hide things from her older sister. But she was doing a poor job of it.

"Why don't you wrap it?" asked Sofie after a while.

"What?"

"Your ankle. Wrap it. It'll give you a bit more support. And then sit down and put it up, for heaven's sake—stop stalking around the house."

Lidia glared for the thousandth time that day, but she obliged, going outside first to find a few sticks and thick pieces of bark, which she used to brace the ankle, then wrapping it tightly with cloth. The women did not go out again, settling into domestic chores, mostly mending, endless mending, as the darkness lengthened outside. After a long time, Sofie began to doze, seated in her chair, leaning back against the wall, her mind taking her to Will again, and the angry words they had exchanged before he left.

~

July 17, 1759. Early morning.
The Light home

Sofie startled awake. The candles had gone out and it was pitch dark in the cave. Lidia had drifted off lying on her stomach on the ground. Before she had fallen asleep, she had been stitching a quilt that Sofie swore the girl had been working on ever since she came to live with them. Now Lidia was sitting bolt upright, and Sofie could feel tension and fear emanating from her. She did not know at first what had awakened them, but then she heard it—someone else in the room, fumbling clumsily in the darkness and breathing hard.

Sofie reached out and caught hold of Lidia's shoulder. She didn't know what half-cocked scheme Lidia was about to launch into, but she knew it wouldn't be a good idea and it would likely result in injury for the younger woman. Lidia was always acting first and thinking later, much later, sometimes never thinking at all. Sofie slowly rose, keeping as silent as she could, and cast about for the torch that she kept in the house, usually near the fireplace. It had to be the boy rustling around, but still her heart hammered with fear that perhaps he had been followed by his own forces, or whoever had shot him, and maybe even now there were invaders, French or Indian, inside her home. She found the torch and flint and the Frenchman's saber, and moments later the cave flickered with light.

The young trooper was on the floor, digging about in the bloody uniform coat that Sofie had removed a few hours before. He looked up in terror at them, trembling, still sweating and pale.

"*Qui êtes vous?*" he whispered, his voice so dry it was barely audible.

"*Nous ne te ferons pas de mal,*" returned Sofie, stumbling over the words.

"*Vous parlez français?*" asked the boy.

"*Un peu. Parles-tu anglais ou oneida ou seneca ou allemand?*"

"*Oui. Anglais, oui.* I speak . . . English." He had an accent, but his words were clear.

"What's your name?" asked Sofie, switching to English.

"Adam-Constant Regnant de Montréal," he replied. Then he turned back to his uniform coat, pawing in it for something, searching among the pockets. He had a distinct tremor to his movements and he seemed almost frenzied in his search. "*La lettre, la lettre. . . ,*" he murmured as he dug through the pockets.

"Adam?"

He froze and looked back up at her, furtive, like an animal caught in a trap.

"What are you looking for?"

"The letter. The letter. I have to warn them," he replied and continued digging through the coat. To Sofie he seemed wildly delirious.

"What letter?" she prompted, but he had stopped, triumphantly yanking a crumpled bit of paper from a pocket sewn into the coat's blue cuff.

"It's here, it's here," he said. "I must go. I don't have much time." He attempted to stand, catching hold of the bed, but the effort was wasted; his legs would not hold him.

Sofie passed the torch to her sister and went to his side, assisting him back into bed. He seemed baffled by his lack of strength, like a little child unsure why they couldn't lift the same heavy rocks from a field that their father could.

"You're not going anywhere, Adam," she said. "You're hurt."

"No, no, I have to . . . I have to go. *S'il vous plaît. Je dois y aller. Vous ne comprenez pas*," He became agitated again, struggling to get up.

Lidia stepped forward, as if to help her sister, but, reaching out, she pointedly pushed into the trooper's wound, pressing hard against the bandage. He passed out.

That was it—as the young man went limp on the bed, Sofie turned and slapped Lidia hard across the face. She felt an instant twinge of remorse for losing her temper as her sister drew back, holding a hand to her face and looking at Sofie in surprise.

"How could you be so cruel?" asked Sofie. "You're a monster, Lidia. He's a hurt young man, nothing more than that. And he saved my life, or have you forgotten that? Don't touch him again or I'll take a belt to you."

"You can't take a belt to me, Sofie. I'm nearly twenty-one years old!"

"I don't care how old you are, if you cruelly torture an injured person in my home, then I will beat you black and blue." Sofie turned from her younger sister back to the trooper, who had briefly opened his eyes but then drifted off again, all his strength and alertness gone. She reached out and took the crumpled paper from his limp hand, smoothing it open and staring at the scrawly French script.

Lidia, despite her sister's vicious reprimand, leaned forward, raising the torch. "What does it say?"

"Give me a moment, my French is poor." Sofie scanned and then rescanned the document, whispering the phrases aloud to help them make sense in her head. She set the letter down, her mind reeling. When she finally spoke, her voice was soft and breathy. "An attack. The French are sending reinforcements against the British besieging Fort Niagara."

"But that will catch the British between the fort and an army!" cried Lidia, her face flushing. "How many reinforcements are they bringing?"

"Nearly a thousand. Indians and French and Canadian troopers and militia."

"We have to warn them!" Lidia exclaimed, so loudly that Adam shifted again, frowning in his sleep. "I can take his horse and ride there."

"You cannot," replied Sofie, already sure of what she needed to do.

"Of course I can. We have to warn them, Sofie. Your husband may be there. We can't just sit and wait. Remember . . ." Lidia choked on her words before her voice strengthened again. "Remember that at German Flatts we had a warning. Our Oneida friends warned us, and we did not listen. We should at least give your husband and the forces outside Niagara the chance our leaders spurned."

"I know, Lidia, I know. We will warn them, but not you. You can barely hobble around the house with that ankle. You cannot ride a horse and support your weight in the stirrups. I'll go."

"You?" cried Lidia, eyes wide with disbelief. "How can you go? Your son is not three months old yet. I can't nurse him, Sofie. He'll die if you leave him."

"I'm not leaving him. I'm taking him with me," replied Sofie, steely determination entering her voice. She rose from the bed and began gathering things—dried porcupine meat, crumbling cornbread that was just beginning to mold, a few early apples, and extra napkins and garments for the infant. Lidia followed her, limping and still protesting.

"You're going to take that child into the wilderness? There are more than a hundred miles between us and Fort Niagara. There are bears, wolves, rattlers, and roving Indians, from clans and nations we don't know, some of whom are allied with the French. You have beautiful golden hair that any warrior would be proud to add to his scalp collection. You can't do this."

"A Haudenosaunee woman could do it. I'll take the wampum belt that clan mother Yako'nikulowanah gave me. Those I meet along the way will see it and know our family's friendship with the Six Nations. I speak Mohawk, Seneca, and Oneida, and I can understand Onondaga well. I can get through."

"You are not a Haudenosaunee, Sofie."

"But I know enough of their fortitude, skills, and strength in the wilderness to survive out there. It's only a hundred miles."

"A hundred miles with a baby on your back in . . . a week? You may have a week, not longer. Even the strongest Haudenosaunee warrior couldn't make such a journey."

"They could, and so will I."

Finally Lidia fell silent, helping her sister pack. They paused as they looked over the weapons in the cave—a hatchet, the soldier's musket, Will's musket, and the saber. Sofie tried to exude calm and confidence for her younger sister's benefit, but inside she felt the same doubts that Lidia had shouted at her in protest. She stared at the weapons uncertainly.

"Take the saber and Will's musket. I shouldn't need any more weapons than the trooper's musket," said Lidia. "I'll keep the wet powder and musket balls from his kit and dry them out."

"I hope not to need any weapon at all, honestly. But the French may be looking for their lost trooper. Perhaps it would be best if you keep the saber."

"One lost trooper? He's not an officer. You saw his uniform—he's nothing but a courier. They probably don't even know he's missing. Take the saber, Sofie. I won't hear of you leaving it here."

Sofie nodded reluctantly. She went to the closet and began digging through the few garments Will had left behind. If she was going to be riding for a week in a cavalry saddle, a skirt would not do. She slipped Will's breeches over her chemise and one of Will's shirts over her head, buttoning a waistcoat over the billowing white shirt. Together, in the gray light of early dawn, the sisters climbed to the paddock, tacked up the trooper's horse, and packed Sofie's belongings into the saddlebags, attaching a blanket roll to the cantle and sheathing Will's musket along the horse's side. Back inside the cave, Sofie fitted herself with the soldier's belt and scabbard, sheathing the saber on her hip. Then she took up her son and nursed him. He would need food before they set out.

Lidia was lingering near her. It was touching, Sofie thought; her little sister was hanging close to her as if she didn't want her to go. It took her back to when they were children, Lidia so much younger than herself, clinging and affectionate, so different from the angry, harsh, reactive young woman she had since become.

"You don't have to leave tonight, Sofie," said Lidia. "You can stay and get some more rest before you go."

"No, you said it yourself, I have a week, maybe, before the reinforcements reach the fort. The sooner I leave, the better. I can rest more along the way if I leave now."

"I still don't think you should go. It should be me."

"Lidia," replied Sofie, her voice gentle. "Your ankle. You're not ready for a journey right now. Let it rest. Let the swelling go down."

"What about him?" asked Lidia, turning back toward the bed and the sleeping soldier.

"He may pull through, he may not. I don't think he's a threat to you."

"But he was taking word to the French of reinforcements."

"And now he has no horse and no weapons."

"He was strong enough to break that wolf's jaw, remember that?"

"Aye, and thanks to that I'm alive. What do you want to do? Bind him so he can't harm you when he wakes up?"

"It will be easier to tie him with the two of us before he's awake and fighting."

Sofie nodded reluctantly, burping her content, satiated infant and then returning him to the cradle. "You're not wrong. Yes, I'll help you, but, Lidia, you have to promise me you won't hurt him or kill him. I owe him my life, and I would hope that a Canadian woman would show the same kindness to my husband if they found him wounded and alone in the wilderness. I know you want to fight, always. But I don't believe it's what Mother and Father would have wanted. You know how they felt about violence, how I feel about violence."

"I won't hurt him," said Lidia.

"You promise?"

"On Papa's beard."

They both grinned sorrowfully at that. Sofie blinked back the moisture that sprang to her eyes, remembering their tall, broad-shouldered father, with his bristling, gray beard that bobbled when he spoke and his merry, shiny red cheeks that matched so well with his ready smile and laugh.

"Well, there's an oath I know I can trust."

They tied the young man's hands behind his back, and, rolling him onto his stomach in the bed, they hobbled his legs as well. Something had softened in Lidia, Sofie could feel it. The anger and deep hatred were not as they had been before, though the girl did draw the ropes around Adam's ankles excessively tight. Part of Sofie still worried that her sister would perjure herself and yet become a murderer, but she pushed that thought away, allowing herself to trust the younger woman, for once.

Once the trooper was tied, still sleeping, Lidia helped Sofie nestle her son in a cradleboard, another gift from the Oneida clan mother Yako'nikulowanah, near German Flatts, years ago, when Sofie had first married Will. Sofie took out the wampum belt, allowing a flash of memories to pass through her mind— memories of her friend and their time together—as she ran her hands over the intricate designs on the belt. Then she bound it around her waist, over Will's jacket. It would be the first thing any Indian in the forest noticed. She stuffed the message from the trooper's coat into one of the waistcoat pockets. Then, after Sofie had attached the cradleboard to her back with the tiny child inside, blinking and looking about in calm bewilderment, the two women climbed back to the paddock.

As Sofie reached toward the saddle to mount, Lidia caught her hand. "It really should be me."

"I know you could do it, Lidia—believe me, I know you could, but you're injured right now. I have the best chance of success. I'm . . . I'm sorry I struck you earlier, and I'm sorry I threatened to beat you. I shouldn't have lost my temper like that."

"That's all right, proves that you're human after all," said Lidia with a brief, half-hearted smile.

Sofie swung into the saddle and looked down at Lidia's expressive face, staring up at her with a look of trepidation. "It's all right, *kleine Schwester*," whispered Sofie soothingly, seeing the first sparks of tears in the corners of Lidia's eyes. "I'll be careful. See to it that you are as well."

Lidia nodded, and Sofie turned the horse north and east and set off into the dark forest and the unforgiving wilderness beyond.

4

ADAM

July 19, 1759
The Light Home

The overwhelming humidity was the first thing Adam noticed when he awakened. There was a thick, musty smell in the cave, and the air was dense and unmoving. The second thing he noticed was the agony lancing through his right side. He had been intermittently awake over the last day, or several days—he wasn't sure how long it had been—but everything was a blur. There were vague pictures in his mind: a wolf snarling, inches from his face; a yellow-haired woman dressed like a man and nursing a baby; someone pressing hard into his wound and sending daggers of searing pain through him. Which of those images were real and which were imagined, he couldn't tell. They were hazy and distant, like dreams. But he felt alert now, and alive. The scratchy wool blanket was undeniably real and the tearing agony in his side was no dream.

What he remembered most vividly from his delirium was the angry face of the German girl as she pointed the musket at his face. He attempted to reach up to touch his head, to confirm it had not been blown into a million pieces, but he realized quickly that his arms were bound behind his back. He twisted in the ropes, finding his legs similarly tied. If he brought his ankles up to his hands he could probably undo his feet, he speculated. He lay quiet for a while, contemplating whether or not he wanted to try it. Then with a jolt, he remembered the letter in his justaucorps' cuff, and his mission to warn the British Army and redeem himself. He found his resolve to accomplish this necessarily final mission of his life had not dulled; if anything, it had strengthened. If he did this one thing, even if it meant death, then perhaps, before the end, he would be able to live with himself again.

The room was dimly lit by beams of sun streaming through the cracks around the door. He darted his gaze into each dark corner, taking in the cluttered, cozy home, garments strewn about, food sitting by the fire, an empty cradle tucked away in the back of the cave. He was alone. His uniform lay piled on a stool by the bed, except for his breeches, which he was still wearing. He writhed, bringing his ankles up behind his back to meet his fingers. The pain in his side from the movement took his breath away, and, within a few seconds of starting his contortions, he could feel the bandages wrapped around his abdomen dampening again.

He struggled on, clenching his teeth to prevent himself from crying out. It took him more than fifteen minutes to unbind one ankle, taking brief rests between his fumbling movements. Once that one was free, he relaxed. He could walk while dragging the rope. He didn't have the energy to keep working in that awkward position. He glanced around the room again. He was sweating, but it was not the sweat of a drunkard in need of his life-sustaining beverage; it was real sweat. The cave was sweltering. It felt like he was being boiled alive. Out of force of habit, he cast a cursory look around for some kind of spirit, but he found nothing that looked likely. He wondered where he was, and into whose hands he had fallen. This deep in the wilderness, he would have assumed an Indian family, but the decorations and comforts were decidedly European. He dismissed the idea of the girl; he had dreamed her. The German girl was dead. That part had not been real, just the hallucinations of an exsanguinating, delirious *ivrogne puant*.

He sat up, slipping his feet over the edge of the bed to touch the stone and earth below. He froze as the world darkened for an instant and the furniture and quilt-covered walls weaved before him. After a moment his vision steadied and the lightheadedness eased. He looked about for anything sharp: a knife, a bayonet, a sword, anything he could use to cut the ropes binding his hands. At last he spotted a rusty knife near the firepit. He staggered to a standing position, wobbling, but maintaining an upright posture. He was dizzy standing, and he was sweating like Corporal Renaud—like a pig.

Getting the knife to his hands was its own challenge. He had to kneel and twist, reaching behind him and scrabbling vainly with his fingertips, unable to see what he was trying to grasp. A noise outside halted his efforts. He stilled. His chest was heaving and every breath caused a stabbing sensation in his flank. He listened, droplets of sweat oozing down his face and chest and back. It sounded as if someone was dragging something. He stretched his fingers out again, frantically, and managed to get ahold of the knife at last.

Quickly he scampered back to the bed and grabbed his justaucorps, then turned and stumbled to the door, unsure if he was swaying or the world around him was. With his hands yet tied behind him, he pushed the door open slowly with his shoulder. Before him lay a world of blazing light, illuminating a nearly dry creekbed that ran through the bottom of a narrow gully. Just to the left of the door was a path leading up the ravine. The sound of scraping and dragging had stopped and he could see no one outside.

After shoving the door open the rest of the way, he caught himself as another wave of dizziness threatened to topple him. He leaned against the wooden wall for an instant, taking slow breaths until the lightheadedness eased. Then he started climbing the trail. He pressed his left shoulder against the rock wall of the gully as he walked, maintaining an uneasy balance with his arms tied, clutching the knife and the coat, trying to avoid tripping on the coattails or the rope still wrapped around one ankle. He had nearly reached the top when he heard a gasp below. Glancing over his shoulder, he saw her—the blasted German girl, that perpetual ghost. She had been dragging a log back along the bottom of the ravine, but on seeing him she dropped it and began limping after him, something clearly wrong with her right leg.

Adam lurched forward frantically, stumbled, righted himself, and tottered up the last few paces and onto a broad grassy meadow above. Then he set off in a wild, careening dash, listening for the sound of pursuit, feeling as if he was drunk from the lack of coordination his body displayed. But if he was drunk, his side would not hurt so horrendously, as if wild animals were digging into his flesh. A few moments into his awkward run, the rope dangling from one ankle caught in the bracken layering the forest floor and he fell, landing heavily. The fall knocked the breath out of him and he struggled to catch it, his bandage drenched anew in blood. When he looked up, the girl was standing over him, brandishing a musket but not pointing it at him this time.

"You must be feeling better," she said in English, snatching the knife from his tied hands as she spoke.

"Much better, *merci*," he whispered in reply, still working to catch his breath. "I have to go."

"You can't go."

"Why are you here? You're . . . you're dead."

She glared. "You'd like to think that, and I'm sure that was your intention when you attacked me at German Flatts. But I survived."

A strange feeling washed over him when she said this, like the warm, heady feeling that whiskey gave him, a brief rush of relief, a blooming as if of life anew. "So you remember?"

"Of course I remember," she spat. "You don't forget the person who murdered your parents."

"Murdered your . . . I murdered no one that day if I did not murder you." He didn't know why he was defending himself to her, but something about her accusation rankled him—her, the girl he had thought he had killed for so long. For the first time in two years, he wanted to defend himself. He wanted to fight back.

"Whatever you say. Now I need you to stand up and march back to the cave. I promised Sofie I wouldn't kill you, but if I tell her you attacked me she'll forgive me for an act of self-defense."

He sat up, still clutching his justaucorps behind him, and then waited as the world reeled madly.

"You're bleeding again," she said, surveying the bandage across his middle.

"Where am I?"

"*Ganadawao* is what they call this creek."

"What day is it?"

"The nineteenth of July."

He cast his mind back to the maps he had seen prior to leaving Fort Machault, but the name of the creek didn't spark a memory. He blew out a slow breath and turned his gaze up toward the girl. "Look, I'm sorry—more sorry than you can possibly imagine—for striking you in the head that day. But you should let me go. I am going to warn the British of the French reinforcements that are coming. If I don't go, they'll be caught in a surprise attack and they'll be slaughtered."

She chuckled. "Are you? Going to betray your own forces and warn the British Army? I know you were heading to Niagara to tell Pouchot of the reinforcements coming. I saw the message."

"No, you're wrong. I am a deserter. And you should either let me go or kill me. They will be looking for me."

"Who will be looking for one lost courier in this wilderness?"

"Lignery. Lignery will be looking for me."

The girl scoffed. "You really think someone as high-ranking as Captain Lignery, commander of the Ohio, will be looking for you? I'm not going to kill you, though if you had asked two days ago I happily would have. But neither am I going to let you go—Adam, is it?"

He nodded. He must have told them his name, though hopefully not his true name . . . or told just her his name? Had there been another woman? The girl had mentioned a promise to a person called Sofie. Perhaps there had been another. The vision leaped back into his mind of the slightly older woman, tall, buxom, long golden hair streaming over the shoulders of a man's shirt and waistcoat, his own saber belted around her, suckling an infant at her breast. There had been another one, at least in his dreams. But what was real and what was a hallucination during the last few days was still pathetically unclear.

"Well, Adam, I need you to stand up and walk back to the cave."

Nodding his head wearily, he struggled to rise, sinking back on his knees a few times before he gained his feet. He stumbled, tripping on the rope around his ankle on his first step, but the girl reached out and caught him. He glanced at her in surprise, but it had only been instinct. There was no kindness nor forgiveness in those blazing blue eyes.

It was a difficult, slow descent back into the gully, the girl walking behind him the whole way, menacing him with her musket. She was limping, as he had noticed when she had first started chasing him. He could see the sticks of a makeshift splint protruding from beneath her skirts. In the brief seconds that he was assessing her ankle out of the corner of his eye, he tripped and slid down part of the path, knocking loose scree that pattered to the creekbed below. This time his German captor did not reach out to assist him as she had before. He righted himself and shakily pressed on, at last sinking to his knees on the rocks outside the cave, exhausted, shivering, and diaphoretic. He dropped the justaucorps that he was still clutching. She waited.

"Do you have the *Anfälle*?" she asked suddenly.

"The *Anfäll* . . ." He shook his head. "I don't understand."

"*Anfälle*, *Anfälle*, the *Krämpfe*," she repeated. "Convulsions. Seizures, that's the word for it. The falling sickness?"

"No, I don't."

"Two days ago, and also yesterday, you seized, multiple times—at least three times yesterday. Writhing on the bed, shaking and stiff, foaming at the mouth. I thought you were dying."

He did not reply, staring mournfully at the trickling brook before him, largely stagnant pools turned rusty red by the sandstone. Since he started drinking heavily, it was the first time he had gone without alcohol long enough to have seizures. He had seen it happen to other men. Some never woke again after convulsing, foaming at the mouth, their eyes rolled back in their heads, gasping and choking on their own spit and vomit and writhing for what felt like hours.

"I wasn't sad to think you were dying. In fact, I'm disappointed to see you so improved today," the girl insisted in the silence.

"You should kill me," said Adam.

"I'd be happy to, but unfortunately, as I told you, I made a promise that I have to keep. Why are you so keen to die?"

He shrugged. Why was he so keen to die? And if he was so keen to die, why had he not ended things himself at any point over the last few years? Instead he had taken part in all the actions that followed the surprise raid on German Flatts, horrible skirmishes and battles, firing his musket wildly into the advancing troops or at the shadows of Iroquois among the trees, wishing one well-aimed bullet from the enemy would end the horror of his waking nightmare. Now here she was, the girl herself, standing over him, alive, real—he had felt the reality of her hands when she had kept him from falling in the forest. He had not murdered her, but instead of relief, all he felt was shame—shame and guilt for being such a waste of a life, and a hankering for a drink to give him that warm, floating sensation, to make that shame melt away. He had known that sensation for an instant in the forest, when he had first realized he was not a murderer, but it had not lasted, and he wanted it back. Alcohol would give it to him. Alcohol always worked.

"I need to . . . relieve myself."

"And?"

"It will be hard to accomplish tied like this."

"So? Who do you think has been helping you with the chamberpot while you've been delirious? You just want me to untie you so you can run and carry your message to the other French bastards at Fort Niagara."

"I won't run. Truly, I haven't the strength to run again. I can barely stand."

She studied him. He could feel himself swaying even on his knees and still trembling. After a moment, keeping the musket ready, the girl took the knife he had stolen from the cave and sliced through the ropes that bound his wrists. He rubbed the feeling back into his numb, cold fingertips, then rose and stumbled behind a boulder. A few moments later, adequately relieved, he stepped out and went to the coat he had set on the ground. The girl was menacing him with her musket as he sought inside the sleeve for the paper, that little, precious message on which his whole redemption hinged. He gradually became more frantic in his search, turning the cuff inside out and tearing at the seams.

"You won't find your precious message in there," said the girl.

He looked up, feeling slow and stupid. "*La femme avec le bébé.* The woman, the woman with the baby, she took it?"

"She took it," replied the girl, and there was a gleam in her eye of cruel triumph. "She's going to warn the British. Then your troopers and your precious Lignery will walk into a trap."

He sighed wearily. Despite his failure, he had still

succeeded. He clasped his hands together and extended them toward her. She eyed them dubiously.

"It's not a trick," he said. "If you insist on keeping me I will not fight you, but if you don't tie me, then I promise you I will try to run again, after I've rested."

"And you're going to just let me tie you now?"

"I am your prisoner."

"Come with me, then, I need to bandage your wound again, and if you were able to get free last time, I'll have to tie you differently this time. And you're not going to sleep on the bed anymore. I have to wash all those blankets and sheets. The mattress is soaked in blood, thanks to you. It's probably ruined."

He walked ahead of her into the cave and sat still while she unwrapped the bandages around his abdomen, revealing the hideous wound along his right flank. After she dressed it—with unnecessary roughness, he thought, though he did not blame her—she let him put on his shirt and stockings. Then she took a sturdy oak walking stick from beside the door and put it through the crook of his elbows, running it like a crossbeam behind his back, before she bound his hands in front. She hobbled his legs tightly again, so that he could only step an inch at a time. Another rope she attached to the stick and fixed to one of the pegs that had been driven into the cave wall to hang quilts on. There was just enough slack in it for him to lie down, though he had to wedge himself tight against the wall to do so.

The position was awkward, lying on his stomach, palms pressed into the stone and earth of the floor. He lay quiet, enervated, still diaphoretic, perhaps feverish, his head aching, feeling as if someone was repeatedly bayoneting his abdomen. He turned to watch as the girl ate. After a long time, noticing his dull, bleary gaze on her, she offered him some berries, but he shook his head, too nauseated to feel hunger yet.

"How did you come to be so far from German Flatts?" he asked, his curiosity getting the best of him.

"Well, after your friends killed my parents, I went to live with my sister here, in the middle of nowhere, away from the rest of my family, my friends, everything I once knew and loved. This is my life now: loneliness, wolves, friendly and unfriendly Indians alike, brutality, hunger, and work. We don't even have a single book to read, not even the Bible. And it's all thanks to you."

"I'm sorry," he murmured, realizing suddenly that he did not know her name. But the exhaustion had already overwhelmed him, and he did not have the strength to ask any more questions, not today. He let his eyes drift closed, and the last thought he had as consciousness deserted him was that the German girl, with her pink cheeks and heart-shaped face and those bright, angry blue eyes, was quite beautiful, in her own hardened, fierce way.

5

LIDIA

~

July 20, 1759
The Light home

Lidia hadn't cleaned the linens on the bed before she'd slept, but had lain on the opposite side from where the soldier had stewed in his blood and sweat for days. She woke slowly that hot summer day and stayed in bed for a long time, eyes closed, waiting for the familiar sound of Sofie moving softly about the cave, preparing breakfast, or of the baby crying, but there was nothing. Gradually the memories of the past few eventful days returned to her and she opened her eyes. She darted a glance toward the pale young man lying on the ground, awkwardly twisted in his bonds, his shirt half-unbuttoned. A beam of gray light leaking around the door frame illuminated his begrimed, youthful face, his dark hair falling across a forehead that was slick with sweat. He would have been handsome if a little fattened up, she thought, then banished that reflection instantly, frowning.

If Sofie were there, she would have scolded Lidia for sleeping past sunrise. But Sofie wasn't there, and the bed felt cozy and delightful after the nights spent on the ground. She nestled deeper into the straw mattress, pressing her cheek into her feather pillow, a luxury she had made for herself a few months back, stuffed with goose down. Eventually, with great reluctance, she slid out of the bed, remembering her injured ankle with a jolt as it hit the floor.

She wrapped the ankle again and then dressed herself, sliding her stays over her chemise, layering her petticoats, and at last slipping into a worn blue gown, tattered along the hem and sleeves from overuse. Adam did not stir as she dressed, braided her hair, and ate a few leftover bits of cornbread. She was determined to gather more berries, and perhaps some chestnuts or apples, maybe *Pfifferlinge* if she was lucky. She took a basket from beside the door and belted the kitchen knife in its sheath around her waist. Before slipping from the cave, she cast one last look at Adam, but he still had not awakened.

In a clearing just beyond the little pasture, she paused to survey the garden. The first of the summer squashes were only a few inches long yet, but the corn was growing well, a little taller than she was, silken gold tresses protruding from each green cocoon. There were fresh green beans as well, juicy and plump, and she resolved that if she still had room in her basket on her return from the forest she would pick some for dinner.

There were things Lidia hated about living alone in the vast expanse of untamed forests surrounding Lake Erie, but these perfect serene mornings she loved. She whistled softly as she meandered through the sparkling dew-wet forest, past the elegant designs spiders had crafted between trees during the night, through ghost-pale beams of morning light. A faint mist quickly lifted, and the heat grew as she limped, skirts soon soaking from the wet grass. She felt lighter and happier than she had in months. There was trepidation in the back of her mind for her sister, but she had every confidence in Sofie's ability to navigate the uncertainties of the wilderness. Before Lidia had come to live with her, Sofie had been alone numerous times, with Will away trapping or trading with the Haudenosaunee. She was a strong woman, courageous and fierce, despite her Quaker-like beliefs about violence. If anyone could make it to Niagara before the French forces, it would be Sofie Light.

It took Lidia more than an hour to reach the berry patch, hampered as she was by her swollen ankle. Despite the lancing pain with each step, her carefree joy only grew the further from home she went. Joy had become almost foreign to her since her parents' deaths on that horrible night in German Flatts, and she wasn't sure what had changed in the past few days. Perhaps it was the closure of meeting the boy who had struck her in the face, of facing him again and being victorious this time. She did not know. But she felt airy, as if she might float away from happiness, and full to the brim with life and exuberance. She startled a deer that raced off, crashing through the trees. She briefly cursed herself for not bringing the trooper's musket, but there was still enough dried meat left from the porcupine Sofie had shot a few weeks back that venison was not an urgent need.

When she reached her berry patch, she lost herself quickly among the green leaves, prickling thorns, and juicy blackberries and thimbleberries. She kept singing softly to herself as she picked. The noise was soothing and would hopefully frighten off any bears that might be munching in the same patch.

"Ein Jäger aus Kurpfalz,
Der reitet durch den grünen Wald,
Er schießt das Wild daher,
Gleich wie es ihm gefällt.

"Juja, Juja, gar lustig ist die Jägerei
Allhier auf grüner Heid,
Allhier auf grüner Heid,

"Auf! Sattelt mir mein Pferd
Und legt darauf den Mantelsack,
So reit ich hin und her
Als Jäger aus Kurpfalz . . ."

Her basket brimming and her stomach full, Lidia hardly knew where the time had gone. The sun had reached its zenith, perhaps even a little past it. She had lost track of the passing of hours, absorbed in her tunes and the endless harvest of luscious black raspberries. She limped a few steps and settled on the grass, her back against a rock, propping her aching leg on a log. A twinge of remorse ran through her. It was past midday and broiling. Her prisoner would need water and to relieve himself, and here she was, miles away, without a care in the world. She assuaged her guilt by reminding herself that he was an enemy, and there was a reason he was tied. He had been a member of the forces that had killed her parents and so many other peaceful settlers. If he was suffering, it was a small price to pay for the injuries he had inflicted on so many others in his short life. With the warm sun smiling down on her, bees and butterflies flitting around the berry patch, and the pleasant din of insects and birds lullabying her, Lidia forgot the troubles of her prisoner and drifted off to a contented sleep.

Her eyes snapped open. An Indian warrior, garbed and painted for battle, was standing over her with a light carbine pointed at her chest. Behind him she could see others, Indians and French troopers alike, all on foot, though a few were leading horses. She cursed herself inwardly. She should have heard them—a party like this, soldiers with horses, guns, clanking metal, they must have made a hell of a racket. The man with the gun shouted at her in a tongue she didn't know. It was not Mohawk, or Oneida, or Onondaga, all of which she had learned in her youth spent playing with the children of those nations. Nor was it Seneca, the most common tongue in that region. She tore her knife from its sheath and leaped up, pushing the offending gun barrel aside. But the warrior was on her before she could do any damage, pinning her smaller frame to the ground, twisting the knife from her grasp. He caught hold of her throat, choking her while she writhed and punched at him. He wrenched her long brown hair up by her braid and released her neck, putting his knee in her chest, and pressing her own knife to her forehead.

One of the French soldiers barked a command and the warrior relaxed the pressure from his knee. He reluctantly let the knife-wielding arm fall to his side but still kept Lidia pinned to the ground, and took hold of her neck again. He began to squeeze as she continued striking vainly at him with her fists. Behind the warrior she heard more orders shouted in French as her vision blurred. Then the Indian released her and she clawed away, backing up against the rock. She reached to her throat, gasping for air, and accidentally spilled her entire basket of berries in her mad scramble to distance herself from her captors. She scanned the faces around her, some curious, some unfriendly, some leering. They were speaking together in French and the Indian tongue that she didn't recognize.

"*Spricht jemand von euch Deutsch?*" she murmured, her voice hoarse, her heart thumping so hard in her ears she could barely hear herself. She continued, offering the other languages she spoke well. "English? *Onödonwa' ga:' gawën:ö'? Ukwehuwehnéke? Kanien' kéha? Onoñda' gegá' nigaweño' deñ' ?*"

For a moment there was silence in the berry patch. Then a tall, almost regal-appearing Frenchman, older than the others, stepped forward, leading a horse behind him. "I speak English," he said. The others backed away when he approached her; they all looked at him with marked respect, and Lidia assumed he must be their leader. There were insignia and medals on his uniform coat, though she did not know their meaning.

"What is your name?" asked the man. He had dark hair with flecks of gray, only a little stubble about his chin, hazel eyes, and a soft, fatherly expression on his sun-worn face. There was something strangely familiar about him.

"Lidia Erghamer," she replied.

"And what is a young woman like you doing alone in this wilderness, Miss Erghamer? Where is your family?"

"I'm not so young," she answered and then, remembering Sofie's mission, she continued, "And I have no family."

"You live alone out here?"

"Yes, alone," she insisted.

"I must apologize for your rough treatment by my forces, Miss Erghamer. These are dangerous times for a girl to be alone in these parts."

"Don't you think I know that?" she hissed and then reached to pick up her knife again. The warrior that had pinned her down placed his foot on the weapon, stopping her. "Your man attempted to relieve me of my scalp and now he's attempting to relieve me of my only weapon to protect myself," she said, then drew herself up tall and continued, "What is your name, oh great commander of such cruel, spiteful soldiers?"

The soldiers stared, wide-eyed. She assumed they were alarmed at the familiar, scolding manner with which a feral-appearing girl they had found in the wilderness was addressing their commander. Even if they could not understand the words, her tone was unmistakably disrespectful. But she did not care what they thought. What she said was just.

For his part, the commander smiled even more broadly, as if the entire thing were a delightful joke to him. Then he said, "I am Captain François-Marie Le Marchand de Lignery, Miss Erghamer. And I hear your reproach, and grant that it has merit. Henceforth I shall endeavor to control my men better."

She drew in a sharp breath at his words and sized him up again. Captain Lignery himself. He looked humble and kind, not how she would imagine a man who had been given command of the entire Ohio Country a few years ago, '56 or '57, she thought. She had heard of him, and that was something, in her isolated world. When Adam had said Lignery would be looking for him, she had thought the young man possessed an extremely bloated sense of self-importance.

"You will forgive me, Miss Erghamer, but in these dangerous times, I cannot leave a woman alone in the forest. I will need to take you under my protection."

"You mean take me prisoner," she retorted.

"I suppose, but a prisoner of Captain Lignery is always protected. No harm will come to you."

"I would prefer to return to my home."

"I am afraid I cannot allow it. If you know we are passing, you may choose to warn others, and that could be disastrous for my forces. We cannot allow you freedom after seeing us. But . . . perhaps you have seen another French soldier out here in these woods? We are only patrolling now looking for a deserter."

"I know where your deserter is."

A strange expression flitted across the captain's face, a mixture of relief and dread. There was something important about Adam to this great captain, that much she could tell. This prisoner of hers meant something. He could yet be useful for her.

"And if you agree to let me go, I will give him to you," she said, enjoying having the upper hand.

Lignery's face took on a strained expression. He spoke to several of the men around him in French; then he turned back to her, spreading his hands wide. "If you can indeed lead us to our deserter, then I can promise you freedom in exchange for him."

"An easy trade." She knelt and busily gathered what she could salvage of her berries off the grass, scooping them into her basket, staining her hands purple as they mashed in her fingers. Then, nodding her head east, she said, "Follow me," and set off into the forest.

The idea of the French knowing where she lived made her uneasy, but intuitively she felt Lignery trustworthy, and besides, she had no hope of escape, limping as she was. If she gave him Adam, he had said he would let her go free. Perhaps she would need to move somewhere else, find a separate safe haven to keep her scalp from being lifted by an enterprising young warrior that might sneak back after Lignery left. But at least she would be free to hide and defend herself in the wilderness and wait for Sofie to return.

She could almost feel the soldiers' impatience behind her as she led them back through the forest with her slow, halting gait. Her ears burned every time they murmured to each other in French or the Indian language. They laughed and she clenched her fists, reaching instinctively toward the empty sheath where her knife had been.

"They do not laugh at you, Miss Erghamer," said the soothing voice of the captain behind her.

She turned, meeting his gaze with her head raised at what she imagined was a proud, haughty angle. He smiled back, a smile that reminded her of her own father, though this war-hardened man could not have looked more different from her bearded, plump, rosy-cheeked German papa. "I didn't think they were laughing at me."

"Then why did your shoulders become so rigid, and your ears turn so pink, and why did you reach for your knife? My ears may be a little dull from many years of listening to gunshots at close range, Miss Erghamer, but my eyes are as sharp as they were when I was your age."

"It was just a sound I heard. You have to be ready at any time out here. Ready for anything. There are wolves, bears. The moose are quite aggressive too."

She could tell that she had failed to convince him. He was shrewd, this French captain. She found herself considering again why such an important commander would bother to come out with a patrol looking for one deserter.

He had called Adam a deserter as well, which raised the possibility that Adam had not been lying about taking that message to the British. She dismissed that thought from her head as soon as it presented itself. It was Adam's fault that she was in this predicament, a captive of Lignery when she should be free. It was Adam's fault that she lived so far from civilization, and she still felt fiercely that it was Adam's fault that her parents were dead. He had been there, after all, among the soldiers that killed them, and she was not about to grant him any dispensations on her judgment.

"How long have you lived alone out here?" asked the captain.

"I have not been alone for long," Lidia admitted bitterly. She had already come up with a lie that mixed in enough truth to make it plausible. "I lived with my parents here before. We had moved here from German Flatts, in the Mohawk Valley. Two winters ago we went back to spend the Christmas holiday with our extended family." She glanced back at the captain and saw a gleam of understanding in his eyes. He had heard of the attack. "My parents died when your troopers attacked German Flatts, surprising families of peaceful farmers, and I was left to fend for myself. I came back here to live."

"I'm sorry for the loss of your family. German Flatts was . . . a truly horrible attack, little better than a massacre. It has left a scar on the Mohawk Valley and on all who were there." He didn't speak again for some time, finally breaking the silence to say, "I am still impressed that you have managed to survive in this wilderness alone for so long. You are a fierce young woman. My own wife is brave, and strong, and more than twice your age, but I don't think even she could survive as you have, out here alone."

Lidia swelled her chest out with pride, even though he

praised her for only a partial truth. She led the soldiers along the dry creekbed, through the sweltering heat of the afternoon, and finally to Will and Sofie's cave, nestled in the ledge wall of the ravine. Here she saw again the captain's admiration of the resourcefulness of her family. But the flicker of appreciation on his countenance was brief. He seemed anxious and distracted, and though she had only known him for an hour, she felt that his distraction was probably uncharacteristic.

Lidia pulled the door wide, a shaft of light falling on Adam, still prone—the only position in which he could find comfort, trussed as he was with his elbows hooked over the crossbeam behind his back and his hands bound in front. He looked toward her with eyes full of urgency, and she felt a pang of guilt at his dry lips and feverish glow. She had been away too long. She might at least have left the chamber pot and some water near him; even a murderer deserved that.

One of Lignery's officers pushed past Lidia, followed by a few other soldiers, the Indian warriors hanging back. The officer went straight to Adam, yanking him to his feet and striking him hard across the face. When the unsteady youth toppled and fell under the blow, the officer began kicking him repeatedly, screaming profanities in French.

"*Arrête-toi, Caporal*!" cried Lignery, and the corporal stepped back. The captain moved forward, not speaking, and Lidia watched as Adam rolled over to look up at Lignery, defiance on a face that had been meek and apathetic before. They exchanged a few words in French. Lidia did not understand what they said, but suddenly Lignery drew his saber and she lunged forward instinctively to stop him. A soldier blocked her path. With a swift stroke, Lignery sliced the rope holding Adam to the peg in the stone wall and then cut the hobbles around his ankles. Adam did not even flinch.

Lignery turned from the deserter to the heap of bloody garments Sofie had removed from Adam. The captain began digging through the justaucorps, checking every pocket, reaching inside the dark blue cuff, finally tearing out some of the lining as he became more frenzied. The corporal, who had taken Adam in hand, slammed the young man against the wall, loudly screaming at him again in French.

"What are you looking for?" asked Lidia, stepping forward to intervene as the corporal raised his hand to strike Adam again. It was instinctive, again, and she didn't like that instinct to protect the bound youth, but it was what Sofie would have done.

"The letter. The deserter was carrying a letter. Perhaps you've seen it?" asked the captain.

Adam clamped his mouth tightly shut and for an instant his eyes met Lidia's. She was sure he was going to tell the captain that another woman had taken the letter. That the other woman was going to warn the British, information that might make the captain more inclined to be lenient in his sentencing of the deserter. But Adam said nothing and received another series of blows from the brutal corporal.

Lignery raised his hand to stop the corporal, a warning look in his eyes though he kept his gaze trained on Lidia.

"I don't know—" Lidia started and then suddenly thought better of it. "Oh! There was a letter, yes. I forgot. It was written in French. I couldn't read it, so I just used it to start a cooking fire a few nights back. The night I found your deserter."

Lignery studied her intently; she could almost feel him

weighing out whether or not to believe her. After a moment his shoulders relaxed, though she fancied there was still a gleam of distrust in his expression. He issued orders to his troopers, who allowed Adam to slide his stockinged feet into his shoes before they roughly shoved him toward the door. Lidia stepped aside, though there was a strange twisting in her gut, an unexpected trepidation. What did it matter what happened to this French boy? She had been intent on killing him herself only three days before, and now he was being marched outside, likely to be hanged from a tree nearby in an efficient military execution. The prospect shouldn't have made her stomach curl into knots. He was nothing, nobody —he was an enemy, and one of those involved in her parents' deaths. But the churning of her abdomen only worsened as she tried to convince herself it shouldn't be there.

As they marched Adam past her, the corporal who had beaten the deserter so viciously grabbed her arm and pushed her toward the door as well. She spun and raised her fist to strike him.

"Leave me alone. You have your prisoner," she snapped.

"You really think *le capitaine* is going to leave you here, after what you've seen?" sneered the corporal in surprisingly intelligible English.

Lidia turned toward Lignery, who was bringing up the rear of the troops as they filed out of her house. He wore a dejected expression and almost looked as if he had forgotten her entirely.

"You said I would be free if I gave you your prisoner," said Lidia, her voice raised, as if daring him to go back on his word.

Captain Lignery sighed. "Yes, free, Miss Erghamer, after the region of Niagara is secured for France. Right now it would not be safe to leave you here. You must travel with us for the time being. When the fighting is over you can return to your home in peace."

"That's not what you said!"

"I'm sorry to have been misleading, *mademoiselle*. Now come, we've wasted enough time and cannot tarry any longer here. We have a long way to go yet."

"You lied!"

A man, one of the horse soldiers, appeared at the door, speaking rapidly in French. Captain Lignery paused and issued a few clipped orders, and the soldier disappeared. The captain turned and scanned Lidia with a look of disappointment. "Am I the only one who lied? My Mississauga scouts have found tracks of a horse leading away from here, they say it was likely mounted. Did you indeed burn the message that the boy was carrying, or did it find a new courier?"

She closed her mouth tightly.

The captain shook his head, his lips drawn tight. "Miss Erghamer, you can come along peacefully and no one will harm you, or you can march tied like a common prisoner."

Lidia paused for less than a second; she had already known the choice Lignery was going to give her, and she had already decided what her response would be. She launched herself onto the captain, fancying that she took not only him but also all of his soldiers by surprise as well, knocking him off-balance so that he stumbled, barely catching himself as she pummeled him with her fists. In a moment, strong arms came at her from every side, restraining her and tearing her off the captain, who dusted himself off and straightened his white justaucorps.

"Very well, then," he said, and gave quiet orders in French to his soldiers.

Within a few minutes they had bent her elbows around a thick pole that ran behind her back and tied her wrists tightly in front of her, the same way she had trussed her own prisoner. The corporal gave her a rough shove but Lignery rebuked him sharply. After a brief discussion with his soldiers, Lignery turned to the bound young woman.

"I am sorry you chose this way, Lidia. My men have orders not to harm you, and rest assured, they will be punished if they do. You march in the back with the deserter, under the guard of this corporal. And, as I promised, when the fighting is over, you will be free, either to return here alone or to go anywhere else you would prefer."

A few moments later, after the indignity of watching the soldiers loot all the stores of food and what few valuables Sofie and Will possessed, Lidia found herself trudging along in the back of the column of soldiers, alongside Adam, her ankle aching with every step. She watched, biting her lip, as the horse soldiers left the remainder of the group, setting off into the forest along the trail her sister had disappeared down a few nights before. She glanced at Adam. He was pale and sweating, and there was fresh blood staining his bandage again, his wound doubtless reopened by the corporal's blows. But he had a new, dogged determination about him and marched without complaint.

During the hike back toward Lake Erie, using the creekbed as a path, the corporal took the liberty of cutting a sharp switch from a sapling and using it to whip Adam around the legs and across his shoulders and back anytime the youth seemed to flag. Lidia winced when the birch sapling left angry red welts across Adam's shirt, exposing his still sickly pale skin, but Adam did not cry out. He seemed determined to show no response at all, keeping his eyes trained ahead, slowly and methodically plodding forward. As they neared the lake, the path became rougher, plagued with large boulders, and slippery from water. At one point Adam, clearly exhausted, tripped and—unable to catch himself—fell, landing face-first with a faint groan. This was the opportunity the corporal must have been looking for, because he immediately leaped forward, laying into Adam, flogging him hard with the sapling as Adam tried, with little effect, to protect himself—making himself small and bringing his shoulders up around his ears, keeping his face pressed toward the ground. The corporal screamed insults at the boy in French as he beat him and the troops ahead of them disappeared around a bend.

"Stop it!" cried Lidia, surprising herself as she lunged forward to place herself between the corporal and his victim. The officer was breathing heavily, dripping sweat, his face red from exertion. "Why do you torture him? He's going to be executed anyway—let him have his last few minutes or hours in peace."

"Executed?" repeated the corporal with an incredulous expression on his face. He tossed back his head and let out a loud guffaw. "He's not going to be executed. He won't even be court-martialed. He tried to kill me and deserted, he's a traitor, but he will face no consequences. You think Lignery will execute his own son?"

"His son?" replied Lidia in bewilderment, looking back and forth between Adam and the corporal. "Adam-Constant Regnant de Montréal is Lignery's son?"

"Regnant de Montréal?" laughed the corporal, shoving Lidia to the side to get at Adam, who was struggling to rise. He spat on the young deserter and kicked him directly over the wound in his flank, a look of pure delight spreading across the man's broad face as Adam turned whiter still, gasping in pain. "Is that what he told you his name is? Just a commoner from Montreal? Pah, dog! This is Adam-Constant Le Marchand de Lignery, Captain Lignery's oldest son. Though the apple, in this case, could not have fallen further from the tree!"

6

SOFIE

~

September 23, 1758
The Light home

It wasn't often that Sofie got angry. She had believed her whole life that anger was a sin, punishable by God, but, even more than that, she felt that anger was a terrible waste. Anger used energy that could be spent on a thousand other things—energy that was desperately needed to survive in the harsh wilderness of America. But that morning in early autumn when Will slipped from their bed and began dressing, she glared at him as if her expression could burn a hole through his back. After a while, finding that he did not respond to her unspoken rage, she sat up and fumbled for the flint. It took a few minutes, but she did manage to light a candle that sat upon the polished stump that served as a bedside table.

As the candlelight sputtered, she glanced toward her sister, asleep on a straw mattress in the corner. Lidia's face, usually so contorted, expressing her every flash of anger and bitterness, was smooth and peaceful, unaware of her sister's ire. It made Sofie even more angry to see her usually passionate sister so blissfully unaware of her own distress. She had been simmering in her anger for almost a month, ever since Will had first begun to talk in his slow, musing way, of joining the British Army—as if it wasn't a serious thought at all, just an idle, flickering fancy.

The first time he had mentioned leaving had been three weeks before—or perhaps it wasn't the first time he had said something about it, but it was the first time she had noticed. Will had a way of talking and telling stories in a meandering fashion, and sometimes Sofie lost the thread of his thoughts before he finished his tales. There were times when she wasn't paying attention; she admitted that, and tried to do better. So the first day she remembered him mentioning anything about it was three weeks before. He had been standing outside with his shirt off, his red beard plastered to his sweaty chest, right foot planted on a hefty log that had so far evaded his efforts to split it. He was chewing idly on a thin splinter. It was the beauty of his stance and his muscled, heaving chest that had caught Sofie's eye, making her pause in the midst of laundering linens in the creek to admire her handsome husband.

Then he had said it: "You know . . . I did meet some of them militia men when I was up trading by Fort Ligonier. Some of those men said they seen what happened at Fort William Henry, described it to me. In detail. Men, women, children, massacred in broad daylight while the French looked on. No one raised a finger, they said. They just let it go on and on. Murdering children, Sofie."

She had shook her head, turning her attention away from his muscular body to the words he was forming. "How awful," she said in a breathy voice, though she wasn't thinking of anything awful just then; she was thinking about how far away Lidia was, and if there might not be time for a little further exploration of what lay beneath Will's breeches.

"That and what happened to your parents and Lidia, Sofie, all that . . . I'd say it's about gotten me fired up. When I think of what might happen if you had a little one and someone dashed its head against a rock . . . that's what they described to me. Women screaming and trying to tear their babies back from heartless killers . . . when they said all that, well, I just . . ." He trailed off.

Sofie had opened her mouth then to share with him that she had missed her last bleeding and there would perhaps be a little one by this time next year. That good news would put him in the mood for a bit of love-making, she thought, but she was cut off before she could tell him.

"You know, Sofie, they're looking for translators, scouts, guides. The British Army, that is. They pay decent too. I heard maybe as much as two pounds a month."

"Oh?" she had replied lamely. She didn't know what else to say. But since that day a thousand things had come into her mind that she should have said, and that she now meant to say, and loudly, that morning in late September as Will put on his patched wool coat, preparing to leave and join the British Army.

As Will swung his pack over his shoulders and reached for his tricorn hat, she slid out of bed. Miraculously, Lidia still did not stir. Will leaned down to kiss Sofie as she approached, but she shoved him away. That one act of power, fierce and defiant, filled her with a heady, buzzed warmth, like one would have after too much *Glühwein* over Christmas libations. The sensation of power and strength dulled as her husband drew back with a hurt expression on his face, his brow wrinkling.

"I'm leaving the musket here with you," he said.

"You're leaving your wife alone in the wilderness and going off to die," replied Sofie. It didn't sound the way she had imagined it. It sounded practiced and stilted. It was practiced and stilted—she had murmured those words to herself dozens of times over the last few weeks. She too felt rage and despair when she learned of the massacres that occurred upon British settlers moving west, but she felt the same rage when Haudenosaunee people were massacred, and the French, and the Canadians. It was all a bloody mess out there, and she had long ago given up ascribing any moral authority to one side over another. Things would always be terrible, as long as the British and the French continued their relentless war over territory that was never theirs to begin with. But the horrific atrocities taking place beyond their doors did not mean Will should sacrifice his own life to try to fight on whatever side he thought was the most righteous. It was not their battle. She had hoped that living with her, a faithful follower of Christ who believed in turning the other cheek and practicing a way of nonviolence, would temper his warlike urges. Yet here they were, three years into their marriage, with him about to go out the door to fight and kill, going against everything that he knew his wife believed.

"Sofie, we've talked about this."

"No, we haven't!" Sofie snapped back, her voice rising. Lidia shifted in her sleep and Sofie took Will's elbow and pushed him out the door, shutting it behind them and moving away down the gully in the predawn gloom. "*You've* talked about this, Will," she hissed. "I haven't said my piece. Not once have you let me say my piece."

"I asked you a dozen times how you felt. You said I should do whatever I believe is right."

"And what you believe is right is abandoning your wife and going off to war to murder people and be killed? You think my father would have consented to your request for my hand if he knew you would just abandon me within the first three years of our marriage?"

"I believe it's right to fight back against the French, Sofie. And you, of all people, should understand that. They killed your father, Sofie, and your mother. They're taking over our country."

"My parents wouldn't want you, or anyone else, going off to kill in memory of them. They believed in peace, Will, and the love of God that can transcend evil, that can transcend violence and hatred. He who kills by the sword will die by it, that's what they would have told you if they heard you talking the way you are."

"Sofie . . ." Will trailed off. There was a mix of surprise, anger, and resolve on his face. The horse above them in the paddock let out a snuffling sound and pawed at the dirt. "I ain't leaving you alone, Sofie, your sister is here."

"My sister whose mind was practically shattered by nearly being killed—"

"By the French! All the more reason for us to fight back! It's a miracle you didn't lose her along with your parents that day! If we don't fight back, how many more peaceful settlements'll be ravaged? How many more children and women and farmers'll be killed? I've got to go, Sofie. If we ever have children, how can I stand before them and tell them that when our people were under attack, when our country was in a war, I just stood by and did nothing, hiding in a ravine in the middle of nowhere?"

"We won't have a child if you're dead, Will!"

He stared back at her, his gray eyes wide. Their panting breaths blew billowing clouds of mist into the crisp early-fall air. She had seen that look of his before, though not often, his jaw clenched, the little vein on his forehead jutting out. Stubborn ass.

"If I'm a coward, then I don't deserve a child, Sofie, and I don't deserve you," replied Will softly, and then he set his tricorn hat firmly upon his head and turned toward the paddock, leaving his wife staring after him with tears of impotent rage streaming down her cheeks.

~

July 19, 1759
Sixty miles south of Fort Niagara

SOFIE HAD LET THAT MEMORY PLAY IN HER HEAD A THOUSAND times, maybe more, since the day Will had gone away, the last day she had seen him. Each time she saw the scene again in her mind, she came up with new things she ought to have said, either contrite pleas for him to stay or angry, snappy retorts. It depended on her mood and on how much she was missing him when the memory came to her. There had been times during the cold winter months while the baby grew steadily inside her that she had regretted everything.

Perhaps, she thought, if she had been softer, kinder, more understanding, he never would have left. They were both the same; that was the great flaw in their union. Mr. and Mrs. Light, they were both slow to anger, but once they boiled over they were equally unforgiving, stubborn, and fixed in their ideas. That day as she rode through the forest with her baby on her back, she thought briefly of all the things she wished she had said, then she shook her head. She didn't need to say all those things. Will knew. He knew she hated war; he knew she didn't believe in violence. He knew how much she abhorred killing, and still he had gone, and she hated him for that. She didn't even know if he was alive. He had sent no letters, nor any of his pay home; there had been nothing from him since the day he rode away.

The baby began to cry, forcing her focus back to the present, to their journey along the winding deer trails, ever northward. The first two days of travel had been pleasant enough. There was plenty of water, berries, and *Pfifferlinge* enough to keep a woman full, without even breaking into the supplies of dried porcupine meat and cornbread cakes she had packed. She turned the horse's head toward a slow stream trickling to their left. The gelding was a reliable animal, used to being pushed by scouts and couriers through the vast untamed land surrounding Lake Erie. She let him plunge his lips into the creek while she dismounted, her feet splashing in the wet sand and rocks, her legs wobbly beneath her. Attaching one long rein to a branch, she undid the cradleboard on her back and swung it to the ground.

The little boy looked up at her with a pathetic affect. His blue eyes were teary, wrinkles running across his forehead, his bottom lip quivering. He had just the faintest dusting of soft strawberry-blonde hair, his cheeks were pudgy, and his arms creased with folds. She was proud of his size. She wanted him to stay plump—it would increase his chances of survival. He was going to be big, that she could tell, like his father. She lifted him out and held him against her chest, soothing him while she undid the buttons on her waistcoat and shirt and pressed him to her bosom. He was so distraught it took him a few frustrated attempts before at last he latched on and calmed. Even then he was unusually fussy, and she noticed with trepidation how warm his body was against hers, as if she were holding a bundle of hot coals.

"There, there, little one, I'm sorry," she whispered, swaying to rock him. "I'm so sorry." She kissed the top of his head, right on his precious soft fontanel. Still he fussed, eating, then bawling, then eating again, his pale face turning lobster red from his sobs.

Feeding the son Will didn't know he had was when she most hated Will, and most loved him at the same time. She hadn't named the child yet. She was waiting for his father to return. When his father came back they could pick a name for him. In the meantime she crooned diminutives at him in German, English, French, Oneida, Seneca, and Mohawk. He did not seem to mind these sweet appellations, nor that he had no name of his own. One didn't need a name to be a person; one only needed the love of another, and his mother loved him more than she loved life. He began to scream again, and this time nothing she did soothed him.

"*Mon chou, mon petit chou. Së:nöh ëhsasdaëh he:awak. Ta'sa:je:h.*" She began pacing with him. "*Ganz ruhig, mein Kind, ganz ruhig.*" He only wailed louder, and he was hot, and they were two days from Lidia and home, two long, hard days of riding. After an hour of trying to calm him, searching him for anything that would tell her the source of his distress—a rash, a mark, a bruise, anything—but finding nothing, she finally changed his napkin, secured him back in the cradleboard, mounted the horse, who was spooked by the sobbing child, and rode on. The baby screamed for hours, his body like a flame against her back, and finally, exhausted and whimpering, he fell asleep as the sun set.

Still Sofie pushed on, consumed by guilt, unsure what else she could do.

That night the summer air was full of mosquitoes and the noise of a million cicadas, katydids, chorus frogs, late peepers, and bullfrogs, and other more haunting cries. There were moments she startled from near-sleep at the dirgelike screech of a fox, or the inquisitive hoots of an owl. Twice that night she heard the sound of something large crashing through the trees and bushes, a bull moose or a bear. The gelding would have spooked more but he was too exhausted. She had no idea what time it was when at last she dismounted and set up a makeshift little camp, unsaddling and highlining the horse. Again the baby woke and cried, barely suckling at all. It filled her with dread when he fell silent, still hot, his fontanel dipping in the middle in an alarming manner. She stretched out on her stomach on her bedroll, resting her chin on her folded hands, staring at the infant, nestled among his blankets in a cradle of tree roots. She wished he had kept crying; at least then she would know he yet had some fight and strength in him. She watched him breathing, eventually falling asleep to the uneven rise and fall of his tiny chest.

She woke to her baby sobbing again in the middle of the night, his voice weaker this time. He was also intermittently coughing, a coarse hacking sound. His breathing had worsened; his body was trembling, and his lips and tongue were dry—so horribly dry. She picked him up and held him close, pacing slowly as he coughed and patting his back. As she carried him, Sofie searched in the darkness for some herb to make a plaster for his chest.

Despite her attempts to quell the ugly thoughts, the way her son looked brought back memories of the Others. She didn't think of them often, but this was the first time—and perhaps would also be the last—that her son had been sick, and she couldn't help but remember them. The images of their tiny faces filled her mind. She had been the oldest, and Lidia the youngest, but between the two sisters there had been the Others. She had watched them, helped her mother care for them, and loved them until they died. Now she felt sure that she too would lose one of hers, perhaps more as well, but this one would live only in her memory; her husband, if he was still alive, would never know the son he had given her. She alone would carry the grief of his loss when he died, like all the little Others.

Her mother had waited to name each of them too, and only three of her mother's children had lived long enough to have names—herself, Lidia, and Martin. She remembered Martin well, only about a year younger than herself. Sickly though he was, Martin had lived. He had been her playmate, her friend, and her worst enemy at times, until he was five and she was six, then she had held his hand as he coughed, breathing like her baby was now, hot as the sun itself, until his breathing stopped and he was gone, just like all the Others. That had been their first year in the New World, the place they had finally settled. A place that was at last supposed to accept the relentlessly persecuted Palatine Germans.

She blamed the harshness of this country for the loss of her little brother. But she blamed herself as well. She had always believed, as she had been taught, that a truly Christlike person would pray and God would answer. With childlike faith she had prayed for each of the Others, especially Martin. But God had not intervened, and with the logic of a child, she could only assume that Martin's death was because of her own lack of faith, her own lack of goodness. She had carried that shame with her ever since, that sense of guilt. The knowledge that she had not the faith Jesus spoke of in the Bible that could move mountains. Reason and maturity had dulled this sensibility, but not eradicated it. There was still a part of her that felt that if she could just attain true goodness, if she could just embrace true virtue and excise from herself all that was evil, then perhaps she could save those she loved, even when they were deathly ill. But she was a violent, hateful person, she felt that keenly. She remembered how only a few days before she had lashed out instinctively against her own sister. No, she would never attain the kind of virtue and faith that could move mountains, or save an ailing child.

She shuddered at the old, half-buried memories of the Others, of her little brother. No one remembered Martin anymore, because her mama and her papa, who had adored their little son, were both dead. She alone remembered Martin, and no one else ever would. They died. Children just died in the New World. She supposed little ones died in the Old World as well—several of the Others had died there —but Martin had died in America, in German Flatts. It seemed more of the babies died than lived in this harsh land. So Sofie had not named the baby in her arms. She remembered Martin best, because he was older, because he had a name. The Others were blurry, less fiercely painful, and she felt that was because they had never been given names. Perhaps she could forget her own little one when sickness took him because he had no name. His memory would not be so vivid and heartbreaking as Martin's memory still was, all these years later.

She walked with her son until he fell asleep again, intermittently coughing still, but sleeping. As the first pale light blossomed in the east, she found herself on a green, grassy knoll, standing before a quiet, chuckling spring that trailed off down the hill in a tumultuous though tiny waterfall. A tall jutting gray stone, spangled with quartz, rose up from the center of the pool above the waterfall. The long grass stretched down into the water, and the ripples gently tugged on the tendrils of emerald, as if trying to encourage the green blades to join the water on its voyage.

Exhausted, Sofie paused and then, biting her lip, she stepped into the cool, flowing water, letting it pull at her stockings and breeches and fill her shoes. A mist hovered over the forest, stretching in pale, ephemeral fronds into the distance. She faced east as the gray light faded into pink, and the dark blue sky ripened to peach and purple tones. A beam of light cast itself across the land as the piercing brightness of the sun rose, setting the dew and mist sparkling like a million twinkling stars. The water around her ankles shimmered and turned to gold.

She reached down and scooped up a handful of water from the pool, letting the dazzling droplets fall slowly on the infant's face, still and peaceful upon her chest. As the water drops touched him, she whispered a name, a name for the baby she had brought into the world and treasured for three months. It was just a phrase in Seneca she had learned some months before from a hunting party, not a proper name at all, but a beautiful phrase. It would be his name for as long as the Almighty let her keep him, a secret, precious name that only his mother would ever know. She whispered again, "*Eodi'nigoiyo-ak.*" *Their minds will be at peace*. When he died she would remember him, and remember him by his name, though no one else in the world would ever know it.

Back at her camp, Sofie saddled the gelding, who was rested and calm. She attempted to nurse the infant a few more times, her breasts sore and swollen, but he took only a few drops from each nipple, and then fell asleep again, his strength exhausted by the fever and the hacking cough. A rash had broken out all across his body, marring his pale skin with red, angry papules, disfiguring her perfect, lusty infant. She wished he would wake up and fight again, and cry with that terrifically loud, undeniable voice of his. Repressing the horrible thought that it was her fault that he was not fighting anymore, her fault that he wouldn't make it to the first anniversary of his birth, she gently packed him into the cradleboard, kissed his head a dozen times, fixed him to her back and mounted the horse again, to press on, further into the punishing wilderness of the New World.

~

July 20, 1759
Forty miles south of Fort Niagara

THEY CONTINUED TRAVELING, ALONG WINDING TRAILS THAT all seemed to blend together with the forest floor, faint traces of dirt barely visible beneath the clustered poison ivy, mayapples, plantain, and five-leaf ivy. Sofie had lost track of the distance they had gone. The infant had not cried for hours, but she willed herself not to think about that.

She did not know exactly where they were. She had been trying to keep to a route that skirted the great falls, passing instead through thick, clustered fens and marshland, where bogs threatened to betray their every step and drown her horse in their bottomless depths, a place where no trail showed the way. She had pressed on through the hot, sweltering days and had become the unwilling sustenance of thousands of bloodsucking mosquitoes and biting gnats. Every moment was heavy with dread at how far she still had to go. She was haunted by the fear that she had already missed her brief opportunity to warn the British, and perhaps her child would die for naught.

Lost in these dark thoughts—lost in guilt for daring this adventure with a child too young to consent to such a risk, and clearly too young and fragile to bear it—she hardly noticed the horse become skittish beneath her. She instinctively pushed him on with her feet, squeezing her calves against his flanks, but, despite her urgings, he continued shifting and stopping, ears twitching, then pinning down to his neck while his nostrils flared. When he spooked for the third time, even waking the sleeping infant, Sofie roused herself to attention. Surely the placid gelding could not have become so distressed because of his rider's melancholy. She glanced up, scanning the thick forest around her, broad oaks and spreading maples crowded among pines and shrubs. There were flies buzzing around, harrying the poor horse, and incessant mosquitoes, biting at all three of them. The baby wailed suddenly, with a voice that was almost strong, a voice that gave her hope, though she tried to brush that away—best not to get her expectations up. Dashed hopes left a terrible abyss behind them.

Then she saw it, the reason the horse was spooked. A flash of looming, hazel eyes, with slitted pupils, hidden among the dense underbrush, and a tawny coat of fur moving behind the thick green leaves. She did not wait. The infant cried as Sofie drove her heels into the horse's flanks, over and over again. The gelding took off through the forest, running like madness. She heard the yowl of the mountain lion but did not look back, crouching as low as she could to assist the horse as it maneuvered among the trees.

The branches whipped at them, striking her face so hard she felt the sting of her flesh tearing. She thought at any moment she would miss ducking and a great maple bough would tear her and her child from the saddle and hurl them to the ground, all but defenseless against the cruel mountain lion. When at last she dared to throw a glance over her shoulder, there was no sign of the beast. They lost interest, sometimes—that was the only saving grace of being pursued by mountain lions, though at other times they stalked and hunted prey for days on end. Will had told her that. They would follow a trapper as he moved through the streams and ponds checking his traps, until finally he was lulled into a false sense of complacency, and then the monster would strike.

The forest grew too close to keep the gelding safely at a lope, and Sofie slowed him to a quick walk, still pushing him all that day with everything she had. The baby stopped crying again, and her guilt rose up, threatening to swallow her very soul. He did not cry anymore, though she could feel him moving in the cradleboard at times. It was nearing dusk when the piercing pain in her own breasts finally forced her to stop and make a semblance of a camp. She had thus far only started small, wispy fires, but knowing the mountain lion might yet be out there in the forest, she took the risk of another person seeing her and built an enormous blaze to frighten the animal away. She piled sticks and bracken near her bedroll, to nourish the fire through the night, and set the loaded musket on her other side.

Sofie tried with some encouraging success to feed the infant, who looked horribly dry. He took more than he had at the previous few feedings but had to be awakened intermittently and reminded of the nipple in his mouth. Finally she set him down and he quickly drifted off. She cooked her last few *Pfifferlinge* over the licking flames and ate them greedily, along with the last of the dried porcupine meat. Then she heaped enough logs on the fire to keep it blazing for at least a few hours. As she lay down, her exhausted gaze flitted around the camp and the trees, every movement of shadow caused by the play of the fire becoming a lion prowling toward its prey. But she was too tired to stay awake.

~

July 21, 1759. Early morning.
Twenty-five miles south of Fort Niagara

THE COALS HAD BECOME BLACK STONES GLOWING WITH BRIGHT red edges when she awakened with a start to the yowling of the mountain lion. She leaped up, grabbing at the branches and sticks she had piled near her and throwing them into the coals, creating a burst of smoke and sparks like the eruption of Vesuvius. The horse reared and neighed madly, and then came a terrible crashing. She lunged forward, calling out, “Wait, wait! Easy, boy, you’re all right!” but it was too late. The gelding broke free of his highline and an instant later he was gone, the sound of him thundering away in frantic terror quickly fading in the darkness.

Sofie spun to see the prowling mountain lion making toward her infant, who was just beginning to awaken. Snatching up one of the burning branches, she thrust it at the animal, driving the predator back from the child as smoke and sparks filled the air. The lion turned its attention upon her, howling and slashing with enormous claws that flashed in the firelight. Baring its fangs, the mountain lion lunged, but she drove it back with the fiery branch again, catching hold of the musket as she passed it in her advance.

She had seconds, not minutes, she knew that. There was no time to think, no time to plan, just time to act. She ran forward again, shouting and waving the branch at the mountain lion, and it backed away, giving her the seconds she needed, the space between them to drop to one knee and raise the musket. The lion yowled again and the child behind her was screaming, and then the lion was rushing at her again—but she had the musket trained on him. She exhaled and time seemed almost to freeze as the cougar pounced and she squeezed the trigger. The animal landed on her, knocking her to the ground, and she flailed madly, angrily. The child was screaming and she couldn't leave him to die alone. But the mountain lion did not fight back. It was a dead weight. She slid the creature off her as she drew in gasping, shaky, horrified breaths.

She had shot true. The predator was dead. But the horse was gone and the flames threatened to set the dry forest around her alight. Her infant was screaming for his mother, screaming to be held. Sofie sat there, staring at the chaos for a moment, wanting to laugh and cry all at the same time. Exhausted and battered, she climbed to her feet and set to making things right. She beat the fire back down and scattered the coals, reloaded her musket, and suckled her sick child. It was not yet dawn when she had her son bundled on her back again in the cradleboard. She packed her blanket roll, the saber, and the nearly empty canteen, and rested the heavy musket against her shoulder. Looking for the saddlebag that had contained what little food she had left, she found it burned to a cinder and kicked it aside. There was no food, and no horse, and she had at least twenty miles left to go, by her estimation.

As the dim light of dawn began to glow far to the east, Sofie found herself ready to set off on foot, for the last leg of her journey. That was when she heard the distant sound of a horse's neigh, clanking metal, and voices carrying through the forest. For a moment her heart leaped with hope, but then she recognized the words were not English; they were speaking French. They would find her encampment, and they would find her and her baby, and that would be the end of her mission, the end of any chance of warning the British soldiers, of warning Will. Swallowing hard, her heart pattering in her chest, she glanced down at the chaos of her camp and then back at the dark forest surrounding her. She squared her shoulders, and then Sofie Light, housewife, farmer, seamstress, mother, and slayer of lions, turned north and began to run.

7

ADAM

~

July 20, 1759
Eighty miles south of Fort Niagara

"This is Adam-Constant Le Marchand de Lignery, Captain Lignery's oldest son. Though the apple, in this case, could not have fallen further from the tree!"

Adam, curled in a ball from the agony of the kick to his wound, glimpsed the girl's expression of confusion, followed a split second later by one of rage. Why was the girl angry that he hadn't told her his real name? Did he owe her his real name? He had been a prisoner. He had every right to keep secret the fact that he was Lignery's son. To be the son of the commander of the entire Ohio Country was to be a target. He really had only the faintest memory of telling her a name at all, in the midst of his delirium. Yet she looked at him now as if he had betrayed her, as if he were an absolute scoundrel for lying to her. She stood back as though to let the corporal at him again. Apparently his one mistake was enough to cost him the brief protection she had offered.

The corporal began kicking him repeatedly, every boot thud sending lancing agony through Adam's body. Renaud wore a grin like a child with a new toy as he drove his foot into Adam's side and back, anywhere he could reach. Adam was tired and allowed himself to disassociate from the pain, letting his reflections wash over him, the same way the beatings did.

It was pathetic how predictable Renaud's behavior was now that he could punish Adam indiscriminately. He was a common bully, nothing more. He had always hated Adam but had little justification to lay a hand on him before. Now that Adam was at his mercy, he was relentless in his beatings. Finally the corporal who had nothing could lord over a man who was in every social distinction higher than him, though his military ranking was lower. Adam obstinately refused to give Renaud the satisfaction of hearing him cry out, though the pain in his right side was becoming unbearable. He found that focusing on that relentless, tearing pain in the old wound helped him to ignore the added stings of the corporal's hickory switch and the thumping blows of the man's boots. Adam settled back into the dull apathy that had gotten him this far.

"*Arrête-toi, Caporal!*" came the familiar, deep voice of his father, cutting through the haze of agony into which Adam was losing all sense of consciousness.

Adam rolled over as the blows stopped raining down on him. He squinted up at his father, who was on horseback—that ruddy mare he liked so much, lots of spirit that animal had, like the German girl; both were always upset and spooking over something. They were both all reaction, no calm, no pause to take in the situation and formulate a rational response. They both always acted in the way Adam felt like acting around his father.

"Wouldn't want the corporal to beat me to death and lose the satisfaction of watching me dangle by the neck from a tree?"

"Adam . . ." His father glanced at the corporal. He had slipped. Captain François-Marie Le Marchand de Lignery had slipped and addressed his soldier as his son in front of another marine. He was finally cracking under the emotional strain of having such a disappointment for an offspring. "Leave us. Take the other prisoner. I'll bring the deserter," Lignery ordered the corporal, who bowed and stepped away, pushing the girl ahead of him.

Adam could almost see his father restraining the overpowering urge to dismount and help him up.

"Perhaps you'd like to take a few shots yourself?" prompted Adam.

"Shut up, Adam. You know I would like nothing better than to untie you and set you free. Do you have any idea what a position you've put me in?"

"If you'd like to untie me, then why don't you?"

"Because I know you, Adam, or have you forgotten that? I know you won't run. I know you want the sublime satisfaction of torturing your father for all eternity by forcing me to give the order to have you executed. You haven't cared about living since German Flatts. But if you could haunt me forever, that would please you, wouldn't it?"

Adam grinned a little and sat up, wincing as he did so. "Did you mean what you said in the cave?"

"Of course I meant it."

"Well, if you indeed wish that I had died and little Daniel had survived his infancy instead, then I guess you're right, it does give me a little pleasure to know that I will haunt you forever."

"Then perhaps I will set you free and tell the corporal he can do whatever he wants to you when they catch you again. Wash my hands of the whole affair."

"It would still be your orders that killed me."

"You're a selfish, stubborn ass, Adam, you know that? What happens afterward won't bother you when you're dead, but those of us you leave behind will hurt forever."

"I'm sure given two or three months of tromping around in the wilderness and fighting His Majesty's endless wars, you'll have forgotten me before winter comes. But . . . whatever will you tell Mother about all this?"

Lignery bit his lip, studying his son. It was not all anger there, Adam had to admit; there was pain in his father's eyes, and not only the pain of disappointment, but the pain of having to hurt someone he loved. Adam dropped his eyes for a second, not wanting to see the brief vulnerability he had caused the hardened captain. He clenched his teeth and raised his leg, digging his heel into the ground and struggling to rise. He made it almost to his feet when he overbalanced and toppled, helpless to catch himself. But strong hands caught him and steadied him before he could fall. Distracted by his attempt to rise and his physical agony from doing so, Adam had not heard his father's rushed dismount, and suddenly he looked up to find the older man's weatherbeaten face only inches away, staring at him with those piercing hazel eyes—eyes that were mirrors of his own.

"Don't you think I've thought of that? If I let them execute you, even if I lie to your mother about how you died, she will still find out. Soldiers talk, and she will never forgive me."

"That's hardly my problem, *mon capitaine*, since I'll be dead, as you said. It won't make much difference to me."

The captain, his face stiffening a little at Adam's callous response, assisted his son to his feet. He kept his hands on Adam's shoulder when he was finally standing steady, though he was sweaty and shivering. "Why are you so bloody stubborn, boy?"

"I'll give you one guess, and it's not Mother."

The captain let out a laugh that quickly changed to a stifled sob. He caught himself though, and though his eyes were shining, he did not cry. Finally he leaned in close to Adam's ear and whispered, "Let me free you. I can tell them you overpowered me. I can tell them to push on and not hunt for you. We need to move fast if we are to maintain the element of surprise. What's one deserter in the grand scheme of the war?"

"Father, even if I wanted to, I cannot run anymore. Walking this far has almost killed me. I have no strength left."

"Take my horse. No one will question me, Adam. I am the commander of this entire force, nearly fifteen hundred men, and they all answer to me."

For an instant Adam saw the curtains pull back, saw the briefest possibility of escape, of a new life of obscurity somewhere in the vast reaches of New England; the chance to forget the past, the war, the death and horror, to live as a man reborn. Then he saw the soldiers coming back down the ravine behind his father and the curtains closed again, this time forever. There was only one path out of his predicament, and that was dangling on the end of a rope whenever his father worked up the gumption to order his execution.

"*Mon capitaine*, is everything all right?"

Lignery spun to face a small company of scouts led by a lieutenant. The captain's shoulders sagged in defeat. "Everything is fine, Lieutenant," he replied. "Have we intercepted the rest of the forces?"

The lieutenant nodded his head, still eyeing the father and son with some suspicion. "Yes, *mon capitaine*. We are just a mile from the lake. I asked them to wait there for you."

Lignery looked back at Adam and there was such sadness in his eyes that Adam felt his stomach churning with terrible remorse. An overwhelming desire for alcohol, any kind of alcohol, rose up inside him. He wouldn't care about any of this if he was drunk, least of all would he care about his father's feelings, the father who had spent most of his son's childhood away fighting wars for a king that cared nothing for the settlers across the sea.

"The prisoner is weak," said Lignery. "Barely able to stand. He cannot be marched another mile. He needs to ride."

The lieutenant nodded and dismounted, leading his horse forward. Lignery turned toward his son and switched to English, as he was well aware that the lieutenant knew none. His voice was low and desperate. "Now, Adam. Now or never."

Before he had time even to be surprised at his father's words, just following his captain's orders, like he had in every battle, Adam swung the stick he was tied to, striking his father in the abdomen. Lignery let out a groan and stumbled back, and Adam thought for a second that either his father was very good at acting, or he really had struck the older man too hard. But there wasn't time for remorse or concern for his father. He darted forward, stumbling toward the ruddy mare. It was foolishness. An exercise in futility. The animal turned tail and bolted. Within a few seconds the hopeless escape attempt was over and Adam was knocked to the ground, stunned by a blow to the head from the butt end of the lieutenant's musket.

The lieutenant yanked him roughly to his feet. Adam was reeling, waves of nausea and dizziness washing over him. "Perhaps he has a bit more marching in him, after all, *mon capitaine*, or would you like me to execute him now? He struck an officer in front of witnesses. Men have been killed on the spot for much lesser offenses."

Lignery shook his head. "No, we will not execute him now. He deserves a court-martial like any other marine trooper." He sighed and turned back toward Adam with defeat in his proud hazel eyes. "But, yes, as you say, if he has the strength to run, you may march him the last mile."

The lieutenant frowned dubiously at the deferment of Adam's execution but followed his superior's orders. He shoved Adam onward, pushing him hard and fast along the last mile of marching before they joined with Lignery's forces, moving in their boats along the shoreline of Lake Erie.

When they emerged from the ravine, it was late in the afternoon. The world had taken on a hazy sepia glow, and across the unending expanse of vibrant blue water, heat waves bounded up, distorting the sky and clouds on the horizon. From the south stretched an incredible multitude of vessels, canoes of every size imaginable, birch pirogues from Presque Isle, and enormous bateaux carrying equipment and soldiers. It was as if the lake had turned into a floating city, bigger and more lively than even Montreal. Adam paused for an instant, catching his breath at the sight as they paused on a bluff above the sandy beach. The lieutenant thrust him forward roughly and he stumbled down through the sand, still gazing in awe at the flotilla advancing toward them. Indian warriors, girded and painted for war, paddled beside hundreds of French troopers, with their white coats and cuffs of green and blue, muskets, sabers, and bayonets glinting in the sun.

His father did not look at him again. During the last mile to the lake, Adam had little time to reflect on the offer his father had made and that last desperate attempt to help him escape. It had been uncharacteristic, wildly uncharacteristic. The bold, stern commander of the Ohio had descended to the level of a common conspiratorial soldier, setting a prisoner free and pretending he wasn't involved. What on earth would prompt such a man to behave in such a way? If Adam had been just a little stronger, a little more recovered, he would have escaped, and then what? He had felt that excitement of possibilities, a feeling he had not known since his father signed his enlistment papers when he was fifteen—the excitement of life opening up for him again. But then it had been over, and there was nothing but a firing squad or a gallows awaiting him now.

He was led aboard one of the barges and shoved to the floorboards in a corner. He leaned back against a crate full of what smelled like rotting fish, and turned to his left to find the blazing eyes of the German girl glowering at him again.

"You lied to me," she said.

"*Mon dieu, femme*," he replied, sighing and closing his eyes. "*Je donnerais n'importe quoi pour un verre de rhum.*"

"I don't speak French."

"What makes you think I was talking to you?" He opened his eyes again and half-smiled at her through a face that he could feel was swollen from Renaud's blows.

"I'm the only one here, or . . . the only one listening."

"She speaks the truth," he murmured wearily.

"What's wrong with you, anyway? You do nothing but mope and jest."

"What else should I be doing?"

"I don't know. You're a papist, aren't you? Don't you people pray or do some sort of last rites before you die?"

"I shall need a priest to perform my last rites, and it seems the captain is going to let me have that honor, as he hasn't let anyone kill me yet." Adam stared out beyond the flotilla at the waves of Erie, cresting and falling and rising again, his eyes glazing over with exhaustion. "He wants to do it all correctly, all perfectly formal, I suppose, as he always does."

"If you're just going to lie there and feel sorry for yourself, then I shall talk to this barrel of dead fish instead."

Adam laughed. It surprised him, and he could see by her face that it surprised the girl as well. "Why should I have told you my correct name when you had me bound and even tortured me in your cave?"

"Tortured you?"

"Deny that you purposefully thrust your hand into my wound to cause me pain."

She opened her mouth and then bit her lip. She was an instinctively honest young woman, that much he could say. Lying did not come naturally to her; it took effort.

"Anyway," he continued, "you never even told me your name. Perhaps you would be so kind as to introduce yourself now to a simple fellow prisoner, doomed to die."

"There you go again, feeling sorry for yourself. You're very good at that. My name is Erghamer, Lidia Erghamer."

"That's lovely. I often wondered what your name was, since the day I thought I killed you."

"It takes more than a musket butt to the head to kill an

Erghamer, or a Palatine in general," she said, as if he should already know that. "We're brave, bold people."

"That I can see," he said. "Well, brave, bold Lidia Erghamer, if you'll permit me, I'd just as soon get a little rest, if I can. It appears I will survive to the gallows yet, but that last march nearly did me in."

"Suit yourself. I'll be awake, planning my escape."

"*Très bien*," he whispered as he sagged back between two enormous barrels and drifted off to the sound of the raftsmen chanting to keep time as they drove their oars into the sand.

~

July 21, 1759
Sixty miles south of Fort Niagara

ADAM AWOKE TO THE NOISE OF A STRUGGLE. IT WAS PITCH dark on their little raft, and it seemed they had come to a stop, the flotilla resting during the night somewhere close to shore. The raft Lignery was using as their prison was one of the supply boats, and aside from himself and Lidia there had been almost no one else aboard, only two laconic guards and a couple of men to row the long oars. Lignery had clearly pushed late into the night, but eventually his weary troops had won out over the indefatigable nature of their captain. The guards were asleep, the oarsmen were asleep—Adam could hear them snoring—but still the scuffling sounded beside him. He rolled over awkwardly and found Lidia struggling madly in the arms of Renaud. The big corporal had one hand clamped over the girl's mouth. She had been partially successful in loosening her bonds, setting her right fist free, and she was using it to punch Renaud repeatedly.

Ignoring the burst of agony in his right flank, Adam pushed himself up and launched head down into the corporal's abdomen. Caught completely by surprise, the corporal released the flailing, angry young woman, and toppled over the side of the boat. He grabbed hold of Adam's neck as he fell, pulling the younger man into the water with him. A resounding splash sounded and then there was nothing but bubbles and gurgling. Adam flailed, kicking his legs, his head briefly bursting up from the water. He saw Lidia running across the raft and heard her high-pitched cries for help. Then the corporal grabbed him with his enormous fists and thrust him under the lapping waves.

Adam had just enough warning to suck in a deep draft of air before the corporal pushed him under and held him down. He knew he should not fight, that he should conserve the little bit of air he had managed to store up, but the impulse to kick out and wriggle away was too strong. Adam felt his feet scrape the bottom, giving him leverage. The corporal's white breeches stood out in the dark, murky water, and he saw his opportunity. With the last bits of air burning in his lungs, bubbles flurrying about his face, he pushed up with his feet, spinning and swinging the stick he was tied to. It struck the center of the corporal's groin with a dull thwack, and Adam himself winced as Renaud released his grasp, reaching for his injured nether parts. Adam paddled his legs furiously and a moment later his head breached the water and he was gasping in great, delicious gulps of air.

Someone grabbed the stick he was bound to and dragged him back to the raft. An instant later he was on solid wooden timbers, coughing up water, panting and wheezing. There was a tumult all around him and the corporal, still purple from rage and pain, was hoisted aboard the boat as well. As soon as Renaud had caught his breath, he began shouting and cursing in French. Then a calm voice cut through the chaos.

"What is going on here?"

Adam glanced up to see his father's face among the melee, lines of worry twisting across his forehead. Adam opened his mouth to speak, but the corporal cut him off.

"They were trying to escape, sir. I tried to stop them, but the whelp knocked me in the water. You ought to kill him now, sir."

"Noted," replied Lignery in a cold tone, enough to remind the corporal of his place. He turned toward the guards. "Is this true?"

Lidia had both arms free of her bonds, but she was restrained by guards that flanked her on either side. The men nodded, dropping their heads in shame.

"We . . . we fell asleep at our post, sir."

"And you'll receive a whipping for it. But we've other things to attend to now. Secure your charges."

"What are you doing prowling around in the night? Don't you ever sleep?" Adam interjected.

"No, and it's a bloody good thing I don't, or you would be dead now," replied Lignery. "Not that I owe you an explanation, but it is almost morning and I was arousing the officers for our next leg of this voyage."

"And couldn't resist the chance to sidle over to the prison bateau and gloat over your son, tied like a hog for slaughter?"

"I heard a commotion."

"The corporal is lying. No one was escaping. Renaud was trying to hurt the girl."

The captain turned toward the corporal, an eyebrow raised. "Is this true?"

"Don't believe the deserter dog, sir," replied Renaud instantly. "They were trying to escape and I was attempting to secure them again."

After a momentary pause, the captain nodded his head. "Thank you, Corporal. Given your special attention to duty, you are now officially in charge of the detail guarding the prisoners."

"No!" cried Adam, lurching to his feet and toward his father. He was immediately restrained and the corporal punched him in the gut, taking his breath away and silencing any further speech.

His father had turned away, but Adam managed to get his attention again, gasping out, "A word, alone, *mon capitaine.*"

Lignery turned and nodded his head and the men drew back, trying to bind the struggling Lidia.

"Take the girl away. Don't leave her here. The men will hurt her," said Adam, keeping his voice low.

Lignery gave him a sharp look.

"You know I'm not lying. You haven't been a common soldier in a long time, but remember what it was to be one. You can say she's under your protection, but she's not, and I cannot defend her, tied as I am. These men are hungry, *Capitaine*, and the girl is beautiful, and helpless in her bonds. You may as well have served her to them on a silver platter with an apple in her mouth and told them not to touch her. You're a fool if you think they won't hurt her. What if she was one of your daughters? Marie-Ann or Marguerite?"

For a long time Lignery said nothing. Behind him the men had managed to wrench Lidia's hands behind her back and bind them tightly. After another moment he spoke in English, addressing the irate young woman.

"Can you ride, Miss Erghamer?"

"Of course I can ride," she spat in reply.

"I will take the girl with me," said Lignery in French, with another glance toward his son. "Find her a horse and tie her to it. I'll lead the animal behind mine."

"What did you tell him?" cried Lidia at Adam as the men began to push her after Lignery. "You told him about Sofie, didn't you?"

"Lidia!" hissed Adam with warning in his voice. "I told him nothing. He's going to protect you, because I can't."

The corporal struck Adam hard across the face. But the voice of the captain stopped him.

"Don't touch the prisoner, Corporal Renaud. I'm going to have this girl with me all day, and if I find out that what the prisoner says is true, I will have you stripped of your rank and drummed out of the marines in disgrace. Mind your orders and don't mistreat the boy. He'll get his punishment soon enough, and not from you."

A strange look came over the corporal's face, a look of fear and also rage. He saluted as Lignery moved away, followed by the guards pushing Lidia before them. When Renaud turned back to Adam, a cold chill ran down the young man's spine. There was such a look of hatred contorting the man's face that if an expression had the power to make a person burst into flames, Renaud's glare would have done so.

"I don't suppose you've got another of those flasks on you?" asked Adam cheekily and watched in satisfaction as the corporal drew himself up as if to strike his prisoner and then deflated and turned away, shouting orders to the raftsmen as he stormed off.

8

LIDIA

July 21, 1759
Fifty miles south of Fort Niagara

The flotilla began moving before the sun rose and before the first doves began to coo. Lignery was riding that morning, rather than floating, and Lidia rode alongside him on a round-barreled, squat little horse. Lidia had noticed the day before that the captain's sorrel mare seemed very antsy on her bateau, her eyes constantly rolling in her head and rivulets of streaming sweat covering her red flanks and neck. The captain explained that he took every chance to ride, wherever the terrain allowed him to keep up with the boats, rather than confine the feisty animal to a barge. A few of Lignery's aides and officers rode with them that morning, and the other commander of the relief forces, Captain Aubry, a brusque, businesslike man who spoke in clipped, rapid French.

A gray mist lifted around the edges of the lake as the sun

rose and the haunting cries of loons carried over the vast expanse of water. A golden light melted the fog away gradually, leaving behind a sullen, oppressive heat, thick with humidity. Lidia watched this all with vague, exhausted interest. She was still processing what had happened during her attempted escape, the assault by Renaud—the knowledge of what might have happened made her shudder, but Adam had prevented it. Adam, the boy she had spent two years hating, had leaped to her rescue and almost drowned for his efforts. She bit her lip, remembering how close she had come to murdering the boy. Boy. She kept thinking of him as a boy, but he wasn't, really. He was about the same age as her, perhaps a little younger. She turned her thoughts away from Adam with effort and back to the two captains. They spoke mostly in French, except about Lignery's deserter; for those discussions they switched to English, the language that few of those around them understood.

"I can give the order," said Aubry at one point when the captains had ridden in silence for some time.

"He's my trooper," said Lignery, and he sighed as he said it.

"He's your son. But what he did cannot be overlooked. Deserting, assaulting the corporal, and doing God knows what with that letter." Aubry glanced darkly at Lidia when he mentioned the letter, then turned back to Lignery. "I heard he even assaulted you."

"My trackers will find the rider who has the letter," replied Lignery, and at that Lidia sat up very straight and attentive. "He cannot have gotten very far. The tracks were only a few days old."

"That is not the point. Your boy has done many shameful things over the years, Lignery, and you do punish him, but leniently, always too leniently. The men notice—

the men talk. Picoté would have been right to discharge him dishonorably after what happened in German Flatts."

"Yes. I see now that I should have let him be expelled from the marines. Better to be discharged in disgrace as a coward than to . . . be executed." Lignery's voice was low and grim and Lidia watched as his face seemed almost to age before her eyes. But he squared his shoulders. "But, no, Aubry, it has to be my order. He is my trooper."

"Suit yourself. My offer stands," replied Aubry. "No one would blame you for deferring such an unpleasant task to another, equal officer. And Lignery, my good man, he has to be executed, you understand that, don't you?"

"Of course I do," snapped Lignery, and there was a note of vehemence in his tone for the reminder. He fell silent, staring at the path ahead of him, morose and sullen. Despite the short time she had known him, Lidia felt this affect was very unlike how the commander usually comported himself.

"And you, young lady, still unwilling to tell us what happened to that letter?" asked Aubry, turning back to her.

Lidia shifted in the saddle, uncomfortable in her bonds. Her brow creased and her lip curled, but she did not reply.

Aubry shook his head, and continued in English with a cruel gleam in his eyes, "You ought to let the Mississauga work on her for a while. She'll sing out what happened to the letter then, who took it and where he was headed." Before Lignery could reply, someone called Aubry over to the shore. One of the pirogues had overturned and caused a wild hullabaloo. Lignery allowed Aubry to handle it and rode on, leading Lidia behind him on her horse. They had ridden together past the midday mark when Lidia's stomach emitted a loud, trumpeting groan, and Lignery looked up in surprise, as if he had forgotten her entirely.

"I'm sorry, I should get you something to eat," he said.

"That and I need to piss," said Lidia crudely, making the captain wince.

"Can I trust you not to run if I untie you?"

She bit her lip, glancing down at her swollen, throbbing ankle dangling out of the stirrup because it hurt too much to push against the iron. "I won't go anywhere. I doubt I could make it far just now."

He untied her wrists, which the men had switched to her front for riding the horse, and helped her slide down from the animal. She let out an involuntary yelp as her foot hit the ground, pain stabbing up into her groin. She almost fell, but Lignery caught her and assisted her with the first few steps, blood flow gradually returning to her legs. After she relieved herself, she sat down gratefully on a moss-covered rock under a copse of pine trees. Lignery's aide, who had hung back all day, probably sensing his captain's mood, hurried forward, bringing up a simple repast of hard cheese, dried and salted meat, and stonelike bread, so rigid Lidia thought she would break a tooth on it. Like a starving wolf Lidia tore into the food, gulping water with each bite to soften the bread. She had finished her first serving when she noticed the captain was not eating. He was watching her with an amused smile, but he had touched none of his own food.

"Aren't you going to have some?" she asked. "The bread is terrible, moldy and hard, and I think I saw a few maggots in mine, but you must be hungry."

"I assure you, my dear, I am not," replied the captain.

"You're still upset about the business with Adam, then?" she continued, not caring how impertinent her questions were. If anything it supported her story that she was a rude backwoods woman, unaccustomed to the etiquette of human discourse. "It can't be helped. A deserter is a deserter."

"Did he tell me the truth about last night? The corporal . . . did he try to rape you?"

Lidia spat, feeling the rage bursting up inside her, sensing that her anger had quickly transformed her expression.

The captain saw the answer on her face and shook his head. "I thought as much. That bastard. Are you hurt?"

"No, Adam . . . Adam knocked him into the water."

This seemed to make Lignery even more sad. He smiled still, but not a joyful smile—rather the kind that looks like it might crack into a sob at any second. "He's a good man, my Adam," he whispered faintly.

Uncomfortable with the strange, deeply vulnerable look in the man's eyes, as she would have been uncomfortable to see her own father weep, Lidia attempted to change the subject. "Do you have other children, Captain?"

"I do. In fact, Adam was one of twins. His brother Daniel died when he was quite small still. I've had nine in total, six of whom are surviving . . . soon to be five." He choked on the last phrase and then stood up. "We must push on. We'll go aboard one of the bateaux for a while. Do I need to have you tied again, Miss Erghamer?"

"You can if you like, but I won't run away, or even swim away now. It's daytime, they would catch me in seconds and I already know what your men like to do with helpless women bound in ropes."

"I am sorry. Corporal Renaud will be punished severely for what he attempted. We cannot countenance that sort of behavior."

"As you cannot countenance deserters?"

Lignery pursed his lips. He helped her up, gave her leave

to use the bushes for a few minutes again, and then, when she emerged, they led their horses down to the shore. One of Lignery's aides had already signaled a large bateau, which was pulling toward them clumsily, its sail raised.

"The French Army runs on discipline, Lidia, as I'm sure the British Army does as well, and the German military," said Lignery as they waited for the vessel. "We give special treatment to one soldier and it will ripple through them all. If a trooper can rape a woman without public acknowledgment and discipline, then they will all take to raping women. They are like animals, hungry and lustful. If a man deserts and is allowed to do so without the appropriate punishment, they will all know, and every mother's son among them that has ever considered deserting will do it."

"So you will kill your son."

Lignery stepped into the water and lifted her easily aboard the vessel. She could see his jaw was clenched, the blood vessels in his neck standing out, though he did not reply to her statement. It took a few minutes before the horses were loaded, with the urging of the aides from behind and Lignery clucking and encouraging the animals from ahead. Lidia removed her boots and settled near the edge of the bateau, her bare feet dangling into the water, gazing out at the flotilla around her.

Sometime later their vessel passed near the one where Adam lay, and Lidia stood, keeping her weight off her injured ankle, straining to see the young man. He was bound as before, leaning against the crates and barrels aboard the raft. For an instant she thought him dead, so pale had he become. A wrenching heaviness churned in her stomach. She stared hard at him, noticing that the captain was purposefully averting his gaze from the prisoner. Lignery knew Adam was there; she could see that in the flush about the captain's ears, and the way he held his back rigidly straight and his shoulders unnaturally square. He kept his gaze fixed pointedly ahead. She glanced back and forth between the unmoving youth upon the raft and the captain.

"He doesn't look well. Do you think we ought to check on him? His wound may have soured."

The captain ignored her.

"Do you hear me? I mean Adam. Adam doesn't look well. Your son, Captain, he doesn't look well. I can't even tell from here if he is breathing. Oughtn't we to check on him? Give him some medical attention if he requires it? I don't think any of your surgeons have looked at that wound since we were captured."

The captain still ignored her, and Lidia craned her neck, looking for any sign of life in the prisoner. As she watched she saw the beastly corporal Renaud, also aboard the raft, moving toward Adam, stalking in a threatening manner, carrying his musket like a cudgel.

"I'm just . . . I'm just going to check on him," she said suddenly, and before the captain or anyone else could react, Lidia plunged over the side of the boat. She ignored the shock of the cold lake water, and struck out toward Adam, her tattered, muddy skirts swirling around her, quickly soaking with water and becoming unbearably heavy. She could feel her face flushing as agony lanced up her leg with each kick. She repressed the urge to stop. She had no idea what she was going to do, but a vague notion of wrestling the musket out of the corporal's hand and bludgeoning him to death with it formed in her mind as she paddled.

"*Arrête cette fille! Arrête-la!*" called Lignery behind her. She tried to swim faster, but her skirts were dragging her down. The brief liberty afforded by the water made her grin, despite her pain, and remember the freedom of racing with the Oneida and Mohawk girls in the forest as a child, leaping into the ponds and swimming alongside her friends, free and wild. How easy life had been, and how unspeakably happy it had been. But now the pulsing agony in her ankle reminded her that she was no longer a child.

Hands grasped her arms and legs, yanking her from the water. She had made it surprisingly far. A sergeant aboard a passing canoe had fished her from the lake, but she was close enough now at least to see that Adam was breathing. He opened his eyes at all the commotion and glanced about, bewildered. His hazel eyes were glazed, and he seemed almost uncomprehending, but his gaze met hers and there was a strange, delirious, grateful expression on his face. Then his lids drifted shut again and he was gone.

She struggled against the soldiers as they twisted her hands behind her back and began tying the ropes tightly, pushing her face into the bottom of the canoe as she fought vainly against them. Lignery's vessel had drawn near and he stood on the deck looking down at her with sorrow.

"Miss Erghamer, you lied to me, just to make me feel like a rake again. I do not want to tie you like an animal."

"Then don't!" she cried, a flash of inspiration hitting her. "If you have a surgeon look to Adam, then I promise I won't run or try to swim away again. I'll keep my word this time. In exchange for medical attention for him, I will be a cooperative prisoner."

The captain's glance flitted between her and Adam. Then he nodded and spoke rapidly in French. The soldiers were unsure at first but assented after a moment, untying her and helping her across to the captain's vessel. She turned urgently toward Adam, who was no longer stirring on the raft.

"You will make sure he's seen?"

"He will be seen by our surgeon. I've sent word already. They'll move him to the surgeon's bateau, the infirmary boat. I keep my word, Lidia, unlike some among us."

"You were just going to let him die," she accused.

"He dies no matter what, Lidia. If he dies of some illness from the souring of his wound, then I will not be the one that killed him."

"You would be still, because your negligence of his condition would have led to his death."

The captain sighed. "None of this is any of your concern, Miss Erghamer, and the boy is your enemy. I don't understand why you care what happens to him."

"He helped me," she blurted out before she could stop herself.

The captain did not answer, but the anguish in his eyes at her mention of Adam's brave attempt to help her spoke volumes. He did not talk to his young prisoner for the rest of the day. There were flurries of reports, canoes joining the captain's raft and then leaving. There were scouts and officers. They gathered around a map spread out on the boat deck. They were planning for the eventual attack on the British forces outside Fort Niagara. Most of the proceedings were lost on Lidia, and she inwardly scolded herself for her refusal to learn French. Sofie had offered multiple times to teach her as much as she knew. She tried not to think about Sofie, what dangers her sister might be facing in the wilds surrounding Lake Erie. But if her sister failed, if she did not bring word of the approaching French reinforcements to the British Army, then that entire region, her home, would become a French holding. She would have to learn French. Who could say if Lignery would return her to her home as he had promised, or if he would sell her off as a slave to an

Indian sachem, or march her back to Montreal to serve a French family as a maid? Nothing was certain.

She had largely kept herself from looking toward the bleak and unclear future. But, with no one to talk to the entire day, just endless miles of sweat, the stink of filthy men, and the constant babbling hum of a language she could not comprehend, she found herself reflecting on the what-ifs that lay ahead with sadness. It was her normal state to be concerned only with the present, and until she became a captive of New France's *troupes de la marine*, it had always served her well. She was always here, everything was always now, never a moment to spare to think about the future, or the past—the awful nightmare of the past. But now, with the present so bleak, she did not want to be a part of it. She could not help but think about the prospects ahead, though there was no hope to be found in those reflections.

That night, well after dark, they stopped to rest somewhere along the lakeshore. Lignery's aides set up his tent, and she crouched in the corner, watching the men talking. There was some difficulty with his Indian allies, some disagreements, but they were not speaking in Oneida, or Onondaga, or Mohawk. She stopped listening after a long time, gazing idly at the canvas wall of the tent, lit by a few flickering lanterns with flies and moths buzzing around their dim glow. They were getting closer to the river, and the bogs and marshes there would slow their progress, at least a little, Lidia thought, with some comfort. A lone woman on a horse might make it through much faster. There was yet hope.

A man entered the tent. He was a good deal older than the captain himself, kyphotic and stooped, with a shuffling gait. He wore a threadbare, matted wig, and his face was lined, pockmarked, and sallow. He looked grave as he waited quietly in the corner, near Lidia, while Lignery spoke with Aubry, a few other officers, and the Indian sachems, all gathered around a map on a makeshift table of logs and stumps. The old man with the wig peered down at her after a while, as if just noticing she was there.

"*Excusez-moi, je ne vous ai pas vue là-bas, mademoiselle,*" said the man, bobbing his head courteously.

"I don't speak French," she replied.

"English, English, how delightful. A coarse language to be sure, but not without its charm. It was my first tongue," said the man, brightening. "Who are you, my dear woman, and what brings you to this dangerous land?"

"I am a prisoner of Captain Lignery, and my name is Lidia Erghamer."

"A good, sturdy German name, to be sure. How quaint. I am sorry to hear you have become a prisoner. I have just finished tending to one of his prisoners and if I had the station to do so I would reprimand the captain most severely for that boy's condition. I do hope you are in better health than he is?"

"Adam? You are the surgeon! You're taking care of Adam?"

"Adam, Adam, yes, that was his name, I think. It was only mentioned to me in passing. I don't always concern myself with names. Which reminds me, my own name, yes, that would be the polite thing. I am Henry Boiford, surgeon for Lignery's forces."

"How is Adam?" It annoyed Lidia how the man blathered on, meandering and changing the subject every few seconds. He had taken care of Adam, and he was a man of medicine and surgery—he would know the young man's chances. She remembered for an instant that she ought not to care, but it was too late. Every time she tried to remind herself of that blow to her face two years before, she remembered the same young man charging Renaud as he groped her, and then came the memory of Sofie, and the youth who had broken the wolf's jaw and saved her sister. Two saves; perhaps it was enough to outweigh one blow to the face in the heat of battle.

"He'll survive," said Boiford. "Long enough, at any rate, for them to kill him. But the boy was in rough shape. I've set him up among my other wounded, on the infirmary raft. Tonight I'm not even moving him to a tent on shore. He's been moved about too much, by far. Needs a proper rest. He was going to die, under the hateful eye of that pig of a corporal, Renaud. You know him? A swine from Marseille. Better for the boy to be under my care. Though . . . I must confess, a good part of me feels it's a waste to use bandages on him. Someone washed that wound out well before I did —was that you? That may have saved his life. The bullet grazed the liver and broke a few ribs. Without the cleansing it had some days back I think it would be sorely infected. I abraded the wound, cleaned it out well, made him bleed a bit more, but it's properly washed now and dressed, and he's a strong lad, though I think a little soured from too much drink, as is often the case among these soldiers."

Lidia let out a sigh of relief and realized with a start that Lignery had moved to join them and was also listening quietly to the report.

"Thank you, Dr. Boiford," said the captain. "I'm sure the boy will be well cared for with you. No danger of him escaping from the infirmary?"

There was a hint of hope in the question, Lidia thought, as if Lignery did not fear Adam escaping as much as he wished he might.

"I don't know what you think that trooper is made of, sir.

He can barely open his eyes just now, let alone attempt an escape. Still, I have kept the guards with him and he is manacled to the bateau. He won't escape."

A shadow of disappointment passed across Lignery's hazel eyes, but he smiled and nodded his head. "I am grateful for your work, Doctor."

"'Tis nothing, 'tis nothing. The infirmary beds are quite empty, just a few particularly explosive dysentery cases now. I had need of a real patient to justify the forty-odd livres the government of France is so generous as to allot me each month for my work. So it is I that should be thanking you, *mon capitaine*. I am pleased to see your other prisoner is in better health than the unfortunate boy."

"It was not I that shot him."

"But . . . if you will permit me, sir, it is you who allowed him to be beaten so severely by your men."

"You overstep, Doctor," replied the captain, his eyes narrowing and his voice becoming dangerously low.

"Indeed, that I do. I only wanted to report to you on the outcome of the detail you gave me. Forgive me, sir, I will retire and continue my care of the prisoner."

The doctor bowed hurriedly and slipped back through the tent flaps into a night spangled with the glow of fireflies. The tent was almost empty by then. Two of Lignery's aides were fussing about to pack up the charts and maps.

"The cot is yours, Miss Erghamer, I will sleep outside, but just outside, so no one can disturb you."

"Thank you, Captain Lignery. I was wondering . . . my clothes are quite torn and dirty—is there anything else I could wear?"

"I am sure we have a few spare uniforms that might fit you, if you don't mind wearing men's clothing."

"I do not, sir. In fact, I think it much more practical garb than women's garments in this wild place."

"Very well, I will have my aide find you something tomorrow that is a little cleaner and less torn. Now, Miss Erghamer, *adieu* and good night."

All night Lidia wandered dream fens, through cattails, floundering in chest-high bogs, calling for Sofie always, and finding her nowhere. Several times she thought she did see Sofie in those murky nightmares, but without her infant, sobbing and beating her fist against a tree, or lying in a sucking pool of mud, groaning and covered in blood. When Lidia finally awakened the next day she found herself drenched in a cold sweat.

~

July 22, 1759
Thirty-five miles south of Fort Niagara

"I'M SORRY, MISS ERGHAMER," SAID THE SOFT VOICE OF THE captain from the tent door. "I know it is not yet daylight, but we must keep going. I have the garments you requested."

She rose from the cot and stumbled half-asleep to the tent flap, lifting the canvas and taking the proffered bundle of clothing. She dressed herself in the breeches, stockings, garters, shoes, and waistcoat of a French soldier, and slipped the heavy justaucorps and her old clothes into a saddlebag to carry with her. Once dressed, she joined the captain outside. In a few minutes the impatient aides had packed up the tent, and she was mounted on the horse she had ridden the day before, her hands untied this time. It was a gloomy morning and afternoon, with a constant dripping rain, no lightning or thunder, but the steady drizzle was enough to make everyone miserable. They reached the mouth of the Niagara River late in the afternoon, the clear waters turning brown and muddy where Lake Erie flowed into the river, and the land becoming treacherous and sodden beneath the horses' hooves.

Lignery waited on the shore, watching for a time as the endless flotilla moved down the shimmering river. His aides set up a makeshift table for him and he seated himself on a log beneath a towering sassafras tree and began writing brief messages in French, one of the aides copying them as he wrote. A group of about six Indians gathered around him to receive the letters. When the captain spoke through his translator, Lidia found to her surprise that the translator was speaking in Seneca. She thought a few of the Indians were from the far west, Shawnee people, and another she suspected was of the Mississauga nation, but at least two of them she was sure were Seneca.

"Pouchot should look to my coming on the twenty-fifth of July, in three days' time, from the south. If he can give us any intelligence on the best way to proceed, the areas most susceptible to attack, where the British are weakest, that would be a great boon to us," said the translator as the young messengers stowed the letters in their leather bags.

"I have spoken with Pouchot," replied one of the Seneca, speaking so quickly that Lidia struggled to understand him. "My brother and I just came from him. The uncle in the fort urges you to advance from across the water, from the west side of the river."

"And you, what did you see of their lines? Where are they weakest?" asked Lignery after the translator relayed the message.

"They are weakest along the southern side, at the portage road along the river they have very few men. But they are scattered all along their line, and with this great multitude of warriors and soldiers that you bring, we could break through anywhere," replied the warrior.

Lignery bowed his head in deference. "Thank you, my brother, for this information. Walk safe among the trees to bring my letter to Pouchot."

The warriors all nodded and dispersed, heading north swiftly, soon lost to sight as they followed the winding portage road along the Niagara River.

The captain had paid little attention to his young captive that day. He seemed content with her promise not to elope, and she kept it. Occasionally she toyed with the idea of riding off into the forest; somewhere out there, Sofie was moving through unknown dangers, pursued by Lignery's men. Lidia hoped that her sister had already reached the relative safety of the British trenches, but one woman, alone on horseback, with a baby on her back . . . anything could happen, and the nightmares of the evening before still plagued her waking thoughts. They rode on, ever northward along the portage road. It was easy to let her horse have its head and daydream, ignoring the seemingly endless miles passing beneath her.

"But the fort is of concern to you."

She startled from her reverie at the sound of Seneca being spoken again. The captain had halted his horse ahead and was conversing through a translator with a tall Seneca sachem flanked by warriors of his clan. Lignery wore a strained, worried expression and seemed more animated than usual. He spoke for a long time in French before the translator hurried to turn the words into tolerable Seneca.

"If Fort Niagara falls, then the British will take all the land surrounding Montreal, all the Quebec territory. They will block the roads to your people, prevent the passage of goods, money, and food. They are not like us—the British are not like us. The French have lived peaceably with your people. We allow you to live as you choose, as you always have. That is not the way of the British. They consume and destroy. They kill men, women, and children. They have no remorse. They will make you accept their ways. They won't let you go on living as you do now. The British are not your friends, Tsa'degëöye:s. You cannot afford to remain neutral in the coming battle."

"We have no fight with the British at your fort. Our brothers among the Six Nations tell us to remain neutral, not to side with either the French or the British in this coming fight," replied the sachem.

"Your brothers have only their own interests at heart. They see only today, not what tomorrow will bring. Today they have good relations with the British. But these British do not understand your people, and they will destroy the ways of your nations. If you stand beside us, if you fight, not only will you bring great honor to your people, with many kills, slaves, and scalps, but you will create a future for your children, a good future; a future like your past."

"We will think upon it, and for now we will continue to travel with you, Captain Lignery. But I cannot promise that my warriors will go with you into battle when the time comes," replied Tsa'degëöye:s. Then he nodded his head and left, taking his warriors with him.

"Trouble with your allies?" asked Lidia impertinently.

Lignery glanced at her, spurring his horse forward again. "So, you speak Seneca?"

"And Mohawk, Onondaga, and Oneida."

"Useful skills to have in this wild country."

"I think so. My first playmates were children of the Oneida and the Mohawk people."

"You think I did not tell them the truth?"

"No, you did. The British do have a way of consuming the Indians, conforming the ways of the Six Nations to their own ways. It wasn't like that at German Flatts. We considered the Haudenosaunee as our brothers and sisters, and lived as such. They gave land to our people when we were exiles. They taught us their traditions, and we taught them ours, but as friends, we didn't expect them to adopt our customs."

"If all relations between people followed that model, what a better world we would live in," mused Lignery, half to himself. "Boys like my son would not have to don a uniform and partake in a horror the need for which they do not understand."

"You regret that Adam joined the marines?"

"It was the only life I had known. My father was a great leader on the battlefield. I joined as a marine when I was fourteen. Adam was reluctant to enlist. He wanted to go to France, to study law. I wanted him to fight. I told him . . ." He trailed off for a moment, as if remembering who he was speaking to. "I told him that if after a few years as a soldier, he still wanted to study law, then I would send him to France. Instead I—"

"Instead you're going to execute him," Lidia finished, aware as she spoke how heartless it was to say the words aloud. "I cannot imagine ordering the execution of my own child."

"It can't be helped. I've been putting it off, but I can only delay so long. After the battle for Fort Niagara is over, then Adam must die. There is no other way."

Lidia fell silent, staring down at the dusky mane of the horse she rode. After a while she glanced up, and whispered, "I'm sorry, Captain Lignery."

"Thank you," he replied, smiling slightly at her. "Tell me more of your family, Miss Erghamer, I would welcome the distraction. Have you brothers and sisters?"

"I think I had many, but before me. I was the last, and my sister Sofie the first, and the others died in their infancy. So the only one I've ever known was Sofie."

"And what is she like?"

"Bossy, mean, better-than-thou about everything. You know, an older sister."

Lignery chuckled. "Indeed, I think my younger ones would say the same of Adam. He is teasing and cruel to them, but I think it comes from a place of love."

Lidia shrugged. "Maybe. I think it comes from a place of arrogance. An Oneida clan mother that adored Sofie used to call her *Yako'nikulatshánit*, it means 'she has a strong will', but if I could give her a name I would've called her *Teyakotele'takályat*, 'she's a nag'. Just because you're older doesn't mean you always know better than your younger sister. I've faced horror and war, after all. Sofie wasn't there the day your troops attacked German Flatts. I was. I took a stand against them."

"I imagine you would have. You do not seem the kind of woman who would hide in the face of battle. Was there no warning of that attack?"

"There was a warning," said Lidia and chewed her lip hard. "The Oneida warned us. They came to our leaders one day and told us of the coming French forces. Our elders laughed at them and turned them away, saying they were not afraid. I often think of that . . . of how different things might have been had we just listened to the Oneida. If only I had made them listen. But I trusted my elders."

"What could one girl do to convince men and women twice her age that the Indians were right? You have nothing to regret in your actions, Miss Erghamer, unlike myself. I, a grown man, who had seen the horrors and evils of war, who knew what he was signing his boy up for, made Adam sign that form and join the marines. He was at German Flatts, you know . . ."

"I know."

The captain's eyebrows rose. "He told you?"

"I saw him there."

"Indeed? And you did not kill him when he fell into your hands along the river?"

"I'm not a murderer," replied Lidia, unwilling to admit that Sofie had been there and made her promise not to kill. She had come as close to being a murderer as one could possibly come without killing.

"After that battle, Adam was never the same," Lignery continued. "He fell to drinking, carousing, getting into trouble. His captain, Picoté, was going to discharge him in disgrace, but I told him I would take him under my command. It was the only thing I thought I could do. He transferred to my command and I've been trying to help him ever since. To little avail. It was Picoté who told me in the first place that the boy should sign up under him, that it would not do to have your own son under your command. I remember what he said: 'What would you do if you saw a wave of soldiers overtaking the wing in which your child fought? What would you do if you saw him cut down on the field of battle? You would behave irrationally—you would have to. And that could cost you and your men everything in a pitched battle.' I listened to him, and I regretted it. Then I took Adam back under my wing, against his advice, and I've regretted that, never more than now."

They rode in silence for a few minutes. The drizzle had melted away, consumed by the fiery July heat. The rain had left no relief in its wake, only an even more intense humidity, broiling the soldiers on the boats and the riders on shore. Finally Lidia spoke up again. "Why do you tell me all this?"

Lignery gave her a wistful smile. "Because I can tell no one else, Miss Erghamer. I apologize for my frankness. Where is your sister Sofie now? She still lives in German Flatts?"

"No, she moved to Philadelphia, with her husband," Lidia lied quickly.

"I know there was someone else at the cave with you, Miss Erghamer. You may as well stop pretending that you lived alone in the wilderness."

"There was no one else, just myself, and Adam after I found him. No one else."

The captain sighed, and for a moment she thought he was going to rethink all his kindnesses toward her, submit her to some awful torture and questioning, but the sound of horses approaching at a trot distracted him, and a few moments later he and Aubry were deep in discussion. Relieved at the captain's attention being drawn away, Lidia turned her own focus back to the troopers on their vessels, watching her with what she thought were hungry eyes. The water was low in the heat of summer, leaving every possible obstacle exposed, and the progress of Lignery's forces down the river had been laboriously slow. The horses were having no difficulty keeping pace with the bateaux as they perpetually caught on rocks, tree branches, and logs. *The river is fighting the French too,* Lidia mused, grinning at the thought of the land and waters of her home taking a side in the war. She turned back to Lignery and Aubry, who were arguing loudly, and found to her discomfort that Aubry was pointing at her, his face red and dripping sweat.

Lignery caught her eyes and then took Aubry's hand and pushed it firmly back against his side. Fuming, Aubry whirled his horse and trotted up the trail ahead of them.

Lidia urged her horse back to the captain's side. "What was that about?"

"Nothing, Miss Erghamer. Nothing to worry about. Aubry thinks you've told a tale."

"About what?"

"He thinks you sent that message on ahead, and that the British will know we're coming long before we arrive."

"How could they *not* know you are coming? You have more than a thousand soldiers tromping through the forest and filling the entire expanse of the Niagara River. The forest is full of Indians of ever-shifting alliances. Your own messengers will probably tell the British before any phantom I've supposedly sent ahead of you through the forest."

Lignery's face remained in a tight-lipped, grave expression. "That's true enough, Lidia. Still, Aubry doesn't take kindly to spies. I suggest you keep your distance from him."

The rest of the day they spent aboard a bateau, Lignery's mare stamping and blowing, the whites of her eyes showing constantly. They pressed on hard, skirting around a portion of the western side of La Grande Île before finally making camp on the island in the evening. Lidia was beginning to understand why the men pushed so hard. Lignery was a force of nature, a driven man, indefatigable, striving beyond the bounds of human strength. His effort set an example among his men. If he could press on through any hardship, through exhaustion, through hunger, through boundless heat that threatened to cook them alive, then so could they.

She fancied the high esteem his men held Lignery in made it all the more imperative that he take the highest road possible and execute his derelict son. But the thought of watching Adam hang from a rope—which only a few days before would have filled Lidia with glee—caused that heavy sensation in her stomach and chest whenever she involuntarily imagined it. The brave, obturate, exhausted youth, with the same determination as his father, though directed quite differently, but still with that same stalwart, stubborn persistence, was doomed to die. The young man that had saved her from the odious Corporal Renaud. The captain seemed to have largely forgotten about that incident, or at least, he was too distracted by the coming battle to ask her further questions about the assault or make any move to discipline Renaud.

Occasionally Lidia saw the corporal among the troops, and he would leer at her, letting his eyes slide over her body with smug satisfaction, with the air of a man who owned the thing he looked at. She rankled at the sight, repressing the urge to attack him outright. It would only get her bound again, and more vulnerable than she already was. She was hot, flushed, and constantly restraining herself as the French soldiers laughed and talked riotously among themselves every time she was near them. She hated them, she wanted to lash out, to fight violently, the way she always had. But it would not do, not yet. She would bide her time and store up her rage for now, letting it fuel her and drive her. At times she couldn't hold her anger inside and swore at the troopers loudly in German, though this only seemed to add to their delight. Bastards, every single one of them.

Late that evening she lay awake in Lignery's tent, camped on La Grande Île, listening to an intense discussion outside in Seneca. Sachem Tsa'degëöye:s had returned.

"Why should we set ourselves against the British for you? You say you will protect our ways here in this land, but the French have shown no kindness to our people. They do not keep the treaties they sign, they do not allow us to follow our ways in peace, they take our land and build and build upon it. The trees they cut down, the elk they slaughter, the rivers are full of your traps, the beavers are vanishing, the beavers! It is not just the British that do this, but the French have been doing it as well, for many years now. Even now the memory of what was before is fading, fading away. Our great fathers, the oldest among us, tell of a time before the white man, of a world that we would hardly recognize now."

"I hear what you are saying—you are eloquent, Tsa'degëöye:s, and speak well. But the white men will continue to come and flourish and overthrow your lands. You have the promise of the French king, of our great father across the sea, that we will keep our treaties with you, and we will protect the Seneca, and all the people of the Six Nations, the people in the western nations, the Mississauga, the Huron, the Delaware, the Shawnee, all the people of this great land, from the excessive appetites of the British to expand and to devour. What you do not see are the many other lands that the British have taken and destroyed across the world. They have ravaged entire nations and languages and ways of life, wiping away the very memory of those peoples. They are relentless, ruthless, and all-consuming. They have no use for the natural world except to exploit it. They will not rest until they have destroyed everything you know and love and made it theirs."

"And you think your house by the mouth of the great river, beyond the waterfall, is the place where it will be decided? You think this battle is of such importance to your people and my people, more than all the other battles that came before?"

"*Si le fort à Niagara tombe, le Canada tombera*," replied Lignery, his voice solemn in the darkness.

"If the fort at Niagara falls, Canada falls," said the translator in Seneca.

After a long pause in which the sounds of night filled the air, the incessant noise of crickets chirping, cicadas singing, June beetles buzzing, and the distant hoots of an owl, the sachem spoke again at last. "I cannot promise my warriors will follow you into battle, Commander Lignery, as I have told you before. But the chain of our friendship remains strong, and we will continue to travel alongside your soldiers down the river. Before the battle we will speak with our brothers who are there, allied with the British, and we will see what we will see."

There was silence for a long time afterward, and then, out of the darkness, she heard Captain Lignery speak. "Lidia, you're awake, aren't you?"

"Yes, I'm awake."

"You were listening?"

"I was. I couldn't help it."

The crickets sounded louder, but after a moment Lignery spoke again. "You say your people, the Palatine Germans of Mohawk Valley, lived at peace with the Iroquois?"

"We did," she said, smiling up into the tent flaps at the memories that came flooding back. "They took my people in when we were exiles with nowhere to go, when we had nothing. They took in my aunt and uncle, and my parents joined them from England when they told them of a good place to live where we could farm in peace and where our neighbors, the Oneida and the Mohawk, were like our brothers."

"That is . . . something. That two such different peoples

could live together in harmony. Is there a secret to such an existence?"

Lidia considered the question, and through her mind flashed images of her feral childhood. Running with the children of the Haudenosaunee, playing and fighting among them, watching her parents and their parents interact. The wampum belts shared freely, the intermingling of each culture's respective holidays. But then came another image, of the Oneida messenger, telling a group of Palatine men sitting at the well of the impending danger. The French were coming, he had said, and they could not hope to resist such a force. How the Palatine men had laughed and mocked the advice, and how dearly they had all paid for that disrespect. Then, more vague and flickering, the memory of their Oneida friends visiting them in their mourning after the attack, holding them and weeping with them. Those memories were foggy at best, for she had been unwell. Her head had throbbed, she had been vomiting many times each day, her vision had been blurred and she had been unable to tolerate light, irritable and in despair at the same time. Her aunt had cared for her tenderly, while she too grieved. But, nonetheless, Lidia did remember how the Oneida had stayed with them and mourned with them for four whole days, as if they too had lost members of their own families. There had been comfort in that true solidarity, great comfort.

"Do you ask because you want to have peace and harmony with the Haudenosaunee, or because you wish for peace and harmony between the French and British?"

Lignery chuckled. "There has not been peace between the French and British people in hundreds of years. You and I will not live to see the day that there is peace between France and England."

"That's very pessimistic."

"English is not my first language, but realistic, I think is the right word, Lidia." Again a beat of silence. It was Lignery that broke it. "Lidia, I meant what I said. I will see you safely back to wherever you want to stay when this is all over. I know you're lying to me about the other person that was living in your cave. I understand. I assume it was your husband or someone else you are close to, and you want to protect them. Regardless, I mean to see you safe at the end of this fight. Once the fighting at Fort Niagara is done, I will personally return you to your cave, if that is what you want. If you want to go somewhere else, even to German Flatts again, I will personally accompany you there."

"That's very kind of you, Captain. I . . ." She stopped herself, a tear starting in her eye, her throat becoming full of thick, choking mucus.

"Yes?" the captain prompted, his voice gentle. He was tired—she could tell he was very tired, but pushing himself to remain awake to hear what she had to say.

"I don't want to watch Adam die," she blurted out.

He did not speak, but there was a change in his breathing that she noticed. It became deeper, slower, more intentional. She listened to it for a long time, despair building within her.

"Me neither, Lidia," he whispered at last, his voice carrying the faintest tremor. "Me neither." Then she heard him roll over and he spoke no more that night.

~

July 23, 1759
La Grande Île

A FAINT MURMUR OF VOICES AWAKENED HER, THE BARELY perceptible muttering of an Indian tongue she did not know. She lay awake, accustoming herself to the pitch black. She thought she could not have been asleep for more than a few hours, but the noises of the camp coming to life again were all around. The darkness was full of the sounds of soldiers gathering their bags, talking softly as they rushed to eat something before the float to Little Fort Niagara, and then the final push, the march on foot along the portage road.

She drew in a deep, joyful breath. It was morning, and she had slept through the entire night without a nightmare. She sat up and instinctively reached for her stays but stopped herself. She was wearing a man's shirt and waistcoat. If there was ever a time to embrace freedom from the whalebone cage, it was now. She rummaged in her bag for her dress, and tore a strip of cloth from the tattered skirt. This she secured around her breasts to keep the nipples from showing through the loose white cloth of her shirt. She slid into her breeches, buttoning them about her waist, pulling on the stockings and gaiters that stretched taut over her swollen ankle, buckling the shoes and finishing off the uniform with the blue waistcoat. It was much too hot to even consider putting on the justaucorps. She stowed the thick wool coat and her old, ragged clothes and stays back in the saddlebag and slipped out into the gray light of dawn.

Lignery was standing a few yards away. She could see lines of fatigue around his eyes, eyes that were red from weariness, or perhaps . . . she dismissed the thought. A captain of the French marines did not cry, not for his son, not for anyone. Still, there was a puffiness under his lids that she could not help but notice. She turned her attention to the men speaking to him. There were two French soldiers and two Indians in buckskin leggings. They were the ones doing much of the talking, with Lignery's translator interjecting with his interpretations as often as he could. The conversation was so animated that the translator seemed to be having trouble getting a word in between the Indian scouts' gesticulations and rapid speech. She thought some of the words were Seneca, but mixed with another language that she didn't know. If only Will were there. Sofie's husband knew every Indian tongue in the region. He would know what they were saying.

In the same instant that she had the brief reflection about Will, one of the Indian scouts reached down and tugged an item from his belt, and Lidia thought her heart stopped. She stared, her eyes wide, unbelieving. It could not be, it must not be, she was mistaken. It had to be some other wampum belt, but the designs were unmistakable. She remembered the day the great clan mother Yako'nikulowanah had given it to Sofie, as a token of her special friendship with Lidia's older sister.

"*Nein!*" she screamed, and all of the scouts turned toward her. "*Nein! Das ist nicht deins! Gib es mir!*" She lunged forward, forgetting her injured ankle, forgetting everything but that beautiful belt the scout was holding and the person who should be holding it. She threw herself on the scout before he could react and knocked him to the ground, snatching the belt from his grasp. Then she began pummeling him repeatedly, screaming loud, profane oaths in German, the kind of oaths that would have made Sofie box her ears or wash her mouth out with soap. Sofie. Sofie!

The Indian scout started fighting back, but Lidia was like a berserker. She caught hold of a stick and began wacking the Indian warrior and the soldiers that were trying to tear her off him. She kept thrashing and screaming, completely incoherent, tears of rage pouring from her eyes.

With their combined efforts, the French trackers managed at last to yank her off the Indian, but then she turned on them. She snarled and snapped, more animal than woman, vicious, unstoppable, no longer in possession of reason. Sofie could not be dead. If Sofie was dead, and her parents were dead, if she had lost them all then she would kill every *Hurensohn* in the camp, or die in the attempt.

She tackled a French trooper to the ground, striking him over and over with her fists. Someone had snatched the stick she had been using before, so she had to make do with her own knuckles. Then, in the midst of her mad rage, as she repeatedly pummeled the French trooper, she heard a voice, a gentle but firm voice, cutting through the madness. The voice of a father, soothing an errant child.

"Lidia, Lidia, you have to stop. Lidia, they'll hurt you."

She spun toward the voice and at the same instant someone struck her head with a musket butt. She tried to swing around and lunge at the person who had struck her, but her legs would not do what her stunned mind told them to.

"They killed her! They killed my sister! *Meine Schwester!*" she shrieked, still trying to fight as the troopers restrained her. The world was becoming dark around the edges. There was only a tiny ripple of light in the middle of the black curtains that were closing before her. She had let them kill Sofie. She had let Sofie go when she should have gone, and now Sofie was dead, and it was her fault, just the way it had been her fault that her parents died. She had not fought hard enough. She never fought hard enough. She should have fought Sofie; she should have refused to let her go. She should have tied Sofie down and gone on her own. Then she would be dead, not Sofie. Not good, sweet, loving, saintly Sofie. Sofie who always took care of others, Sofie who never fought. Sofie should still be alive. And the baby, the baby! "*Wo ist das Kind?*" she murmured, continuing to struggle, tears pouring down her face. "*Das Kind?*"

Vaguely through the madness she could hear the voice of Captain Lignery and the surgeon Boiford speaking, as if far, far away. They were only getting farther away, as the bright spot in her vision grayed, fading into the blackness. They were speaking in English, perhaps to spare her the shame of having her situation discussed openly in front of the soldiers.

"A state of severe hysterics . . . some terrible shock . . . she really ought to be under my care . . . like the other. A dose of something sedating . . . should do the trick . . . get through the worst of it."

Bastards—she did not need them and their sensitivities, speaking in English to spare her feelings. Pigs. They were all pigs, and she would kill them all, or they would have to kill her. She kept fighting, writhing and twisting and kicking as the last flickers of gray light in her vision faded into nothingness.

9

SOFIE

~

July 21, 1759
Near Niagara Falls

It was useless. Stupid. Hopeless. Sofie knew she could not make it. She had been running for miles with a steady, shuffling gait she had learned among the Haudenosaunee. If she kept jogging at this pace, she could go on for many hours. She stayed off the overgrown portage road, keeping close to the river. She had lightened her load as well, to almost nothing. The first thing she had jettisoned from the few belongings she still had was Will's musket. Dropping it made her feel as if she had lost a thousand pounds at once; it made her feel faster.

She tried to hide her tracks, running through streams for as long as they lasted, swinging on low hanging vines, and following meandering deer trails. But she knew the grass and the earth would show the marks her passing made to any Indian tracker with an ounce of skill. Her mad ride and now wild, desperate run to the fort would be for naught.

About midday she found a stony ravine—the first bit of luck she had encountered since she heard her pursuers. She let hope surge anew at the sight of the bare rock—bare rock that would show no prints. She kept to the stones for as long as she could, more than a mile, enough perhaps to throw the trackers off her trail, at least temporarily. They would follow the ravine and look for the place her prints went back into the forest; it would slow them. But she did not let her rising spirits at this stroke of good fortune overwhelm her sense of reality. She knew the trackers were not far behind, and even at her slow, jogging gait, she could not go on forever. She was exhausted. She had already ridden hard with barely any sleep for days, she was carrying a sick infant that still had sufficient strength to whimper for food, and her breasts ached, heavy with milk. She was spent. Every time she paused, even for only a second to catch her breath, every time she even entertained the idea of feeding the infant, she thought she heard the sound of her pursuers. Horses—they had horses. They could overtake her easily on the flat, though in the thick, tangled closeness of the forest she had a slight advantage.

She pushed herself through snarls of poison ivy growing in vines as big around as her arm, through brambles that tore at her breeches, and clambered over rocks that pierced her shoes. There were dense copses of pine, with low branches that raked her skin, and places in the wood so tangled with bracken that she stumbled and tripped with every step. She passed through groves of ash, oak, and maple that grew so thick that she practically had to crawl to slide beneath their overhanging lower limbs, taking care not to let the branches tear her child from his cradleboard.

The fear of the pursuit was a distraction from her infant's health. She knew he was alive; sometimes he moved, sometimes he let out a faint yelp. She had been running since the battle with the mountain lion. She had not had even a second to take the cradleboard off, and she did not know if he was improved, the same, or worse than he had been. The terrible knowledge that this adventure would kill her child oppressed her, slowing her run with stifling, overwhelming despair, a far heavier burden than Will's musket had been.

At last she burst out of the trees and found herself upon a rocky cliff, a bluff, overlooking a vast expanse of forest. The foliage of the treetops spread like an impenetrable floor below her, far below. To her left she could hear the powerful roar of Niagara Falls, still out of sight. She drew in a gasping breath, her heart hammering in her ears, panting, exhausted. Frantically, she scanned the steep rocks for a way to climb down. The child on her back let out a pathetic, feeble cry and Sofie sank to her knees, then onto her hands, sobbing and shaking and retching.

Her strength gradually returned and she removed the cradleboard from her back. The child did not look better, but neither did he look worse. His eyes were still bleary, his rash red and scaly, but, to her relief, he took her nipple. Both breasts had begun to leak earlier in the run, soaking her shirt and waistcoat with milk. The baby ate greedily, enough to loosen the tension in her chest, and then he fell asleep. Briefly she again entertained the idea that he would live, that he was going to survive. Then the memories of the Others came rushing back, the haunting faces of the babies, the haunting face of little Martin. The infant would die, and she would be the one who had killed him, killed him to save his father, as if his life mattered less.

From this dark reverie, crouched over her child upon the precipice, she looked up, catching sight in the distance of a rising cloud of vapor. The falls, the mighty falls. She remembered breathlessly the first time she had journeyed to Niagara Falls with her Will, how he had watched with laughter and pride in his eyes while she sobbed on her knees, whispering prayers and hymns to heaven at the awesome glory of the endless water. There had been immeasurable tons of water, thousands and thousands of tons, pouring from above, weight enough to crush an entire village, weight enough to crush the world, and beauty enough to drive the hardest, coldest soul to their knees. A mist settled upon her eyes at the precious memory: how she had not been able to stand or look away for hours, and how hard she had prayed, and the feeling of Will's strong arms wrapped around her as she wept.

"If I can just get you to him before you die . . . ," she whispered aloud, looking down at the infant with the faintest hint of red in his thin golden hair. "You would love him, *Eodi'nigoiyo-ak*. You would love him so much, and he would love you."

Sofie looked up again, as the sun began to set beyond the waterfall, orange light spilling from the horizon, piercing and brilliant, casting a glorious aureate mantle over the world and softening the edges of the wilderness. The orange beams of light turned to pink and amber waves in the purpling clouds. Involuntarily she began singing softly. As she sang she put the child back in his cradleboard. He opened his eyes again, gazing up at her solemnly, as if he knew the meaning of the words.

"Und wenn die Welt voll Teufel wär'
und wollt' uns gar verschlingen,

so fürchten wir uns nicht so sehr,
es soll uns doch gelingen.

"Der Fürst dieser Welt,
wie sau"r er sich stellt,
tut er uns doch nicht;
das macht, er ist gericht't;
ein Wörtlein kann ihn fällen."

Something moved in the corner of her vision and she stopped singing, turning just as two French troopers and two Indian scouts emerged onto the grassy bluff where she stood. They paused, staring at her, as if trying to make sense of what they were seeing. She almost smiled as she glanced down at the spectacle she had become: a woman in the middle of nowhere, perched on a precipice, the sun setting behind her, dressed in men's clothing, her shirt stiffened from dried milk, her breasts exposed, her golden hair matted, and a swaddled infant lying in a cradleboard at her feet. The troopers started toward her. There was no time. No time to think, no time to find a weapon, no time to negotiate. There was no time for anything. Sofie yanked the cradleboard onto her back and turned toward the cliff just as the men broke into a run, shouting in French at her.

"Arrête-toi! Halte! Ne saute pas!"

But Sofie wasn't listening. She glanced down for only a second at the dizzying distance to the ground and then swung her legs over the edge, determined to make the harrowing descent if it was the last thing she ever did. One of the soldiers darted forward, grabbing at her. He caught the wampum belt wrapped around her waist, holding her for a second as she yanked away. The belt tore and beads flew in every direction, and then she was falling.

She flailed, reaching out to grab for anything she could, loose wampum beads cascading past her. Her fingers closed around a shrub and she slammed hard against the rock wall, the breath knocked out of her. She clung with both hands to the little bush that had saved her and her son's life. Gasping for air, she caught hold of a stronger sapling growing from the rockface and dangled there. The men above were shouting incoherently, their voices nearly lost in the din of the roaring waterfall. The infant was crying, crying strongly. Her milk had strengthened him. Biting her bottom lip, she cast a brief glance at the treetops below her and then began to ease her way down, hand over hand along the sapling's trunk, toward the cliff wall. She could hear the hubbub above her getting louder, but when she looked up, she noted gratefully that a jutting stone blocked her view of the soldiers. If she could not see them, they likely could not see her, and did not know that she had survived the fall.

"*Së:nöh ëhsasdaëh he:awak, nö:koh i:yë's sano'ëh. Still, Kleiner, ruhig. Alles ist gut*," she whispered and hummed breathless snatches of Luther's hymn to calm the infant. After a moment her son was quiet. For a few heart-stopping seconds, she stretched her feet out, swinging on the sapling, finding nothing but air, and then her toes touched a solid ledge. It was narrow, but it was enough. She waited there, feet on the stone, hands clenching the sapling, as the last light of day faded from the sky. She surmised that the soldiers would attempt to make it down around the rock face and look for her body at the foot of the precipice, but not until morning. There would be nothing to find in the darkness, and it would take hours for them to descend, following the treacherous rise down in the east and then back west along the base of the cliff. She had time. She had all night.

The climb down in the darkness was so treacherous and slow that it was nearly dawn by the time Sofie's feet, attached to legs that felt as if they were made of spaetzle, touched the ground. She was trembling uncontrollably and sank to the stony earth at the base of the cliff, taking off the cradleboard and lying supine, sweat dripping down her back and chest. She rolled onto her side, bringing her sweaty breasts to her infant's mouth. He drank with a little more strength than he had at the top of the cliff, but he was feverish again; she could feel the heat exuding from him. The gray predawn light illuminated the rash on his hands and face. She lay beside him, letting him suckle, drifting in and out of dreams herself for nearly an hour, then, while her body groaned in protest, she struggled to her feet.

Her arms ached. Her legs were still trembling and seemed unwilling to carry her, but there was nothing else for it. The fort yet lay ahead, and time was running out. She changed out the baby's soiled napkin with a strip of cloth from the hem of her shirt, packed the infant into his cradleboard and onto her back, and set off once more on legs that quivered with every step.

~

July 22, 1759
Niagara Falls

DESPITE THE URGENCY, SOFIE COULD NOT HELP BUT FOLLOW the foot of the cliff west, toward the wonder of the falls. The falls that would sing their song to generations long after the war she found herself taking some small part in had been forgotten. It was comforting to think in that way as she walked, glazed and exhausted, toward the ceaseless roar that called to her. Toward the place where the Haudenosaunee legends spoke of a maid who threw herself from atop the rapids, sacrificing herself for her people. But the brave maid did not die; she was rescued by the thunder god, saved to live a long life and bring honor to her people.

As she trudged along, a faint speckling of rain dripped gloomily upon her from the cloudy sky. She found herself mulling whimsically over the idea of the thunder god, wondering what such a god would look like. Perhaps the thunder god had no physical structure; his only form was sound, the endless rumbling song of the waterfall, audible for miles across the quiet of the wilderness.

Sofie had lost track entirely of what day it was. She thought it was the twenty-fourth, perhaps the twenty-fifth. Her stomach growled and moaned, but there was no food, no saber, no musket to hunt with. There was nothing but endless marching toward her destination. Even her canteen was gone; she had left it at the top of the cliff. It felt to Sofie as if she had been on this journey since the dawn of time. Lidia, Adam, Will, her parents, they were all a dream, a distant hallucination. In her journey, the rest of the world had faded away. Perhaps the world beyond her had actually disappeared, and the only real people left in the universe were her and her child and the thunder god of the falls. The infant coughed, a terrible, rasping sound, reminding her that soon he too would be gone, and if in fact they were the last ones left on earth, then she alone would be left of the human race. Alone on a pointless walk to nowhere.

She stumbled hard, catching herself against a tree and waiting as a wave of nausea and weakness passed over her. The world faded briefly, and then steadied. She was delirious and it was making her stupid. She attempted to ground herself in reality by pinching her skin. She was lightheaded, dizzy, hungry, and thirsty. She scolded herself in her head and perhaps whispered snatches of her reprimands aloud, she was not sure. If she was going to make it, she needed to snap out of her bumbling, hazy dream and put one foot in front of the other, purposefully and speedily.

Then it was there, stretching out above her—the vast waterfall, taking up her whole field of vision. The water sprayed and cascaded down, making rainbows of light in the growing sunshine from the east. The droplets cooled her overheated body, though the infant began crying fitfully again. Despite her exhaustion, Sofie gasped, gazing in awe at the falls, the way she had when she first looked upon them. She turned slowly to show the boy.

"Look, look, little one, Niagara Falls. *Tetwa'suh'tha*. Here is where the thunder god lives. *Tehsatkahkwalísi!*"

As if he understood, the child calmed and the crying ceased, though she could not see if his eyes were open. In her empty gut, something twisted and cavorted, and then the image of Will appeared before her. He was standing beside her, gazing at the falls, watching her as she wept uncontrollably, like a child herself. Will . . . if she kept going at this rate, she would see him tonight, or perhaps tomorrow. Will . . . the man who had left so stubbornly, so coldly, so many months before. He seemed more a stranger now than the man she had bound her life to a few years before. She reached down and touched her stomach, as if to quiet the churning unrest. She was ready. She would say the right things this time. She had rehearsed them under her breath a million times since the day he had left.

As she stood, preparing the words in her mind that she would tell her husband, allowing her sick infant to stare in awe up at the falling water, she saw a movement out of the corner of her eye, far in the distance. She blinked, turning to look east, rubbing at her eyes and staring. But this was no mirage. There were two Indian scouts moving along a narrow path toward the base of the falls, toward her. They were too far away for her to make out any distinguishing marks, or paint, or garments. She immediately turned and began her shuffling, slow run, north, always north. She was still lightheaded, hungry, weak, barely sweating because she had become so dehydrated, but she had to press on. The last push. If these Indians caught up to her and were unfriendly, then she would be done for, and the British would not be warned. Her Will would not be warned, and she would never be able to tell him all the things she had longed to say since the day he had left.

And then Sofie broke into a desperate sprint. From the base of the falls there were fifteen miles, give or take, between her and the fort. Fifteen miles. She knew she could make it, if the Indians did not catch her first. Perhaps they were friendly, but she could not risk it. She did not have the safety of Yako'nikulowanah's wampum belt anymore. She bore nothing that would commend her to them if they did not speak Mohawk, or Seneca, or Oneida, and her bright golden hair was a scalp any warrior would be proud to bring home.

She did not look back as she ran, switching eventually to the slower jog, keeping her gaze fixed ahead. Looking back would make no difference. Even if they were catching up, she had no strength to go faster. For five miles Sofie ran without stopping, one chapped, blistered foot before the other. The faint drizzly rain of the morning had faded into a disgusting, suffocating humidity as she ran, and she longed for the gentle coolness of the raindrops to return.

She wondered fleetingly if perhaps the scouts had not seen her, perhaps they had not found her tracks. Perhaps there was yet hope. She smiled as she ran, the stupid, fey smile of a dying woman, she thought, a dying idiot of a woman in a hopeless situation daring to believe that she was going to make it, when all chances had long ago been lost. Keeping to the narrow path that followed the river north, she eventually came to a wide clearing, a space where there was no coverage from trees or bushes. She pushed herself with the last strength that she had left, and began to sprint toward the cover of the forest on the other side of the meadow. Behind her she heard the excited cries of the Indian scouts. They had caught up to her and they were giving chase. She increased her pace as a wave of despair rose up like a tsunami to engulf her.

She had just entered the cover of a copse of pine, the ripe, comforting smell of the needles and resin all around her, when they caught her. A heavy body struck her from behind and she lurched forward, tumbling and catching herself with her hands. She struggled to get up, but someone strong was pinning her down and tearing the cradleboard from her back. Taking her baby away. Her baby! She tried to roll over, lunging at them, fighting to get to her infant. One of the scouts was holding the cradleboard; the other thrust his knee deep into her chest, pressing her to the ground. He batted her desperate, flailing arms away. Then he took hold of her golden, matted hair and yanked it up, stretching her neck out taut and raising his hatchet with his other arm.

"*Sëni:hë:h! Sö:ga:' dayögyenö:wö's!*" she screamed at the top of her lungs, but there was no sign of recognition of the words in her attacker's eyes. He was a warrior, and he had caught his prize, and he would take her scalp, and her baby.

A loud thwack split the air, and the warrior looked down in surprise at the thick dogwood arrow protruding from his chest. For an instant he kept Sofie pinned, his hatchet raised, and then he toppled forward onto her, gurgling as the light left his eyes. The other scout turned and began to run, still holding the cradleboard containing her child. Sofie scrambled to get out from under the dead scout, and lurched to her feet, racing after the other Indian warrior. Another twang and thwack sounded from the forest, and the second scout dropped with an arrow in his back. Sofie ran the last few stumbling steps that her legs would bear her and dropped to her knees beside her infant, who was crying feebly within the cradleboard. In a few seconds she had him free and pressed against her heart.

Sofie could hear soft footsteps approaching her, but she did not run. She had no strength left to run, and no strength left to fight. She had traveled more than ninety miles in five days. She had nothing left to give, nothing left at all. She had failed, but she would die or be taken captive with her child in her arms. She was determined never to be separated from him again, for as long as she lived, even if it were only for a few more moments.

"*Sešnye's onödowa'ga:' gawë:nö'?*" asked a voice above her.

She nodded, turning, still on her knees, and looking up with eyes blazing, clutching her child to her chest. "*Do:gës.* I speak the tongue of the People of the Great Hill," she replied in Seneca. "And the People of the Standing Stone, and the People of the Flint, and even some of the language of the People of the Hills. They were all friends to my people, friends of my mother and my father, in the valley of *Ganyë'geh.*"

The Indian studied her for a long time. He was a handsome man, perhaps a few years older than her husband, with a thoughtful face and keen brown eyes. Finally he asked, "Who are you? And how do you come to be alone in this region?"

"I am the wife of William Light," she replied, breathless, hoping with wild desperation that this lone Indian knew her husband.

His eyebrows rose and his lips parted. After a moment he said, "You are joined with William Light, the man with a thousand tongues?"

She nodded.

"William Light is a great friend to all the people of the Six Nations. I owe him my own life, from battles past. You are the Sofie of whom he has spoken."

"I am Sofie." The Sofie of whom William Light had spoken. He was not dead, nor had he forgotten her in the many months since their bitter parting. A warm, almost painful sensation filled her chest, and she felt her eyes burning, but she was too dry to shed tears. She rallied, swallowing against a chapped throat. "I have a message that I must get to William Light's commander. That is why I have come. Please, let me continue unhindered."

"I will take you to him," replied the warrior. "My name is Kanęhsawéhte, of the Tuscarora Nation."

"*Nya:wëh sgë:nö'*, Kanęhsawéhte. If you can take me to my husband, then I will owe you into eternity, beyond what I already owe you, for you have saved my life this day, and the life of my child."

"I heard you call out in the language of my father's people," replied Kanęhsawéhte. "I could not turn away."

"And for that I thank you," she whispered.

Kanęhsawéhte studied the infant in her arms. "Your child is not well, Sofie. Is it the offspring of William Light?"

"He is. He is the son of William Light."

"*Ne:' waih ho'nih shöwöye:ëh.* Your husband will be overjoyed to see you and the child."

"Yes, and I to see him. Come, it is getting toward night, and we have still miles left to go. Let us not wait here."

Kanęhsawéhte nodded and they set off down the narrow trail, beside the rushing waters of the mighty Niagara River, as the evening gathered around them, Sofie wearing the infant in his cradleboard. As they walked, Kanęhsawéhte was quiet, watchful of the forest, and Sofie appreciated his silence. She had traveled for so long alone that the sounds of the forest had become all she knew. The quiet was soothing. Her clothing was ragged and torn, her body covered in dirt. She craved the healing flow of rain. There was a tense crackling in the air and distant black clouds that made the gathering evening darker than it should have been, and far, far away in the ominous sky, heat lightning flickered.

She tripped over a stone, barely able to lift her feet anymore, and Kanęhsawéhte caught her arm, steadying her.

"Sofie, you need food, and water, and rest," he said.

"I . . . have to keep going. Have to get the message to the soldiers. If I don't, many British soldiers will die. I have to keep going. We're so close."

"Sofie, Sofie, there's time. Whatever message you're bringing to them, there is time enough to eat and drink."

He unslung a canteen from his back and handed it to Sofie, who stared at it, dazed, almost uncomprehending. Then she drank all the contents in a few gulps, greedily slurping it down, water running down her face and across her chest, cool and refreshing.

"I'm sorry," she said, staring blankly at the empty canteen.

He took it from her and smiled. "It's all right, sister. It's all right. You needed it more than I did."

"Thank you. Now we must keep going."

"You need food to strengthen you as well, Sofie."

"What are you, my mother?" she snapped back, surprising herself with her vehemence. For an instant the memory of when she had struck Lidia returned to her. It was not something she did; it was something Lidia would do, strike another person when she was angry. But not her, not soft-spoken Sofie, with her firmly held beliefs about the evils of violence. Yet she could feel the rage building inside her again. "I'm fine, Kanęhsawéhte, I'm almost there. Once I'm there, once I've given them my message, then I can eat and rest."

Kanęhsawéhte let out a sigh, and it irked Sofie. What did he know of what she had been through? What did he know of the importance of her message? What did he know about anything? Yes, he had saved her life, but it did not give him the right to dictate what she should be doing. She clenched her jaw and continued walking, stumbling again over an unseen rock, but not letting the warrior catch her this time.

"You're stubborn, Sofie, obstinate, like your husband," said Kanęhsawéhte as he followed her. "At least let me carry the child for you."

She reflected on the offer, her mind dull and numb, though her resolve was still sharp. She finally nodded, stopping to remove the cradleboard from her shoulders—shoulders that were raw and aching from the many miles carrying the weight of the baby. She fed the child, noting blearily that he was more alert than before, coughing less, looking better, looking for the first time in days as if he might survive, as if he would not be like the Others. In fact, she thought wryly, the sick child probably looked a good deal better than she did. Putting him back in the cradleboard, she secured it to Kanęhsawéhte's back and they pushed on.

Gradually the grayness of twilight faded into the blackness of night, and still Kanęhsawéhte led her. Around them the light of fireflies glowed and floated like stars that had come to the forest floor. Sofie began to think perhaps she had entered a dream, or she had been killed by the Indian scout with the hatchet and this was the afterlife. It was a peaceful place, full of the beautiful, haunting sounds of night, and the twinkling of otherworldly green and yellow lights. It would have been pleasant if not for the soreness and fatigue plaguing her. She wanted nothing more than to lie down and close her eyes and stay that way for days, perhaps weeks, perhaps forever.

"Who goes there?" came a youthful voice from the darkness, the voice of a boy attempting to sound like a man, Sofie thought.

"Kanęhsawéhte of the Tuscarora," replied Kanęhsawéhte in halting, uncertain English.

"Passcode?"

"'And when life's sweet fable ends' . . ." Kanęhsawéhte paused. It was clear he did not know the meaning of the words, he had just learned the sounds. After a moment, he continued, "'Soul and body part like friends; No quarrels, murmurs, no delay; A kiss, a sigh, and so away.'"

Sofie chuckled involuntarily, stupidly.

"Who's that with you?"

Kanęhsawéhte turned toward Sofie and she could see that he was floundering to find the English words to express himself.

"I am Sofie Light, the wife of William Light. I've come with a message of great importance to the commanding officer here."

She heard the sentry fumbling in the darkness and then a dull glow illuminated them. The sentry had lit a lantern.

He was a boy, with the faintest hint of stubble on his chin, dressed in an ill-fitting red uniform. He puffed out his thin chest and drew back his shoulders, in a poor effort to look older and more important. She smiled at him and wondered how much she resembled a demon raised from hell.

"I can have someone take you to your husband. He's on the western flank, with De Lancey's light infantry," said the boy after studying her for a few minutes.

She shook her head. "If you have the best interests of your forces at heart, sir, you will take me directly to your commanding officer. The safety of your position and all your troops depends on me getting through to him. After I have spoken to him you may take me to my husband."

The sentry exchanged a glance with Kanęhsawéhte, who said nothing. He probably had understood very little of their exchange, Sofie thought.

"I cannot leave my post, ma'am. But Kanęhsawéhte is a trusted emissary of the Tuscarora. He can take you to Massey's camp, or to Johnson himself."

Sofie relayed this message wearily to Kanęhsawéhte, who again nodded in assent.

"Hold on, what do you have on your back there?" asked the sentry, stepping forward and raising his lantern. Kanęhsawéhte instinctively drew back but then allowed the boy to see the sleeping infant, his pale little face covered in red papules, but he was peaceful and unaware of anything happening around him.

The sentry glanced between the baby and Sofie, and there was a look of wonder in his eyes. "How far have you come to bring your message, Mrs. Light?"

"I, and my son, have traveled more than a hundred miles. I left the Ganadawao creek early on the seventeenth of July."

The boy's eyes widened still more and he whispered a curse word under his breath, then instantly apologized, blushing. He stepped back, almost bowing as Sofie passed, following Kanęhsawéhte.

They weaved their way between small encampments of snoring men and were challenged by six or seven more sentries before they approached the tent of a commander. It must have been past midnight, Sofie reasoned, as they faced the last sentry standing between her and the delivery of her message. The air crackled with humidity and fingers of heat lightning illuminated the black clouds above them. There was a storm over Lake Ontario, she noted, far, far away, where the lightning flashed with mad intensity, and faintly she could hear the rumbling of thunder, barely discernible, like the distant roaring of the god of the falls. But alas, there would be no rain for her tonight, no rain over the bloody trenches that she had at last found, no rain to wash away the grime of her journey.

Everything had become so blurry she hardly noticed them arriving anywhere, but suddenly a man stood before her, his colonel's jacket thrown loosely over his shoulders, his wig askew. He was flanked by others, both Haudenosaunee and British, a few of them holding lanterns and looking at her with curiosity. They were standing in front of a large tent. The flaps lay open, but the inside was dark, like an open maw gaping at her. She stared at the officer and swayed on her feet.

Kanęhsawéhte spoke sharply with one of the other Indians in a tongue Sofie didn't know, and that Indian translated his words into English for the colonel.

"He found this woman and her child on the road to Fort Niagara. She says she has brought a message and refused to speak to anyone but a commander, sir."

"Did she?" asked the officer, looking at her with a questioning expression. "I am Lieutenant Colonel Massey of the 46th Foot. I am one of the commanders here. Whom do I have the honor of addressing?"

"Sofie," she said, her voice hoarse and grating. She swallowed what little saliva she could produce to wet her throat. "Sofie Light. I am the wife of William Light, who I believe is a scout and translator under Captain De Lancey here." There were murmurs, looks of astonishment. Sofie noticed them and stood taller. "I bring word of French reinforcements coming from the south, under the command of Captain Lignery." She reached into the pocket of her grimy waistcoat, and withdrew the letter she had taken from Adam what seemed a hundred years ago, and passed it to Massey.

The lieutenant colonel scanned the letter for a long time. When he looked up again, his face was grim. "If this is indeed true, Sofie Light, you may have saved all the British forces here. Lieutenant Philpot, will you go and rouse Colonel Johnson? We have heard rumors of possible reinforcements before now. If this letter is correct, then we haven't much time, and it looks as if Lignery will be bringing an immense force against us."

There followed a bustle of activity and Sofie found herself pushed to the side while men hurried about in the darkness with their lanterns. In a matter of minutes the lieutenant colonel's tent was fully illuminated, a table set up with charts laid out, and disheveled, dirty men began appearing like specters from the forest and crowding around Massey.

Sofie was shaking, exhausted, hungry—no, starving. Her stomach was nothing but a void in her abdomen. She felt herself swaying again and the new light all around began to fade to gray, while the fireflies seemed to multiply, becoming sharper, brighter, like little bursting stars in her vision, and then she felt hands guiding her down to sit at the base of a tree outside the tent. She leaned back against the solidness of the rough bark. After a moment her vision steadied, and she could see the outline of Kanęhsawéhte's features, and then the shape of her infant's sparsely haired head. The child was sleeping, so peacefully. He was so perfect, so beautiful.

"*De'sadögwe:ta'.* You said if I took you to the commander you would rest, and you would eat," whispered Kanęh-sawéhte in Seneca, and she felt something solid, the crust of some sort of bread pushing against her palm.

She nodded. "I would eat now, Kanęhsawéhte, I would eat. I am so grateful that you took me to him." A moment later she struggled to consume the dry bread. It was some form of hardtack against which her chapped palate was useless. Kanęhsawéhte thrust a canteen into her hands, saving her in her battle with the desiccated, rocklike substance. The Tuscarora warrior disappeared for a few minutes and then returned with more items—dried pork, cornbread, blessedly soft in comparison to the hardtack she had eaten, which lay like a heavy stone in her stomach. She only managed a few bites of this relative feast before she felt she might vomit and pushed the rest away, touching her abdomen as if to quell the waves of nausea rolling over her.

"Would you like to see your husband, Sofie?" asked Kanęhsawéhte, his voice soft, gentle, almost as dreamlike as everything else had become for the exhausted woman.

She nodded. "*Nya:wëh.* If I could . . . I still hardly know if I believe he is alive."

"You don't have to believe, I will show you," he replied. "Can you stand?"

"Of course I can stand," she snapped angrily. "I've come

more than a hundred miles on these feet. Don't treat me like an invalid."

"I do not mean to offend you. You don't look well, Sofie."

"Well, thank you very much. That's so kind of you to say."

"Should you like to wash or refresh yourself before I take you to Will?"

"If Will can't accept me as I am now, then I have no desire to continue our marriage beyond this night," replied Sofie. She regretted her words immediately, but she was having trouble stopping herself from her irritated retorts. She was exhausted, it was late, and the food she had so longed for only made her abdomen hurt. She needed rest. She was going to have it out with Will and then heaven help anyone who tried to deny her sleep after that.

She followed Kanęhsawéhte in a daze, keeping her eyes fixed on the soft fuzz upon the sleeping head of her son as the Tuscarora warrior moved ahead of her. Twice she walked directly into a tree; once she stepped in a hole, some half-dug trench, and fell, landing on her hands and knees. For a moment she lay there, and the dark branches swirled madly above her when she raised her head. She vomited and felt a bit better. Kanęhsawéhte reached down to help her from the trench, but she shoved him away. A hundred miles. She had come a hundred miles. She did not need the chivalry of the Tuscarora man. She didn't need Will. She didn't need anyone. She stumbled to her feet, half-sleeping as she took a few more steps, until a voice stopped them in the darkness.

"Who goes there?"

It was as if an icy hand had reached down from heaven and ripped her heart right out of her chest. She stood in shock and defeat, wishing that the voice would speak again, the deep, slow, studied voice of the man she had once loved so well, or had she? Had it all been a dream?

"Speak up, who is it?" asked Will again, and then switched to one of more than a dozen Indian languages that he spoke with perfect ease. The man with a thousand tongues, that was what Kanęhsawéhte had called him. The man with a thousand tongues. Into Sofie's memory burst the pleasant memory of the taste of that man's tongue in her own mouth. Kanęhsawéhte was looking at her with something like trepidation, as if he knew she would be cross again if he dared speak first.

"It's me," she said, her voice a little stronger than it had been before the lieutenant colonel.

There was a sharp hiss of rapidly intaken breath in the darkness and then fumbling, shaky fumbling. A flint struck a few times, a spark flashed, and then a lantern glowed and she was looking into those warm, disbelieving gray eyes that she remembered so well.

"Sofie . . . ," Will said, more of a question than a statement or a greeting. He was staring at her as if in shock. "Sofie . . . I . . . how . . . ?"

"Yes, it's me. But I didn't come here for you, Will. I came to bring a message to Lieutenant Colonel Massey. When I found out you were here I decided I would pay you a visit, out of courtesy. That's all. I didn't know you were here before, since you haven't seen fit to send word to your wife of your whereabouts, or even if you were still alive." She found it taxing to maintain the angry state she was in, and reflected with detached amusement on how exhausted Lidia must be all the time, to always be in a rage. She longed to wrap her arms around the big man standing over her, one of the few men she had ever met who was taller than she was, and by a head. She wanted to feel those muscular arms gripping her, those hands the size of bear paws tight upon her hips, the pleasure of him inside her, filling her, making her feel whole and strong and brave and godlike. She quelled the mad rush of emotion, passion, and lust, swallowed, and stared up at him, jutting her jaw out the way Lidia always did. She would not soften before him. She would not melt into his arms. He would earn her back with contrition or not at all.

"Sofie . . . I . . . Sofie, I'm sorry. I . . . after what you said the day I left I . . . didn't know if you would even want to hear from me."

"That's stupid."

"It's . . . is it stupid? Do you remember what you said when I left?"

"Do you remember what *you* said?" She wanted to break. She wanted to weep. She wanted to tell him she was sorry. But she would not. How could she tell him that in her head she had replayed the words they had exchanged thousands of times a day since their parting? How could she tell him that she had regretted them? How could she forgive him? "You knew what I felt, you knew what I believed, about war, about killing, about you leaving. And still you left. You didn't even send money back."

"Because I haven't been paid yet . . . I . . ."

"Haven't been paid yet? Why on earth would you stay here and not return if you hadn't been paid? What's the point, unless you enjoy killing? You left me alone in the wilderness and haven't sent word, and stayed out here with these forces, without pay, for months? For almost a year? How could you not at least send word? How could you forget me so completely? How could you be so evil? Did you . . . did you never love me?" That was it. Her voice broke, and a rogue tear spilled down her cheek despite her attempts to remain a cold, impenetrable stone.

"Of course I loved you! How could you even ask that? You're my wife, Sofie. My wife."

"And a wife deserves to know if her husband is alive or dead. A wife deserves to have her husband send word to her once a year."

"Sofie . . . I . . . I'm sorry."

There were more tears, scalding hot tears burning down her face, the tears of wondering for months where he was, what he was doing, whether or not he was dead. The tears of the loneliness of that winter and spring carrying his child, not knowing if he would ever meet the little one, ever take part in the joys of parenting alongside her. The tears of the agony of not knowing if she would be alone forever after he left. The pain he had put her through by being a selfish bastard. She felt as if there were more tears pouring down her face than the amount of water thundering over Niagara Falls.

Will started toward her in the darkness as if to embrace her, but she drew back, trembling with anger. In that moment the infant let out a muffled cough and Will turned in bewilderment toward Kanęhsawéhte, switching with perfect ease to Seneca.

"Why are you still standing there, Kanęhsawéhte? This is clearly a private matter between husband and wife, and whose baby is that you have?"

Before Kanęhsawéhte could speak, Sofie was behind him, removing the infant from the cradleboard. She turned back to Will, whose chest was heaving, eyes wild with alarm, as if he already knew what she was going to say. She extended the infant toward him and the child wriggled with real, beautiful fight again, with strength born anew from the ashes.

"He's your baby, William Light. Your son. Though you wouldn't know that since you never came back and you never sent word."

"My . . . my . . ." Will, stolid, steady, stubborn Will, the man with a thousand tongues, was at a loss for words. His gray eyes were enormous, darting back and forth between her, the infant, and Kanęhsawéhte.

"Your son," she said again and thrust the infant into his arms.

Will fumbled and dropped the lantern, which sputtered and went out, throwing them all into complete blackness. It was Kanęhsawéhte who retrieved the lantern and relit it, illuminating Will again as he stood awkward and uncertain, holding the infant and staring at his wife, as though terrified. Then Sofie saw it. Will had let her put the infant in his left arm, his enormous hand cradling the child's bottom, and then, to steady the child in his grip, he had lifted his right arm, putting it around the child, but where his right hand should have been was only a sharp, bony protrusion of skin, a hideous scar, the hand and wrist gone completely. Will's gaze shifted from the infant, following her look, and his breathing was deeper still, and stifled tears shone in his eyes.

"I . . . I couldn't write, Sofie. I would have, but I . . . I didn't . . . I couldn't do it with my left, and I didn't know how to tell you . . . I didn't know how to . . ."

She lunged forward and then she was holding him, their infant pressed between their chests, like a shared beating heart. Her arms wrapped around him, his stump reaching behind her shoulders. His stump. She gasped, and felt the last great pain pierce her chest.

"Will," she whispered and then just kept saying it, over and over again in a soothing, gentle voice, a rhythmic lullaby. His name. His beautiful name. Her Will. "Why didn't you have someone else write to me for you?"

He drew back, and she took the infant from him. Tears had coursed their way down his face and glittered in his red beard in the light of the lantern. "I didn't know how to tell you, Sofie, to tell you that your husband was a cripple. If I'd had someone else write you'd have known it wasn't my hand. I couldn't tell you, I just couldn't do it. You know what I thought on the battlefield the moment this happened? You know the first bloody thought that came into my head when I looked at that awful, mangled mess that was once my hand? It wasn't the pain, it wasn't the horror, it was just 'goddammit, Sofie was right. She'll never let me hear the end of this.' That was the first bloody thought I had. I just didn't know how to tell you. Honest, I just didn't know what I could say. I'm sorry. I thought you . . . I thought you wouldn't want a cripple for a husband, Sofie, I thought . . ."

"You thought that if you died in another battle and I took your widow's pension it would be better than if you returned home to me a broken man."

Will let out a faint, agonized moan. "You . . . you know me well, Sofie. I ain't saying you're wrong on that. I knew I couldn't come back to you like this. Worthless. Useless. I knew you deserved better than that, better than this. Now that you see it . . ."

"Oh, Will, how could you think that I would reject you because you had one hand less than you did when you left? How could you think me so cruel?"

“Because you were so cruel before I left, Sofie! Can you blame me?”

“I’m not going to reject you because you have only one hand. We’re married, William, I am your other hand. I always will be. Wasn’t that what our vows said? In sickness and in health. Isn’t that the same as in ability and debility? It meant that for me, whatever those words meant for you.”

Then, once again the infant was pressed between them, but this time Will’s lips found their way to Sofie’s, and for the first time in nearly a year, she felt the delicious power of his tongue, the moisture of his lips against her own dry, chapped mucous membranes. She smiled slightly as the distinction blurred between where her lips ended and his began. The man with a thousand tongues indeed. His left hand grasped her waist, pulling her into him, though still gentle enough not to crush the infant between them. When Will drew back from her there was a smile on his face, a smile nearly lost in his thick red beard. He gazed down at her with all the warmth, the awe, and the love that had shone upon his face the day they were married. Then he shifted to look down at their son.

“He’s perfect. What did you name him, Sofie?”

“He doesn’t have a name,” At least, he did not have a name she ever meant to share with anyone but the infant himself when he was older. “I was waiting for you before I named him.”

Will bit his lip, and she could see there were tears threatening to spill down his cheeks again. He reached out with his stump, then remembered himself and switched to his left hand, gently touching the face of his son. Warmth and beautiful agony rose up in Sofie’s chest, threatening to swallow her. A tidal wave of the most exquisitely painful love she could imagine.

"I've regretted leaving you every day. Regretted how stubborn and stupid I was," said Will after a long time. Then he seemed to remember something, looking up and around. "But it's not safe for you to be here, Sofie, this is a battlefield. You and the boy should be home. I can send someone, a friend from among the Cayuga or the Oneida, to escort you back. There's a great many of them that would be more than happy to do that as a favor for me."

"I cannot go south, Will, the French are advancing from that direction. And when I do return I'm bringing you home with me."

"I can't just leave, Sofie."

Her brow furrowed and her eyes narrowed. "You're coming back with me, William Light, or I'm not leaving. I'll stay here beside you. I'm not going back to that cave to be alone for years on end while you kill people in a fight that isn't yours."

"I can't just leave Sofie, that's deserting. I'm a soldier now."

"You were a husband before you became a soldier, or have you forgotten that? Your first duty is to me, Will, to me and to your son."

"That's not the way my commanding officer would see it."

"Then, if you are indentured to the British crown, I will stay beside you, march beside you, camp beside you, until you are free again."

"What about your sister?"

Sofie choked, feeling enraged and disgusted. She stepped back, yanking the infant from Will's tender, gentle caresses, all the anger pent up over the lonely months coming back like a cyclone. "So that is the standard? I must stay in that cave forever for my family, until I die, but you can be out here, risking your life, and killing for as long as you like? Abandoning your family and playing war games in the wilderness? Don't forget that I know you're a murderer now. I know you've killed, and broken the laws of God and man."

"This is a war, Sofie!"

"And it's not our war, it's not our fight! If the French and the British want to squabble over territory that was never rightfully theirs to begin with, what business of that is ours?"

"Sofie—"

"Don't 'Sofie' me. I thought you had changed. Kanęhsawéhte," She turned abruptly to the Tuscarora warrior who had stayed near, though he had backed away from the bitter anger of the couple. He wore a confused and alarmed expression, his eyes darting back and forth between the two of them as they spoke rapidly and vehemently in a language he did not understand. Sofie softened her tone, switching back to Seneca. "Kanęhsawéhte, I am sorry you had to witness this."

"You do not need to apologize. The match is splitting apart? You will go to find a new husband?" asked Kanęhsawéhte.

"I . . . no, I just . . ." Sofie paused, her mind racing. She glanced back at Will, her Will, with his one hand, looking at her like a man who was about to break in two from anguish. "I just need time. And the baby needs a surgeon, a doctor—can you take me to the surgeon for this regiment?"

Kanęhsawéhte nodded, offering the lantern back to Will, who shook his head. With a last sorrowful look at Will, the Tuscarora warrior turned to lead Sofie away. Sofie made an effort not to look back at her husband, keeping her head held proud, chest heaving with each deep, dramatic breath.

But, despite her anger, she could not help herself. Her eyes flitted toward him in the last few seconds that the light from the lantern still illuminated his face. She saw her husband lift his one remaining hand and his stump to cover his face and bow his head, and then the darkness swallowed him as Kanęhsawéhte moved away with the lantern.

10

ADAM

~

July 23, 1759
La Grande Île

At night when Lignery's forces camped, Dr. Boiford either kept his patients in a separate tent, or made them stay aboard the bateau. In Adam's case, given his status as a prisoner, he was kept aboard the vessel with his leg manacled to the deck. Boiford enjoyed his work, as far as Adam could tell, and liked to keep the patients that needed his care apart from the other soldiers, but he was quick to dismiss anyone he suspected of shirking their duty. He had initially seemed intrigued by Adam's condition, but as his young charge had speedily improved, his interest had waned. Now the old man had a new case to occupy him.

They brought Lidia to Boiford's bateau, struggling madly, her face scrunched in rage, screaming and fighting like a wild animal caught in a snare. She cursed vehemently in German, spitting and snapping at the four men carrying her, one to each wildly wriggling extremity. The puttering old surgeon followed behind, tut-tutting, clucking, and constantly murmuring in English.

Adam watched as they tied her to the cot beside his own. Within a few seconds she managed to collapse the whole thing with her struggles. He wondered with trepidation what could have brought on such a spell. Still, seeing her fight so fiercely, he couldn't help but smile a little through his concern. Lidia was strong. Unstoppable. She had the sort of energy and strength that he found it impossible not to admire. To keep going with such effort when no hope of overcoming her captors remained—he only wished he had such vivacity.

The doctor managed to wipe a substance on Lidia's lips, receiving a vicious bite for his efforts. Adam grinned broadly at that, remembering the teeth that had torn through the flesh in his neck two years before. She was truly unstoppable. Boiford, his spectacles askew, stood back, sucking on his injured finger and peering down at the young woman.

"Took on a patient that was too much for you, Doctor?" asked Adam glibly in English.

"What? Oh, you. You're looking better today. Too much for me? I should think not. The girl just wants a little sedation until the hysterics subside. That laudanum should do the trick, and if not . . . well I do have more."

"Won't you need that in the coming battle?"

"I said I have more, didn't I? Impudent boy. I dare say you're looking fit enough to paddle today."

"If you discharge me from your care I will paddle, and happily. But I should probably save my strength. I'll have to walk down the portage around the falls anyway."

"Perhaps I will discharge you . . . later," said the doctor, his eyes glancing back and forth between his two patients. He switched to French. "The girl trusts you, doesn't she? You seem to have some mutual understanding. She was very concerned about you before."

"Only because she didn't want me to die of a gunshot wound and rob her of the pleasure of watching me swing from an elm," replied Adam.

"Is that right? I fancy that she holds some other tender feelings for you, but what do I know? I've only been doctoring humans for more than forty years. At any rate, see what you can do while we float these last few miles to the portage. Perhaps you can talk her off the cliff, so to speak."

"Off the cliff? Wouldn't that be counterproductive? I thought you wanted me to help her."

"Oh shush, boy. You're impossible. The more you improve, the more I understand why your father is going to have you executed."

Adam drew in a sharp breath, then smiled again. "Is it decided, then? I thought the old man was having some guilt."

"And so he is, and probably always will, but I've heard a rumor that it's settled. Because of your condition they had a court martial in your absence. The captain just wants to wait till after the battle. Probably he'll execute you in Fort Niagara proper, with a large number of troopers in attendance, Pouchot's men as well as his, to make the most of the opportunity."

"Yes, wouldn't want to squander the chance to show the soldiers what might happen to them if they encourage their own sons to enlist. Perhaps, one day, they too can attend their son's execution."

"The *troupes de la marine* run on discipline, boy, and you

have none. Your end has been only a matter of time from the day you joined, of that I'm sure."

"Indeed, well, I'm sorry you've wasted so much time and energy on making me well, then."

"No need to apologize, my dear boy. If you want to express your thanks, then you can help me get this girl calmed down."

"Order received, sir," replied Adam, sitting up on his cot and swinging his legs over the side, his manacles clanking as he moved. He felt a wave of dizziness pass over him at the sudden change in position, but it faded after a few moments. When he had first been enrolled under Boiford's care, he had fainted every time he sat up, to the point of absurdity. He was much improved after two days under the surgeon's constant vigilance, improved enough to make the final push to Fort Niagara on foot.

The portage road began just above Niagara Falls at the site of Little Fort Niagara. There was a particularly steep section called the escarpment, but, other than this portion, the road was reasonably flat and straight. The soldiers would be dragging and portering nearly all the equipment from the flotilla along that road to the fort. Adam had traversed the portage several times, but never with a full army and all their accoutrements. It was almost worth it, being a wounded deserter and not having to participate actively in the chaos and backbreaking labor that lay ahead. Lignery would have the entire advance planned and calculated, down to the finest detail, of that Adam was sure. His father was always ten or twelve steps ahead of everyone else; that was what made him such an effective commander. Unlike his son, Adam mused, though he felt he should give himself some credit—he was always thinking a little ahead, at least two or three snifters of rum ahead, at any rate.

Though he wasn't craving it like he had before the wound, he had asked the surgeon for whiskey a few times, and been roundly scolded for his weakness.

"Alcohol is the real killer of men, you know, not bullets," Boiford had said.

"Don't you use it to preserve specimens? That's all I'm doing, trying to preserve my organs, Doc."

Boiford had frowned at that and cursed the young trooper for being a disrespectful drunkard with no prospects in life. This was a rather obvious observation for such a learned man, Adam had quipped. His only prospect in life now was the end of a rope, once his father worked up the gumption to give the order.

Adam shook off his amused thoughts and studied the girl beside him, as the raftsmen cast off their moorings and they began drifting downriver with the rest of the flotilla. Lidia had quieted at last, though she still occasionally yanked at the ropes tying her to the cot. She appeared almost asleep but jerked awake every few minutes, hopelessly struggling against the effects of the sedative, like a small child trying to stave off the natural progression of sleep. She was not crying but there were tearstains on her cheeks. The flesh on her wrists and ankles was raw and torn, making Adam wince.

He calculated how to approach the situation for a long time, then he asked flippantly, "What's set you off, Lidia?"

It was perhaps the wrong tack to take. She turned toward him, her face scrunched and livid, blazing crimson with purple tones, and then, quite unexpectedly, she spat at him. Adam ducked, wincing in pain at the sudden movement.

"My sister's dead, you bastard. You think this is a time for levity? They killed her, and if I can get free I'm going to kill them. And if you try to stop me I'll kill you too!" She went back to writhing and bucking in her bonds, almost overturning the cot again before she quieted, unable to sustain her energy with Boiford's laudanum still settling into her system.

"I'm sorry to hear that," replied Adam, making sure his normally mocking expression was not present. He was sorry. Very sorry. He liked the girl, despite all her passion and rage. He liked her a great deal. He still felt intense, overwhelming guilt that he had been involved in the attack that had destroyed her home and killed her parents. A thought flickered into his mind and he aired it, with caution. "You think trying to kill all these troopers and getting hurt yourself would be what your sister would want?"

Then the tears began to flow down the young woman's face, a face twisted in anguish. She rolled in her bonds, not as fiercely as before, the slow tugs of a trapped creature that knows it cannot get free, but must keep trying or die from the despair of quitting. She choked on a sob and then turned her head toward him, eyes blazing again amid the tears. "You didn't know her. You wouldn't know what she wanted."

"You told me she made you promise not to kill me. That doesn't sound like the sort of woman who would want you trying to kill an entire army on her behalf."

"Shut up."

He bit his lip and waited for her ire to calm. Gradually the dramatic heaving of her chest eased to a slower, more even tempo. Adam considered what to say next. So far every word he had uttered had only enraged her more. And she was right to be upset, deeply upset. The loss of a sister, her friend and companion, that was no small thing. Even more upsetting for him was the idea that if the woman called

Sofie had failed, if she had not made it to the forces besieging Niagara, there would be no warning. It would be a slaughter. Lignery was a master of the surprise attack. He had been fighting in the wilderness of New France for more than forty years, learning every trick the Indian warriors could teach him. He would outflank the British and destroy them, dashing them against the walls of the fort, against the pikes of Pouchot's men inside.

When Adam opened his mouth to speak again, he found that Lidia had succumbed to Boiford's medication and was fast asleep. Her face was still tear-streaked, but calm and peaceful for once. He watched her sleep for a long time before he too lay down and drifted off upon his cot, not awakening until the roar of the falls was thunderous around them and the yellow-orange glow of evening had fallen upon the world.

He half sat up. Troopers were darting about the vessel, bringing her up to tie to the raft ahead of her, mooring her along with all the other boats in an inlet above the great falls. All around them, men were moving equipment to shore, shouting and struggling with some of the heavier packages. Six guards came to unbind Lidia, though she was still sleepy and did not fight them. He was unchained as well, and the two prisoners were pushed across the tied vessels to dry land.

Upon the shore stood the burnt remains of Fort du Portage or Little Fort Niagara, burned as the French troops garrisoned there had fled the fighting at the great fort beyond. It was nothing but a blackened frame of three blockhouses and fencing around a great stone hearth. Adam studied the standing walls, roofless and scorched. It had been so freshly burned that there was nothing green within the boundary of the walls. The small fort had become an empty, barren monument to the fighting beyond and to the bleak future that awaited all that country, as long as the British and French kept fighting over it.

Adam's guards shoved him into the charred remains of the little fort and knocked him to the ground before the stone chimney, his hands bound in front of him. Lidia crouched beside him, staring about with wide, confused eyes. All around them was noise and chaos as the troops worked to secure their equipment, shouting and arguing. Some packages were secured into canoes that would be hauled down the portage about seven miles and then placed back into the water. Other equipment was loaded onto the backs of soldiers, stooped and tottering from the weight, to be carried by men the entire fifteen miles that remained between Lignery's relief column and Fort Niagara.

"You're tied in front, just your hands," said Lidia suddenly. "Why don't you untie me? I can run on and make it to Fort Niagara before your father does. I can warn them that he's coming."

Adam looked down at his bound wrists. He rolled to a sitting position, wincing involuntarily and glancing around to assess the feasibility of Lidia's half-formed scheme. The surgeon was gone, busy directing the men who would be carrying his delicate instruments and medicines. The two prisoners were alone, save for the distracted guards that stood a little way off. Adam reached across and began tugging awkwardly at the ropes binding Lidia's hands behind her back.

She kept her head twisted to watch him, studying him with those bright blue eyes—made brighter by the red vessels so prominent in the sclera from her crying—surveying his every move, her expressive face unreadable, for once. When he had freed her wrists, she reached down and began frantically tearing at the ropes around her ankles. As she worked she said suddenly, "You're coming with me, of course."

"Lidia, I'm not coming with you. Indeed, if I'm being quite honest, I don't think it's a good idea at all for you to be running off into the wilderness by yourself. You could get hurt, or killed, and you're still not fast on that ankle."

"My ankle is fine. And I won't be running off into the wilderness by myself, I'm taking you with me. If I leave you here they'll kill you."

"I'm not coming, Lidia. I'm done running away and hiding from judgment."

"Judgment?" she scoffed at him, and she was back, the girl he had met twice now pointing a gun at his head on two very different occasions. She was full of her old anger and determination; she would not be gainsaid. "What judgment? Because you ran away from a life of killing people for a king you don't know to have money and power he doesn't need?"

Adam laughed. It was the second time she had made him laugh, and it hurt his abdomen like a bayonet through the gut. "No . . . I've done terrible things in this war, Lidia, I've killed and killed and killed again. The massacre at German Flatts was my first action, but I've been in many more since then, battles, skirmishes, ambushes. I am a terrible, brutal man, and I deserve to die. You, of all people, should understand that."

"And you will have your wish," said a new, familiar voice from behind them.

Adam spun as Captain Aubry approached, flanked by his soldiers, including the tall, leering form of Corporal Renaud. In a few moments, despite Lidia's protests and bitter punches, her wrists were secured again. The men pinned Adam to the ground. He only struggled for an instant, then one of the men shoved his hand hard directly into the bandage across his abdomen and the pain shocked him into stillness. Adam, panting and dripping sweat, looked up at Aubry.

But Aubry did not return his gaze; he was standing over the bound young woman, his arms akimbo and his face contorted with anger. "You lied to Captain Lignery, Lidia, and he may have become soft and sentimental, but I promise you that I have not. You promised not to run if Lignery sent the deserter to the infirmary to receive medical care, and yet here you are, trying to make an escape, again."

"You and your precious Captain Lignery had my sister killed," retorted Lidia.

"We did not order her killed. Lignery sent his trackers after a suspected spy, someone we thought might be taking word of our approach to the British. She fell from a great height when his trackers caught up to her. They tried to save her—that's how they came into possession of that wampum belt."

"Well, it's my belt now, if my sister is dead, and you should give it back to me." Lidia's lip was trembling, her hair askew, even tied as she was, Adam thought she looked formidable, unafraid, vengeful, like the fierce Athena of the Greeks.

"You are not getting the belt back. You are not getting any special treatment. You told the captain that you lived alone in the cave, but your sister lived there with you. You sent your sister to warn the British. You broke your promise that you wouldn't try to escape, more than once. You are as much our enemy as the men waiting for us outside Fort Niagara. So you will be tied like an animal until we defeat the British. And afterwards . . . well, I know many families in Montreal that could use a serving girl, and I know many

Mississauga sachems who would love to add a slave to their collection. Now I need you to tell me the truth this time. Where was your sister going? Was she alone? Was she taking Adam's message to the British?"

"What does it matter now if she was? She's dead! She's no threat to you," spat Lidia in return. "I'm not telling you anything."

Aubry's face paled, ever so slightly, and his jaw tightened. It was an expression Adam knew well, all too well. He had had dealings with Aubry many times before, a friend of his father, and an accomplished commander. Aubry was a disciplinarian, more so than Lignery. The captain turned, still avoiding meeting Adam's gaze, and nodded to the guards standing over the deserter.

The soldiers yanked Adam to his feet and lifted his tied wrists above his head, looping a rope through the bindings and securing it to a charred but sturdy supporting pillar of the former fort's missing roof, forcing him to stand on his toes. He saw Renaud unroll a coiled object from under his arm as he moved around behind Adam, out of his line of sight. Adam did not struggle. Glancing over his shoulder, past the corporal, he saw Lidia peering at him, bewildered and alarmed, not yet aware of what was happening. Perhaps the laudanum was still dulling her mind a bit. He gave her a faint smile of encouragement.

"Don't tell them anything, Miss Erghamer," he said, feeling suddenly quite brave and strong, his voice soft and soothing. Then the whip struck his back and he arched in pain, biting his lip to stifle a cry.

Over and over again the lash cut into his skin. It felt as if a farmer was taking a plow to his flesh, the leather creating new, bloody furrows with every swing of the corporal's wrist. Renaud was a brute with the whip; Adam had seen him at it before. He was fast and he struck hard, and he was using the extra vehemence he bore toward Adam in particular to fuel the beating. Adam sagged in the ropes, drawing in slow, deep breaths between gasps as each blow cut into him. The world was beginning to fade blissfully around the edges, not so blissful as when liquor dimmed the lights, but at least the line between consciousness and unconsciousness was blurring. He gritted his teeth, staring into the blackness as it grew in his field of vision. Soon the pain wouldn't be there anymore. Then Lidia's shrill voice cried out and the corporal stopped, his hand raised for another blow, panting from the exertion of his flogging.

Adam glanced over his shoulder, trying to shake his head, trying to offer Lidia that same smile he had given before. It was an expression he hoped looked brave and encouraging, but perhaps it just looked like the grin of a stupid clown tied to a post with his back shredded into bloody ribbons.

"Stop! Stop it. Arrit! Or whatever the hell you say. I'll tell you, Captain Aubry. Sofie did take the message Adam was carrying and she was going to warn the British that you were coming. She was alone. Alone except for the baby she was carrying." Lidia choked on the words as she said them.

"She traveled nearly a hundred miles alone in the wilderness with a baby?" asked Aubry, sounding both surprised and impressed.

"Of course she did, because she was a bloody hero, and now she's a stupid bloody dead hero."

"If you aren't lying this time, then at least we can feel secure that the British do not yet know of our approach." Captain Aubry turned and stopped, staring at Adam's bloodstained back, and Adam watched the man's cheek spasming in turmoil, his teeth grinding. Finally he said,

"Cut him down and tie him properly, so he can't free the girl. We'll bring them down the portage trail last."

"Why don't you just finish me?" cried Adam in French, his voice a harsh, painful growl. "You've gone this far, why not end it? Respect for Captain Lignery?"

The whip cracked loudly, tearing across Adam's rib cage. But Aubry reached out and caught the corporal's arm before he could raise it again.

"'*Sir.*' You've gone this far, '*sir*,'" corrected the corporal with a sneer at Adam.

"What are you going to do if I disrespect my officers?" returned Adam. "Kill me? I have nothing to fear anymore."

"Enough!" snapped Aubry. "The prisoner will die in Fort Niagara, in front of all the assembled troops, once the battle is over. He will not die here and he will not die now. His father issued the official sentence this morning." With that parting shot, Aubry turned and stalked from the ruins, bumping into the surgeon.

"What in heaven's name is going on here?" cried Boiford, pushing past Aubry and his soldiers and running to Adam's side as he was released from the post. He began immediately to poke at the new wounds on Adam's back, making the young man jump and pull away. "I leave for an hour, not more than an hour, and you come and brutalize my patients?"

"Mind your addresses, Doctor. This is the last time I'll forgive you for not giving due respect," snapped Captain Aubry before he departed.

"The boy was trying to free the girl. We caught him, and the captain needed information from the girl—" began the corporal.

"*Silence! Chut!*" cried the surgeon, both hands covered in blood from Adam's new wounds. "If you're going to tie the boy down, then do it so his back is facing up, and have a care, be gentle."

In the tumult and fuss that ensued, Adam felt himself fading in and out of consciousness as waves of pain washed over him. He kept his head turned to the side, watching Lidia as they laid him on the ground and twisted his hands behind his back. She had not taken her eyes off him since the whipping. There was distress in that lovely, expressive face, and he hated it. It made no sense to him at all. Why did she care now? She had tried to kill him herself, and now suddenly she wanted him safe and uninjured. She had even avowed her sister's mission in defense of him. It was likely the result of her emotional state, he reasoned, having just lost her sister and niece or nephew. He wasn't sure if the baby he had seen in his delirium was a boy or girl; they all looked alike at that age.

After Boiford had cleaned Adam's new wounds, he turned to the young woman and reached out to check her arms and wrists, bruised and raw from fighting her bonds as Aubry's soldiers had brutalized Adam. She drew back, snapping at him with her teeth.

"Don't you bloody touch me," she hissed. "Keep your stinking salves and your fucking sedatives away from me."

The surgeon sighed and shook his head. "As you wish, my dear. You're a right fierce woman, no mistake about that. I'll let you be for now." He rose and shuffled off. A detail of soldiers was still working to pack up the infirmary and everything it contained, and they were making an enormous mess of things.

Lidia's eyes had left Adam for a moment, glaring vehemently after the surgeon, and he missed those bright blue pools. "You know, Lidia," whispered Adam, receiving a thrill of satisfaction as her glance darted back to him, "things would be much easier for you if you stopped fighting all the time and let other people help you."

"What do you bloody know about it? You haven't let your father help you with anything, and now he's going to kill you. Where do you come off lecturing me? I don't need anyone's help, I don't deserve—" She cut herself off and then switched her tone to something more haughty and distant. "I'm fine on my own. I'm sorry I offered to take you with me. Clearly that was a stupid idea. If you had just finished untying me quicker you wouldn't be in the state you're in. What happened to you isn't my fault. I tried to stop them."

"Of course, you're right. But what were you going to say about receiving help? That you don't deserve it?"

Lidia bit her lip, and he could see from the anguish in her blue eyes that his guess had been correct. He did not speak again but waited—giving her the opportunity to answer.

"I didn't save my parents," she said after what felt like an eternity.

"You didn't save them?"

"You and your troopers came, and I stood up and took that gun and went out to fight, but they killed my parents. I didn't save them."

"You were a girl."

"I was nineteen."

"You were one girl against an army of trained marines. What do you think you should have been able to do?"

"I should have saved my parents, or died in the attempt."

"And you nearly did die in the attempt."

"And Sofie." The tears began sliding down her pink cheeks again. "I let Sofie go. I should have gone. If I had gone she wouldn't be dead."

"How were you going to ride a hundred miles on that ankle, Lidia? Sofie had a choice. She didn't have to take that risk. She could have stayed in that cave with you. She could have let you go. You didn't force her to go, she chose it, Lidia, because she was a brave, strong woman, a hero, like you said." He paused, watching the young woman's face for any effect his words might be having. Her cheeks stretched taut and her lips trembled. He went on, "She was a hero, like you, Lidia. You're a strong, brave woman too, very brave, and I don't want you to forget that. You deserve help, you deserve honor, you deserve a beautiful, full life, unscarred by bitterness, unscarred by the horrors of war. By this time tomorrow I'll be dead and you can forget me, the monster that tried to smash your face in two years ago. But don't forget what I'm telling you. You're a hero, Lidia, a brave, bold hero. Do you understand?"

Lidia looked at him, a startled expression on her face, but they could speak no more. The troopers had returned and it was time for them to start the last leg of the journey, down the portage road to Fort Niagara.

11

LIDIA

~

July 23, 1759
Niagara Falls portage trail

The troopers pinned Lidia down as they released one limb at a time, moving her arms to her front for balance and binding her wrists again, while freeing her ankles. She was still fighting, but with little spirit, feebly swinging her fists and yanking away when she was touched, but more as an afterthought than with any real ferocity. She allowed the surgeon to come back and resplint her ankle, and all the while she kept gaping at the young man with the bloody back—the young man she had hated so much only a week before.

Her first reaction to Adam's words had been anger and disbelief, that this *boy* would presume to lecture her, the way Sofie used to. But the earnest look deep in those hazel eyes had calmed her rage. He wasn't a boy. He was a man, and he had meant it. He had meant what he said. Kind, encouraging words after she had let him be whipped so brutally. The corporal had struck him at least fifteen, perhaps twenty times before she stopped him. Yet Adam looked at her with soft, worshipful eyes, no blame in his expression. Her chest tightened as the men began pushing her with her slow limping gait through the ruined fort, back toward the portage. She glanced for a second over her shoulder to see the troopers escorting Adam, calm and cooperative, then she lost sight of him as she joined the column of Lignery's forces.

Her guards shoved her along a dusty, broad path, partially overgrown with grass, nettles, and poison ivy, toward the roar of the waterfall. Soon it was difficult to hear anything above the sound of millions of pounds of water thundering into the river below. Dr. Boiford was fussing as soldiers descended the trail with his instruments crammed into their packs. He ran about in a tizzy, shouting and waving his arms in alarm as troopers jostled his equipment and medicines, and misplaced his specimens. The heady, buzzed sensation from the laudanum persisted, dulling Lidia's senses and making her feel as if she were walking in a dream. The ankle didn't hurt like it had before. The medicine's effects had turned the pain from sharp jolts to a dull, throbbing ache.

A little while later, as she was beginning to awaken more, a soldier tied a rope around her middle, taking the other end in his hand. At first she did not understand why she was being put on a leash, but then she found herself descending along the steep escarpment; the rope was to catch her if she lost her footing. In many places she was forced to go backwards, groping awkwardly with her bound wrists and reaching with her feet, slipping and sliding in the rocks and scree. Every time she stepped on loosened stones she would fumble, scrabbling at the dirt and causing a small avalanche of shale to fall on the soldiers below her. She could no longer think of Adam, or of Sofie, or of anything, save her slow, careful descent. All her energy had to be focused on staying upright, and not tumbling down the slope, nearly sheer in places. Each time she lost her footing —and there were numerous such instances—the rope yanked hard around her middle, rubbing her flesh raw beneath her waistcoat.

The descent seemed like utter madness, stupidly steep, the shells of fallen packs scattered in the shrubs and rock, men sweating and panting all around. The moments when the grade lessened, she cast a glance toward the falls, barely visible in the darkness of the looming night. But there was yet a faint shimmering of rainbows cast by the fading gleam of the sun setting behind the falls. Even what little she could see of the waterfall was beautiful. Unbelievably beautiful. Breathtaking. Sofie had told her of Niagara Falls before, but she had thought her sister touched the way she had so absurdly romanticized a bunch of water. Now that she glimpsed those falls herself, Lidia felt Sofie had done no justice to their magnificence. The thoughts of Sofie kept coming to her mind, and with them a wetness to her face, and Lidia knew she was too far away from the falls for that dampness to be the spray of river water.

It took hours for the entire column to reach the bottom of the escarpment and Lidia sank to the ground, not caring about the dirt on her breeches, panting, exhausted, shivering in the darkness. She darted her gaze around, looking instinctively for an escape, like she always did. The laudanum had worn off and her ankle throbbed, and appeared twice the size it had been at the top of the steep trail. It felt wobbly and unstable. She turned her attention away from her sprained joint and toward the falls again, almost invisible, largely obscured by the forest. But the waning crescent moon illuminated a hazy mist far away, at the base of the waterfall, rising above the trees. There were only about fifteen miles from the base of the falls to Fort Niagara, if she remembered correctly. They were getting close, desperately close.

She felt, for an instant, a mad urge to run and jump into the river. If she jumped in she would be swept away; perhaps she would die at the whim of the current and the rolling rapids, but if she lived, the water would take her swiftly to the British, and she would complete Sofie's mission. The mission Sofie had died trying to accomplish. She heard the sound of men yelling and rose, looking up to see Adam, still far up the steep trail, stumbling and weary. When he turned to look down the escarpment, his face glowed gray in the moonlight. The blood on his back stained his white shirt dark, and she remembered his exhortation that if she ran she must leave him behind. Her jaw tightened and the muscles in her neck tensed; she clenched her fists, useless in their ropes. Then she felt someone yanking the rope around her middle, tugging her up and murmuring at her in French.

She rose, jerking away from the soldier holding her leash, taking a few steps on her own, her ankle teetering beneath her. Despite the lateness of the hour, the column was still moving steadily north. A vast, unstoppable force, winding like a white-blue serpent along the portage road. She shot one more glance toward Adam and then allowed herself to be led on, falling in among the marching, exhausted troops.

Finally they reached a broad, flat area, a glade among towering walnut trees. The men began setting up a quiet camp, without fires or tents, simply unrolling their blankets and collapsing into snoring repose. There were six guards around her who led her off to the side of the camp, toward a tree where she assumed they meant to tie her. She resisted, glaring at them, looking back in the darkness for any sign of Adam, but he had long ago fallen far behind.

"Does it take so many French troopers to guard one German woman?" she asked scornfully, and the soldiers stared at her with blank expressions—not an English speaker among them.

"*Le capitaine demande la fille*," said another voice, loud in the relative quiet of the camp. She spun to see one of Lignery's aides riding toward them.

A trooper reached out to grab Lidia, but she kicked at him and turned, yanking on the leash around her abdomen.

"Easy, easy, you can't just throw her about like a sack of moldy potatoes," called the familiar voice of Boiford, speaking in English. He pushed the French troopers out of the way and switched to rapid French speech and then back to English. "Apologies, Miss Erghamer. These uncivilized barbarians from Canada could make sure you understand what's happening, but instead they choose to frighten and intimidate you. The indecorousness of it all, I tell you. Captain Lignery requests your services as a translator further up the road."

"My services as a . . . doesn't he have a translator? Why would I translate for him after all he's done? He has condemned his son to die and I just watched his fellow commander have Adam flayed alive and now he wants me to serve him?"

"You can address your inhibitions to perform his request with Lignery himself, not me," replied the surgeon, his tone brusque and annoyed. "From my standpoint, your hysterics have subsided and you are safe to perform whatever duties the captain requires of you, whether you choose to comply or not."

Begrudgingly, Lidia allowed the men to lift her onto the horse in front of the aide, who turned and spurred the animal up the road, winding through the sleeping figures that lay scattered everywhere. Lignery had stopped further along the portage. He stood with a contingent of Indian warriors. She recognized the Seneca sachem Tsa'degëöye:s among them. The aide let her slide to the ground. She steadied herself against the horse's shoulder and then turned to face the captain, drawing herself up as tall as she could, wishing that she had been granted the impressive German height her sister had borne with such grace and power.

"Your lackey here tells me you want me to translate for you, but I'm not going to do it."

"Lidia, the only translator that speaks Seneca has gone on far ahead, with Captain Aubry, but I believe you speak it well."

"I do. I've learned to speak it well, living alone on the shores of Lake Erie. But I'm not translating for you."

"Why is that?"

"I just watched Captain Aubry brutalize your son, only a few hours ago. You did nothing. Don't tell me you didn't know. And after all the fine things you said about loving Adam and hating all this, you had him whipped."

"I'm having my son hanged, Lidia. Hanged. I did not know that Aubry had him flogged, but the whipping won't kill him, and indeed, compared to some of the punishments he's received for his drunkenness in the ranks, it was probably nothing. Compared to some of the punishments I received as a young, stupid soldier in the ranks, it was probably nothing. To be in *les troupes de la marine* is a brutal life, Miss Erghamer. Adam knows that well."

"It wasn't nothing. Aubry tortured him to make me talk —to make me tell him about my sister, about what she was doing in the wilderness and whether or not she was alone. You're both monsters. Adam is right to despise you."

Lignery's face seemed to tighten as he studied her intently. "You've said your piece, Miss Erghamer, but hear me now. I will not hesitate to have the boy flogged again if you refuse to translate for these warriors."

Lidia's eyes widened as she struggled to reconcile the loving father who had confided his pain to her, and the brutal captain now threatening to torture his son so she would cooperate. Baffled and angry, she turned to Tsa'degëöye:s.

"I will translate for this French uncle," she said.

Tsa'degëöye:s bowed his head to her gratefully. "Tell the great uncle that we have spoken to all the sachems among our brother nations and we have determined not to go into this battle with him. It is better for our people to remain neutral in this fight."

Lidia translated this into English and Lignery frowned.

"The English will outlaw your way of life and push you westward, into unfriendly territory, forcing war upon you from all sides. If you do not fight alongside us, you risk the death of all your people, not today, not tomorrow, but soon, and forever. The Seneca will be obliterated from the earth by the English, their ways and their languages forgotten, and it will be so for all the other nations in this land as well."

Lidia turned, darting her gaze back and forth between the two men. She spoke hesitantly at first, having hardly formed her intentions before her mouth opened. "Your people are making a foolish choice for which you will suffer greatly. The French have been your friends, protected your way of life, fought alongside you. They have guarded the chain of your friendship as if it were more precious than their own children. But you show yourselves cowards by refusing to fight with us in our hour of need."

The sachem drew back, his brow wrinkling. "Are these the words of a friend?" he asked, scanning Lignery's impassive face. Then, returning his gaze to Lidia, he went on, "We will continue to travel alongside your forces. But if the insults persist, rest assured, the chain of our friendship will break, and we will not enter the fight at the fort alongside you, nor hazard any of our lives ever again for the sake of your great king over the sea. What do we owe the French?"

Lidia artfully translated the words to English, altering the language just enough to hide the offense she had given in her translation.

"We appreciate you continuing alongside us in the march to the fort, and when the time comes I trust that you will change your mind about fighting alongside us. There will be much honor and many scalps to be taken."

"The French father is glad you are not fighting alongside his men. He says that you are cowardly curs and the French would be ashamed to fight at the side of lazy pigs like yourselves."

For a few minutes after this translation, the warriors spoke heatedly among each other, and several of them even reached for their weapons, but Tsa'degëöye:s raised his hand. A wise move, thought Lidia. There were too many Frenchmen for his small band of warriors to effect anything save their own deaths if they turned against Lignery now.

"Your insults will not be forgotten," said Tsa'degëöye:s

coldly and spat on the ground before turning and walking away.

"He did not take my words well," mused Lignery. "Do you think they'll fight alongside us in the end, Miss Erghamer? Most of the time, even when they show reluctance, their warrior spirits cannot resist the heat of battle—the joy of killing and taking scalps. There is too much renown and honor in it for them to miss an opportunity to show their prowess in battle."

"I suppose they might. They do continue to travel alongside you, after all. That is something."

Lignery went to his horse, issuing orders to his aide, who reached down to catch hold of Lidia, but she pulled away. Seeing her struggle, the captain turned back and spoke again in French to the aide, who relented, releasing Lidia's arm.

"The men, as you have seen, are taking a few minutes' rest, but we are not camping here. You may ride with me, Miss Erghamer, and unbound, if I can again have your word that you will not run. You have lied to me twice now, but I am willing to give you another chance. I do not like to see a young woman tied like an animal."

"I'm not going to run," said Lidia. She had found a better way to succor the British and defeat the French, using the languages she had learned in her youth. Adam had been right. Her ankle throbbed with pain, and every step was agony; to run now would be foolhardy in the extreme and would help no one. Her best position would be at Lignery's side, mistranslating for him and impeding the already tenuous alliance between the French and the Haudenosaunee. Cooperation was her one chance at defeating Lignery, and Adam's only chance at survival. That last thought, the thought of saving Adam, surprised her immensely. But she could not deny the desire. The memory of him attacking the corporal on her behalf mingled now with the memory of the corporal's whip upon his back—of how every slash felt like it had torn into her own flesh.

Hesitating, the aide finally obeyed his commander's orders and cut the ropes on Lidia's wrists. She rubbed them, noting the raw, swollen skin. Then she turned back to the captain, who extended a hand, pulling her up into the saddle behind him. She wrapped her arms around his middle and he spurred the horse up the trail, taking a winding deer path, keeping mostly out of sight of the troops lying all along the road.

"I'll let them rest a bit, but then we must move on. We'll be in front of the fort tomorrow, easily," he said after a while, more to himself than to her, she thought, but speaking in English.

"And then what?"

"There will be a battle, and we will win. There are more British there, but they are scattered, stretched out. They cannot hope to stand against a force like ours in their current position, if Pouchot's messages are to be trusted. We so far have the element of surprise; despite your sister's and my son's ill-fated attempts to warn them, it seems word has not gotten through after all." He was quiet for a few moments and then said, "I am sorry about your sister, Lidia. From what little I've gleaned from the trackers' reports and from you, she must have been a very brave woman, as brave as you are."

"Much braver than I am," replied Lidia and felt the hot rush of tears starting down her cheeks again. Her voice had a muffled, choking quality to it that she didn't like at all. She did not want to seem weak before Captain Lignery.

"I am also sorry that Captain Aubry subjected you to the

torment of watching him harm someone you seem to care about, for whatever reason. Is he . . . ?" He did not finish the question.

"He's all right," said Lidia. "A little bloody, but nothing compared to the wound he had. I . . . I should have spoken up sooner, though. Fifteen, maybe twenty lashes they gave him before I told them what they wanted to know. Perhaps I'm the monster, after all."

"After a while, war makes monsters of all the men and women so unlucky as to be caught up in one," replied Lignery.

"Then I look forward to untangling myself from this war as soon as I can."

"Very soon. By this time tomorrow we will have raised the siege, and you will be a free woman, Lidia. I keep my promises."

"And Adam will be dead."

His answer was slow, almost painful. He repeated the words she had spoken exactly, one by one, as if they were dragged from his mouth by a team of horses. "And Adam will be . . . dead."

"I'm sorry," she burst out, then quieted herself. It was a brief flash of empathy for the captain, but she had to quell it. She could not afford to care for this man, this man who was going to murder his own son. She was going to betray him. She was going to keep pushing the Indians away. She was going to save Adam from the brutal laws of military discipline. She was going to avenge Sofie's death, if it was the last thing she did. But somewhere inside, despite her resolve, she found herself caring about this father, caught up in a war he didn't cause, like her, and made a monster by it, just like her.

"Adam had a twin, when he was born, you know."

"You told me that, yes, once before."

"Daniel, his name was Daniel. They were as alike as two peas. Indeed, to this day I'm not sure if Daniel is the one who survived or if it was Adam. But we believe Daniel died when he was an infant, little more than a year old. I told Adam, that day that you brought me to him in your cave, that I wished he had died and Daniel had lived. I . . . I regret those words immensely. I wish they both could have lived and flourished and grown into fine young men. I wish more than anything that . . . that Adam was going to survive tomorrow."

"I cannot imagine losing a child, let alone multiple children."

"It is the way of life here. A father is incredibly fortunate to have more of his brood grow to adulthood than the number that die in childhood. Such is the life we choose to lead—the strong die, the weak perish, no matter how you try to save them. In Old France it is not quite so brutal now as this."

"Have you thought about returning there?"

Lignery did not respond for a long time, so long, in fact, that Lidia thought perhaps he had not heard her question. But, at last, he spoke. "I would go to France, bring my wife and my children to a safer life in that old country, if I could. But I cannot leave here. Perhaps I am selfish, Lidia, but the vastness of this wilderness, the harshness of it, I think there is no place more feral and ferocious and beautiful on earth than New France. I think the brutality of it makes it all the more unspeakably beautiful. Unlike France, where the natural world has been tamed and twisted to make it serve man. It would kill me to leave all this behind: the waterfalls, the mountains, the rivers, the gorges, the impossibly vast lakes, like oceans unto themselves. The sun sets more brilliantly here than it has over France for hundreds of years, I think. I have often felt that in New France it is possible to touch the very face of God."

To touch the face of God. Lidia mused on that phrase as the horse moved through the trees in the pitch blackness. She heard the calls of the sergeants rousing their men, and soon she and the captain were followed by the sounds of marine troopers marching along the road, tins clanking, the panting of labored breathing; the soldiers of Old and New France, pushing hard into the last stretch of harsh, unspeakably beautiful wilderness that lay between them and Fort Niagara.

~

July 24, 1759
Three miles south of Fort Niagara

THE WINDING ROAD, FOLLOWING THE RIVER'S EDGE, WAS overgrown with vines, sumac, five-leaf and poison ivy, and grass yellowed by the relentless summer sun. Lignery had paused again as morning began to dawn slowly. They were close, very close. He had been dispatching men and conversing with Aubry all morning in a flurry of constant activity, orders, and long discussions in French that were lost on Lidia. The soldiers were lying at ease, trying to nap wherever they could. Lidia thought that if she could just climb to the top of one of the towering oaks, she would be able to see Fort Niagara in the distance. She had been anticipating the sounds of cannon shots, the chaos of a long-standing siege, but the forest was quiet that morning, save for the French murmurs all around her and the soft cooing of mourning doves. The busyness surrounding the commander gradually abated and she watched as Lignery stood alone by a fallen log that he was using as a table, staring down at a chart where scattered pebbles, acorns, and walnuts were distributed to signify the positions of various forces.

Despite the early hour, the July heat was already rising. Lidia dashed sweat from her brow, studying Lignery, who still did not move, standing quiet, waiting. He looked calm, detached, and resolved, his eyes intermittently closing. He seemed to be listening to the sounds of the forest around him. The expression on his face was somewhere between excitement and sorrow.

"Have you ever seen the French marines march into battle, Lidia?" he asked, unexpectedly.

"No. When German Flatts was attacked it was night. I saw only scattered shapes, fire, and chaos."

"When you see my column of men in uniform marching into battle, you may understand why men go to war. Why men march bravely into the face of death. There is a greatness in it that you must see and feel to understand. It cannot be explained."

"My sister and my parents believed that to kill was the greatest sin there is—that war was utterly evil."

"And you, what do you think?"

"I . . ." Lidia trailed off. "I think sometimes it has to be. Even within the same families people fight. People who grew up in the same way, speaking the same tongue, having the same values instilled in them, still they fight, and sometimes bitterly. In fact, I think the most dark and bloody battles happen inside shared homes. If even families can't be at peace, perhaps fighting is just in our nature, a part of who we are. But it would be better if war didn't have to be. It would be better if men and women knew how to have peace and how to keep peace when they do have it."

The popping of distant gunshots, followed by whoops and horrific screams, split the quiet morning, echoing across the forest. Lignery looked north in alarm, issuing orders to an aide in rapid French. The man, with a glance of trepidation at his captain, turned and started off through the trees, in the direction of the disturbance. The gunshots died away, but still there were cries, some joyous—the battle cries of Indian warriors—but most the shrieks of men in unspeakable agony.

"What is happening?" asked Lidia, breathless, her eyes wide.

Lignery shook his head. "The scouts in the area must have found someone. But those gunshots will alert the British that we are here."

A little while later, as the muffled screams faded away, one of the Seneca men returned with Lignery's aide. In his hand the warrior held a matted, bloody scalp of reddish hair. Lidia shuddered and averted her gaze, but Lignery waved her over.

"Lidia, I still need you to translate," he said, and turned back to the warrior. "Sir, I would have you tell me what has transpired in the woods beyond."

She translated.

The warrior drew himself up tall, turning away from Lidia and toward the captain. "There were soldiers in the trees, a small group of soldiers. They are dead now, save a few that have been taken down the embankment for our warriors' sport."

Lidia shuddered at the idea of the sport they might inflict upon a captive. She knew well the stories of torture and slow death wrought on prisoners of war. The lucky soldiers were the ones who had fallen in the forest. She translated to Lignery.

"The British will know we are here from the sounds of your attack," said Lignery.

"The British already know we are here," replied the warrior. "Nearly a hundred and fifty of them lie in ambush blocking the road to the fort. They've built a bulwark there."

Lidia's heart rate increased, thumping at what felt like a thousand times a minute. She turned to Lignery, quelling the excitement within her, trying to keep it from showing on her expressive face. So damn expressive. She spoke slowly and evenly in English. "They may have heard us firing, but there is no movement from them still. They do not come against you, and my men are satiated for now. They longed for blood. Too long have we been marching quietly in the forest with your womanly, domesticated soldiers."

Lignery shook his head, frowning. "As you say, sir. Then we can count upon your warriors in the coming fight, if they are hankering so strongly for battle?"

"We will speak with the members of the Six Nations that are allied with the British soldiers, and then we will let you know our final answer," replied the warrior, then, not waiting to hear Lidia translate his words, he turned and disappeared into the forest.

More than an hour passed before the Indians returned to speak with Lignery, and by then one of the other translators had joined them. Lidia would have to be very careful if she was going to continue mistranslating. She could only hope that she had already done enough and the Indians would not bring up the soldiers waiting in Lignery's path again.

"What have you and your brothers of the Six Nations decided?" asked Lignery, exuding patience and understanding, not allowing any emotion to show on his face. Aubry stood at his side, his whiskers trembling with anger at the reluctance of their allies to join in the coming fray.

"We have spoken to our brothers that are allied with the British. We will not go into this battle alongside your men," replied Tsa'degëöye:s. "This is not our fight."

"Fort Niagara protects your people and provides supplies to your clans all throughout this region," snapped Aubry angrily when Lidia had completed her translation. "Where would you be without the French? Those of you who are wealthy would be poor and crawling in the dirt."

Lignery placed a hand upon Aubry's arm. He turned solemnly to the sachem. "We would be honored to fight alongside your warriors, as we have in many past battles. Are your men not hungry for action and blood, for the honor that comes with warfare?"

"They have scalps from the sortie in the forest a few hours ago," returned Tsa'degëöye:s. "They have drawn blood and honored their families. They are content, for now."

"Then so be it. We will march without your people, and you will wait upon us here, in the forest."

The sachems nodded and moved away, back toward the river where the distant screams had finally faded.

"Ungrateful bastards," said Aubry, speaking in English, Lidia assumed to prevent his discontent with the Indians from being heard by the surrounding officers. It would be poor form for a commander to foment mistrust with their allies. "We've supported them and helped them all these years, then when it comes to a decisive battle they withdraw."

"We don't need them," replied Lignery. He switched back to French and Lidia understood nothing else that was spoken. A few minutes later orderlies were dispatched in all directions and there was movement down the waiting column lined along the forest road. One of Lignery's aides took hold of her elbow, as if to escort her away.

"*Attendez une minute*," said the captain, and he stepped toward her. In that moment, more than ever before Lidia thought he had a kind, fatherly face. "I will leave you with the other prisoner near the rear of the advance, close to the battle, but behind all my troopers, where you'll be safe. If you try to resist or run, they will bind you."

"I won't try to run," replied Lidia, shoving the aide's hand away from her. "My translation skills may come in useful in the battle ahead, Captain Lignery, perhaps you ought to keep me close."

Lignery smiled, lines of merriment crinkling the skin around his hazel eyes. "Your offer is most courageous and noble, Miss Erghamer, but I have already importuned you more than enough, and you know the Indians will not be joining us in the battle. It is better if you wait behind, with Adam. Selfishly . . . I think your company would be a comfort to him, and I don't want him to be alone, on this of all days."

Lidia allowed the aide to push her away, back toward the rear of the forces, but the captain called to her one last time. "Lidia . . . if things should go awry in the coming battle, I want you to know that it was an honor to have met you, here in the wilderness, whatever our differences have been."

Lidia stopped and the aide allowed her to face the captain once more. All around them was the glinting of gun barrels and bayonets and the sound of men readying themselves for battle. "I . . . would say the same to you, Captain Lignery. It has been an honor to know you." And then, with one last smile at the commander of the French *troupes de la marine*, she let the aide escort her back toward the place where Adam waited.

12

SOFIE

~

July 23, 1759
The British trenches outside Fort Niagara

It was late afternoon. Sofie sat in the dirt beside her sleeping infant in the regimental infirmary tent, a hellish place full of groaning, wounded men. The child looked lusty again, his fontanel less sunken, his skin less pale than before beneath the fading rash, and a fresh, healthy blush around his cheeks. He had eaten ten times that day and filled nearly as many napkins, and she was afraid to step away, lest he awake and squeal for food yet again. The surgeon had hardly spent any time with her the night before, seeming annoyed with the interruption of the sick baby among his wounded and dying soldiers.

"Is this your first one?" he had asked in distraction. When she had nodded, he had let out a loud, exasperated sigh. "They get sick, you know, they all get sick. Sometimes they die, but more often they don't. Did your mother never tell you these things? If the child lives it will be because you fed him enough to keep him nourished. Feed him, every time you think of it, every time it crosses your mind, every time he cries out. Hell, excuse me, but hell, wake him up to feed. Your milk is the medicine he needs. He's dehydrated from fever and cough—look at his fontanelle, sunken nearly through his head. Poor blighter doesn't even make tears. You'd think there would be a course of study women were prescribed before they had children." He had looked at her then and stopped talking.

Sofie had felt hot tears brimming in the corners of her eyes. She had known. She had known very well that her focus on her mission was killing her baby, but she had pushed on anyway, because she was a monster. The guilt, once confirmed, had felt as if it would make her die, her gut and heart had ached. Under the reprimands of the surgeon she had cowered like a wilting scolded child, full of shame.

"Now, now, my dear, your little one looks like he is already recovering. Feed him and I think he will survive this illness. No harm done, really. Just feed him. You can wait here in the infirmary tent. It's not a beautiful sight, but it's out of range of the shots from the fort's mortars."

She had waited through the night at her baby's side, and after a while, watching the indefatigable medical man as he worked, she had lent her own abilities to his efforts. The night passed in a horrific nightmare, moving among the wounded. Some bore simple lacerations, some were already dead in every way save their continued breathing and their beating hearts. Some had hideous wounds in their abdomens and their chests from earlier in the siege that were already soured, and they waited, rotting and in agony, for death to end their suffering. She assisted the surgeon when he sawed the leg off a man much younger than Will, a man the age of the boy Adam. He had screamed and cursed and begged for them to set him free, writhing in the grip of the surgeon and his assistants, intermittently passing out from the severity of the pain. That was a memory that Sofie knew she would never be able to forget—the feel of the boy's sweaty, slick body, struggling in her arms and the sound of piercing shrieks over the slow grinding of the saw through bone. No amount of laudanum could have helped his suffering, and the infirmary was running low on that commodity.

She had been right. She had been right all along. War was evil. Battle was evil. The killing and destruction of men was evil. Her parents had been right all along, and it only filled her with new anger at Will. Will was wrong. Fighting was not the answer. Taking up arms, murdering and dismembering others, was no way to change the world. It only made the world worse, not better. But he stubbornly refused to come home, even now, after the loss of his right hand. That had been the worst part in assisting with the amputation, imagining the same thing happening months ago in some lonely, bloody tent in the wilderness, to her Will. And she hadn't even known.

"They're moving my regiment about a mile away, to set up a bulwark along the road and watch for the French reinforcements. I guess they've had additional word confirming what you told Massey," said a voice, startling her from her grim thoughts.

She looked up to see Will standing over her. He was weary, dirty, and thin, now that she saw him in the light of day. The marching and fighting, the poor food and illness that were forever running rampant among the troops, had blighted her husband to a smaller, more fragile man over the months they had been apart. When she did not answer him, his gaze moved to the sleeping infant on the ground beside her.

"He looks better," he said, his voice soft. "I worried about him all night. I . . . until yesterday I didn't even know he existed, and now I'm worrying about him, Sofie. Staying awake all night worrying about him. What is that?"

"It's love, I think," replied Sofie, feeling her anger softening a little. He was not so confident and strong as the man who had left. The man she had married had been sure of himself to a fault, stubborn and set in his ways. Here was a man who had traveled through hell and probably had no idea how to wrap his mind around that experience. "You love him, Will. You need to come home. Don't go with your troops to the road south. Just come home with me."

"I can't desert, Sofie. I'm a soldier. I signed their papers. But . . . my enlistment period, the year I committed, ends in a few months. If I'm still alive then, I won't reenlist. Does that satisfy you?"

Sofie frowned. "It satisfies me only a little, Will. Particularly the part where you said, 'If I'm still alive then.' That I don't like at all. There are no guarantees in this business. The surgeon himself was telling me about how your own grenadiers blew off your own colonel's head in the darkness, just a few days ago. There is no certainty in war, Will, no promise that you will be alive tomorrow, let alone in three months' time."

"No, no certainty in that, sure. But I'll be hanged for a deserter if I leave now, Sofie. There's certainty in that."

She drew in a slow breath and finally nodded, looking up at him. "Then you stay until September, but that's it. If this war drags on, Will, it drags on without you. We need you at home. Your son needs you, I need you, even Lidia needs you."

Will grinned. "I do miss that wild sister of yours, now that you mention her. Is she all right?"

"She was when last I saw her. I left her guarding a prisoner, a young French soldier that we found carrying the letter I brought to Massey. He was sorely wounded, though. He likely died the day I left."

"You left her alone with a French soldier? Of course he died! Lidia probably killed him as soon as you left. She hates them. That girl hates the French more than anything in the world."

"She promised me she wouldn't kill him."

Will chuckled at that. "I wouldn't trust Lidia's promises as far as I could throw her."

Sofie stood up, dusting herself off and reaching for the cradleboard that lay beneath the cot. In a moment she was swaddling the naked infant into his dress again.

"What are you doing?" asked Will.

"Getting ready. You said we're moving a mile away?"

Will caught her arm. "I didn't say we were moving away. I said my regiment is moving about a mile away, to watch for the French."

"Where you go, William Light, I go, or was that not in the vows we said to each other?"

"Not exactly—"

"It was implied! I'm coming with you."

"There's a good chance of battle, Sofie."

"And you'll need someone to load your carbine, with your arm like that. I can do that."

"I'm not letting you come, Sofie. It's too dangerous."

"If it's not too dangerous for you, then it's not too dangerous for me! Why are you more expendable than I am? Because you're a man, that makes your life worth less than mine? I'm coming with you and your troops, Will.

That's final." She said it in the voice her mother had used many times with such good effect on her father, the voice of a woman who will not be gainsaid, and she saw Will relent. His jaw, fixed in that stubborn way of his, slowly relaxed, his lips parted slightly, and the firm set of his eyes softened into reluctant acceptance.

"You'll be putting bullets in a gun that I use to kill men, Sofie. Doesn't that go against everything you've said you believe?"

"I will be standing beside my husband and supporting him, and God is honored in that. I will not be killing anyone, but I will be by your side through the danger that's coming. I'm not going anywhere, Will. When will you accept that? We're married, forever. Till death do us part."

"But the boy?" asked Will, a pleading expression on his face, his brow wrinkling.

"He comes with me," replied Sofie. "We don't even know if there will be a battle where you are. They may come along the eastern flank, or they may cross the river and come over by water into the fort itself. I'll keep the boy safe."

"I don't want you to come with me into battle, Sofie. I don't want you to bring our child into it either."

"I know . . . and I didn't want you to go into battle either, but you did. I'm coming with you. That's final. I'll reload your carbine at your side, and if worse comes to worst, we'll die side by side, the way God intended a marriage to end."

Together the little family made their way through the thick forest, winding among the dense trees. Sofie darted glances toward the fort as they walked, silent in the daytime, no mortars sounding from the silent, ominous stone walls. The land between the British and the fortress was ravaged by burns and enormous scalded, scarred trenches that the British forces had moved slowly forward, building up bulwarks and digging in again with each short advance, leaving empty, gaping holes in their wake. Sofie still wore the garb of a man, hanging loose around her. She had found a new tricorn hat in the piles of garments taken from dead soldiers and tucked her long yellow hair into it. Nonetheless, some of the men startled and looked hard at her as she passed; she presumed more because of the cradleboard mounted on her back than any resemblance to a female that she yet bore after her trials in the wilderness.

As they approached the light infantry, she heard a voice call out, "Mr. Light, where have you been? I've been looking for you. Needed you to translate an hour ago. Shirking your duties?"

"No, sir," replied Will, stiffening and moving in front of Sofie. "I asked leave of my lieutenant, sir."

A youthful, handsome British officer blocked their path, his face smeared with dirt and sweat. He studied Will and then adjusted his gaze toward the woman standing behind his translator, and his eyebrows shot up. "Who is this? Is this a woman, Mr. Light?"

"This is Sofie Light, sir . . . my wife, sir," replied Will.

"And what is she doing on a battlefield?"

"I brought an important message to your commander, if you must know. And I am going to be reloading my husband's carbine if we do end up in a battle." As Sofie spoke, she pushed past her husband to stand tall before the young man.

The officer studied her for a long moment. "Highly irregular, Mr. Light. Though, I will admit, not without precedent. Mrs. Light, my name is Captain De Lancey of the 46th Light Infantry, and if you were indeed the messenger that brought word of the French reinforcements, then we are indebted to you. But we do not pay our debts by subjecting women to the horrors of war."

"You're not subjecting me to anything. I've spent the night in the infirmary. I've seen the horrors of war. I'm choosing of my own accord to fight alongside my husband. And if you think you can talk me out of it, or order me out of it, you're wrong. I'm not your soldier, Captain De Lancey."

De Lancey's eyebrows stretched even higher, practically touching his shock of brown hair, and for a moment he did not respond, gaping at her. Then his gaze shifted to Will and he almost smiled. "Your wife is a force to be reckoned with, Mr. Light."

"You've no idea, sir," murmured Will. "I've already asked her to stay away from the line of battle, sir, several times, sir."

"Very well, then. We do, on occasion, allow women to support us from behind, loading guns, bringing water and bullets and suchlike. But it will be upon your own head if you come to harm, Mrs. Light, and please, for God's sake, keep the fact that you are a woman as disguised as possible. I don't need my men distracted by any chivalric urges."

"As you can see, I am already doing my best to disguise myself as a man," replied Sofie. "Thank you, sir."

"Well, if you reload Will's carbine it will only make him fire faster. Will is a keen shot. Any help you can offer him will be a boon to our cause and the success of our efforts," replied the captain. "It is I who should be thanking you, ma'am, for your courage. And . . . the child?"

"He stays with me, no matter what happens," replied Sofie, firmly.

"Very well. The men are still digging in here and building a bulwark. Pitch in. And, Mr. Light, keep to the west side of the line. I'll know where to look for you if I need a translator."

"Aye, sir, understood, sir," replied Will, standing at attention as the young captain moved away through the ranks. The light infantry was digging into the ground of the forest floor, building a wall of bracken above their shallow trenches, facing south, toward the narrow road that led back toward Niagara Falls.

All afternoon and evening they dug themselves deeper into the earth, becoming nearly invisible among the fallen logs and jumbled brush. While at first Will seemed stiff and reluctant to accept Sofie's aid in his work, he gradually relaxed, allowing her to lift heavy timber alongside him and to pick up branches that he accidentally dropped. Word spread quickly that the wife of the light infantry's honored scout and translator had joined the battle line, along with word of her heroics in bringing news of the advancing French reinforcements.

"Brought a lady to fight your battles for you now, Mr. Light?" called one of the men, a broad grin on his face. "Why you even stayin' out here if she's here now? She could probably kill twice the men you did with two hands."

"Damn you, Ellis," replied Will cheerfully. It was the most cheerful he had sounded since Sofie returned. She did not know if his improved mood was from the playfulness of his fellow troops—his brothers for months now—or if it was because of the prospect of the coming battle. It wasn't just him either; everyone along the line seemed glib and constantly quipped and laughed as they worked, though occasionally an officer would pass through and remind the men to be quiet.

As evening fell, Sofie nestled close to her husband on the western flank of De Lancey's line, wedged in an uncomfortable hole in the ground, shoulder to shoulder with Will. On her lap she cradled the baby. His eyes were open and he stared up at both of them, solemn and curious. Will leaned down after a moment, bringing his bearded face close to the infant, wearing a big, stupid grin that made Sofie's heart glow.

A light burst out of the darkness, a flash and a roar of sound beyond them, and when the bright glow faded the world was plunged into a much blacker night than it had been before. But before they could become accustomed to the pitch dark again, another blast of colored light and sound flashed in the distance. Sofie pressed herself closer to Will, watching the deadly mortars bursting over the fort. She felt Will's arm wrap around her waist, pulling her into him, and her heart began to beat fast. How she had longed for this day, the day she would be wrapped in the arms of her husband again, and how little she had anticipated the actual circumstances of their reunion. In her wildest dreams she had never imagined lying in a trench beside him, on the eve of a terrible battle.

There was another blast of impressive light, white like the hottest fire, and then, in the darkness that followed, they heard a different sound, strange but somehow familiar. For an instant Sofie glanced around, and then she saw Will looking at their son with a warm, delighted expression on his face. She looked down to see their infant smiling up at them and wriggling with pleasure, letting out little barking yelps of baby laughter. He giggled for a long time, renewing his chortles whenever another mortar exploded, and the fear inside Sofie melted into fascination, and a profane appreciation for the incredible beauty of the explosions, colored lights illuminating the forest, filling the world with their unearthly glow. The child's laughter gradually died away and he drifted off to sleep.

"Why are you doing this, Sofie? You hate war, you hate killing. You've told me a thousand times how you feel about men killing men. Why are you insisting on helping me tomorrow?" asked Will during a brief pause in the gunfire and mortar shots.

"I haven't changed how I feel, if that's what you think. War is evil, Will, in every way. To take a life is the greatest sin a person can commit. It's unforgivable. There is no justification for killing, none. That is what my parents believed, and that's what I believe."

"You know I've killed people in this fight, Sofie. I didn't want to, but that's what war is, war is killing. It's nothing more than that, I don't think—it's just about killing before you get killed. So I've had to kill or let myself die. How will you forgive that, Sofie?"

Sofie waited, quiet, unsure how to respond, unsure why she felt she had already forgiven Will, now that he was here, human, alive, pressed up against her, breathing with her as one, their hearts beating with the same rhythm. Another bright flash, like lightning, but red and vibrant, burst high above them. She sighed as she watched the light fade.

"I never would have thought war could be so . . ."

"Beautiful?" Will finished her thought for her. "It is beautiful, sometimes, Sofie. But if you stay by me tomorrow, you'll see that it's also exactly the hell you think it is, probably worse."

She turned, keeping the sleeping infant balanced upon her legs but managing to press her chin against her husband's chest. "I'm not going anywhere, Will."

13

ADAM

~

July 24, 1759
Three miles south of Fort Niagara

They were bringing Lidia back, pushing her through the ranks to where Adam sat with his hands bound in front of him, his knees drawn up, and two guards standing over him. Despite her limp, she moved with a strange, wild grace, intermittently yanking her arms away from her escort when he dared to catch hold of her elbow to guide her. Adam grinned. Lidia had lost none of her spirit. So much ferocity in one small package—as volatile as a mortar. When she saw him she sped up, dashing the last few steps to kneel at his side, reaching out toward his back, covered by a scratchy shirt that scraped over his new lacerations. He pulled away, torn between his desire to have her touch him and fear of the pain that her fingers would inflict.

There was a slowness to everything that surprised Adam. An acuteness to every second and every detail around him. He was noticing things he had never noticed before: the folds of the shirt that was too big for Lidia as it fell in coiled waves of white about her arm, her exquisite, slim wrist and the strong hand protruding from it, the mud packed under her nails, the buzzing of every single fly around them, the green of the leaves with just their edges burnt to pale yellow by the relentless heat. Everything had become more real than it had ever been before, and somehow more significant. Time had slowed, but not stopped. No, time kept marching on toward his inevitable execution.

By the end of this day, Adam would not be a part of that world anymore; he would be gone. It made him happy, in a strange way, intoxicatingly happy. He smiled at Lidia, his dear ghost, this young woman who had haunted him and driven him nearly mad. She would still be living in the world when the sun set, and that was a good thing, a wonderful thing. It was something worth rejoicing over. Everything was moving slowly. So slowly. He felt he had all the time in the world, because every moment was so immediate, so acutely, deliciously real.

"Are you all right?" Her voice came as if from far away, as if it took years for each word to reach his ears.

"I'm fine, Lidia. Never better. You?"

"I was so worrie—" She stopped herself and a confused expression crossed her face, as if she was surprised by her own words. "I mean, I thought they hurt you very much when they flogged you. It looked beastly. Brutal, really."

"What, that? Oh, no. It was nothing. Stings a bit. Not the worst I've had, thanks to you. You didn't have to tell them anything, Lidia. It doesn't matter what happens to me now."

"Stop saying that," she snapped, and anger flashed in those wondrous, perfect blue eyes, anger and exasperation.

Adam shrugged. "As you wish, *mademoiselle*. But if I stop saying it that will not make it less true. Are the men advancing into battle?"

She nodded, biting her lip and turning her head back toward the front, toward the lines of soldiers gathering in a columnar formation on the narrow road to Fort Niagara. They were standing in rows of twelve, their bayonets and musket barrels shining as bright as fire in the morning sun. Adam was thrust back for an instant to a memory of a street in Montreal, and a small boy waving at his father as he rode by at the head of what the boy had thought was the finest, noblest column of soldiers in all the world. Their uniforms were fresh, new, and starched, their heads held high, the colors of their garments and banners so vibrant. Here, a few miles from Fort Niagara, was a sight just as beautiful as that day, perhaps more beautiful, for this was not a parade for show; these were men going into battle, and some of these brave men would join Adam in death in a few hours' time. He inhaled slowly, filling his chest with precious, delicious air. He would be proud to march through the gates of death into that other world beyond beside these men, these fearless soldiers.

"Are you crying?" asked Lidia, startling him back to the present.

Adam felt it then, the warmth of liquid on his lids, not dripping yet, but forming around the corners of his eyes. "Tears of joy, Lidia, just tears of joy," he mumbled, feeling drunk, but in a happy, stupid way, drunk on the liquor of his last few hours of being alive.

"Joy about what?"

"I am going to rest today, but it's beautiful. It's so beautiful, and I am so grateful for all the time I've had, Lidia, for the life I've been given. The life I never deserved to have."

"Why are you so easy to give up about everything? Why?"

Adam shrugged, still grinning. "Not much use in fighting, is there?"

"I guess I don't feel that way," she replied, scanning the guards standing over them. The two guards were facing toward the troops as they began to march away. "I think we could take these men. Then we could run and join the British."

"So that when the British are defeated we can be taken as prisoners again?" scoffed Adam, pleasantly amused by her insistence on fighting. Always fighting. "We'd just be back to where we are now if we tried that."

"Then you can stay here. But I'm going to run, just as soon as they are properly distracted," she said. She crouched, poised, like a cat on the hunt, her eyes trained on the guards.

The two men assigned to guard them were antsy. Adam could almost feel their guilt at not taking part in the battle. They had been chosen, out of all the troopers, not to have to risk their lives today. Their comrades would face the guns of the British without them, while they guarded the condemned son of their captain. But there was also an undeniable sense of relief in them as well. Adam settled himself back against the maple tree trunk that shaded them, gazing up into the shimmering green leaves. The sun poured delightful rays of warmth upon him and he closed his eyes, basking in the dappled light as it filtered through the foliage. He had forever before the end. Forever. And this was his forever: the warm summer sun, the angry young woman at his side, the twittering of birds in the treetops, the sound of men marching into battle. The rest could wait, the mystery of what came after could wait.

A gunshot sounded, then another. Adam opened his eyes to see the startled look of the guards, staring away into the distance. Just a few scattered shots, nothing more. He felt hands touching his wrists and looked down to see Lidia tearing at his bonds, trying frantically to undo them while the guards were still distracted. There were more scattered gunshots, but not a proper volley yet.

"Lidia," he whispered. "It's not worth it. If you must run, then run now. Don't try to free me."

"I'm not leaving you here," she said, her jaw set and her eyes almost crazed. "They'll kill you, Adam."

"I know that, Lidia, and it's fine. It's better if I die."

"Stop it. Stop fucking saying that. Do you hear me? I'm not leaving you here."

Adam closed his mouth. There was a dangerous warning in her words. She was ready to fight. Eager to fight. Looking for an excuse to fight. The knots and ropes binding his wrists were cruelly tight and she struggled to undo them. Then there was a cry of alarm in French, in a familiar Marseille accent. Adam's head snapped up and Lidia spun, trying to block what she had been doing from the approaching corporal.

"Stupid idiots!" cried Renaud, laying into the guards with the flat of his sword. The men, seeing what had prompted his ire, turned and pounced on Lidia. "I was sent back to guard the prisoners, and relieve you two, and not a moment too soon, it appears. Bind the girl to the tree. Then you are both dismissed back to your companies in the front. Stupid, useless oafs. Imbeciles."

Adam thrust his knees into the ground, striking at the guards with his bound arms, but one of the men whacked his head with the butt of his gun, knocking him to the side, stunned and useless. When the world stopped spinning, he felt Renaud's foot pushing into his neck, pinning him to the earth. He looked up to see the corporal's blade pressed against his chest.

Helplessly he watched as they tied the struggling German girl to the tree, winding the rope around her a dozen times and yanking it so tight that Adam could see her fighting for a moment even to breathe, her face purpling. But she wasn't staring at the men binding her, though intermittently she snapped at them with her teeth. She kept her eyes fixed on him, and the enormous man with his foot on Adam's throat. There was anger in those wild eyes, but also a strange flicker of uncharacteristic fear. The guards stuffed a kerchief into Lidia's mouth, wrapping a cord through her lips and around her neck to secure it in place.

When Adam struggled, Renaud jammed his foot harder into his neck, crushing his trachea. Adam wheezed desperately for air but found none. He kept fighting and the pressure on his throat grew worse. It was hopeless. He could not help Lidia. He could not even help himself. He hadn't the strength to fight anymore, nor the oxygen. He writhed as the edges of his vision became dim, and then the world faded to darkness. In the blackness he heard the men speaking to Renaud in French.

"Don't kill him. He is the captain's son. He will not forgive you for harming the boy."

"He's going to be executed. Why does it matter?"

"He's not going to be executed," said one of the soldiers. "The captain will not kill his own son. He'll be dismissed from the service and hidden away, like all the boys of the nobility when they transgress."

"All the more reason that I should suffocate him now, so justice can be done, eh?"

"Sir, don't do it. The captain will have you executed."

A rush of air entered Adam's lungs unexpectedly, and his vision began to return, stars bursting around him. He coughed and reached up with his bound hands toward his bruised neck.

"Who asked you, Phillipe, hmm?" snarled Renaud, spittle flying from his lips, his face flushed. "Go to the front-line, those are your orders. Now. Rejoin your company. I will guard the prisoners."

The men glanced at each other uncertainly, then they picked up their muskets and set off through the trees in the direction their marching comrades had disappeared only a few minutes before, leaving Adam alone under the maple with the corporal and the bound and gagged Lidia. Adam tried to sit up, receiving a hard kick to the stomach that knocked the breath from him. As he curled into a ball, he heard Renaud chuckling.

The corporal approached Lidia and stood back, one hand on his hip, the other fondling his groin, a lewd smile on his face. Lidia's eyes widened and she fought against the ropes. Renaud laughed again, and taking his hand from his hip, he reached out, running his fingers down Lidia's cheek and into her shirt, groping her breasts and grinning more broadly as she struggled, grunting through her gag.

"My sweet German dumpling doesn't even have her stays. She has already prepared herself for my pleasure," Renaud said tauntingly, and then he began to undo the buttons of his breeches, while Lidia fought harder against her bonds.

Adam lurched forward, struggling to his feet and toppling in a haphazard way at the corporal. Renaud didn't even turn, easily sidestepping the injured young man's desperate attack. In his wild lunge, not coming up against the solid mass of the corporal as he had anticipated, Adam lost his balance and tumbled, landing in a heap. Then Renaud began to rain kicks upon his back, rekindling the fiery pain from the whiplashes. But the corporal was distracted, he wasn't touching Lidia anymore, so Adam did not fight against the beating.

"You scum," hissed Renaud. "Worthless piece of shit." He reached down with one of his enormous hands and yanked Adam to his feet. "It's time to die, Adam de Lignery. If your father won't let you face justice, then I will." He began pushing Adam ahead of him with his musket, while Lidia fought madly against her bonds, letting out muffled cries in which Adam thought he recognized his own name. He allowed Renaud to push him away. He was going to be murdered by this man, but at least distracting him from Lidia might help her. His death might give her time to free herself and escape.

"Why not just shoot me here?" he asked.

"Because your father will know I did it. No, we go to the battlefield. I will tell him you ran and it will appear you died among the other soldiers as an accident. A casualty of the battle as you tried to get through to the British that you apparently love so much."

Adam stumbled ahead of the man, still hearing Lidia's attempts to cry his name through her gag. His mind was racing. He would have to fight Renaud when they reached a distance away in the forest; there had to be a way of keeping him from returning to the girl and hurting her. There had to be a way. But the only way he could see was a vain, hopeless attempt to challenge a much bigger man, and at a severe disadvantage, wounded and with his arms tied. Letting Renaud kill him would only leave Lidia in the same vulnerable position.

"Why do you want to kill me so badly, Renaud?" he

asked, trying to keep the man distracted by talking while his own mind raced. "I will be hanged before the sun sets today, even if you do nothing."

"You know that isn't true!" cried Renaud. "Your father comes after me because you told him I tried to have the girl. But he won't kill you. They would never execute the son of a captain. He'll forgive you and send you back to France, send you to school, and find you a new life. Make you disappear from the records. You'll be forgiven and in ten or twenty years no one will speak of what happened. But I'll be disciplined based on the testimony of a deserter, a traitor to his country and his regiment."

"You'll be disciplined based on the testimony of the girl, not my word. I was a witness, but Lidia suffered at your hands. She can testify to your attack herself."

"Suffered? She suffers nothing. I will give her delight and pleasure like no man ever has before. She'll be grateful for my touch. Perhaps I'll make her into my own little American wife, how would that be? Fill her with children and put her to work in my kitchen."

"You're a pig, Renaud. Don't you dare touch her again."

"Or what? What will you do if I dare to touch her again?" asked Renaud, scorn evident in his tone. "You'll be dead, boy, you'll do nothing. She's mine."

"She will murder you herself if you hurt her. You underestimate her."

"And you overestimate her. Say I make her my wife, I will tie her and beat her until she sees the happiness I can bring her. I won't keep her living alone in a cave in the wilderness like her family did. I'll give her a warm home and babies to keep her company. She'll learn to appreciate it."

"You're delusional! I'm warning you, you cannot tame

Lidia Erghamer. You have already hurt her enough that she has marked you for death. You hurt her more and you'll only earn a more hideous and cruel death at the hands of a rightfully vengeful woman."

"You talk like a fool," replied Renaud, spitting on Adam's back. "If she keeps fighting I'll bash her bloody head in after I've had my way with her. It doesn't matter what I do to her. She has no family, no one who will remember her or come after me. She ought to be grateful that I deign to give her attention at all. Why do you try to defend her anyway? Just because you want her soft, warm cunny for yourself. You're a spoiled brat. Like all of them. Do you know that in France I drank heavily like you do? One day I stole food from the officer's mess—not alone, I stole it along with a rich, spoiled brat. A boy who had everything handed to him in life, everything served to him on silver platters. Do you know what happened to him after that? Nothing happened to him. His transgression was buried; no one believed that he had been involved. He's a captain now, do you believe it? While I was given the choice to leave the service—to leave my livelihood! —in disgrace, or to go to New France forever, and serve there."

Adam's eyes widened, the way in which the corporal had always treated him making sense suddenly, abruptly. Because he was the same as the young noble in France, treated differently because of his connections, while the commoner from Marseille suffered like a commoner from Marseille. Like a nobody.

"You're wrong. If you give my father time, just a few more hours, you'll see that not all those of a higher class escape punishment the way that noble did in France. He'll follow through, Renaud. Lignery will kill me."

The big corporal scoffed, shoving Adam forward again.

Then Adam heard it, the pattering of gunshots, then a proper volley mingled with cries and shouts. The battle had begun in earnest, and they were close, very close. He felt his heart begin to thud heavily, the way it always did before a battle, and sweat started down his brow and chest, making his shirt cling to him. He always had a good few drinks before a battle, always, and went in fortified by whatever disgusting alcoholic beverage he had consumed—but not this time. This time men were killing each other just a few hundred yards away, and he did not have the liquid courage he needed to face that horror. But he knew what he had to do; it hit him as suddenly as the idea he had only ten days before to betray the French. The image of Lidia's lovely face flickering in his mind, her rage and fear as the corporal groped her body, helplessly bound against the maple tree. He could not let the corporal touch her again, whatever else happened, and now there was but one option, one way he might be able to save her from the greedy lust of Renaud.

He glanced over his shoulder at the big, sweating man.

"What are you looking at? Keep going," Renaud growled, shoving out with his musket.

But Renaud's gunstock didn't hit him this time, because Adam ducked under the blow and ran toward the man with his head down, striking the corporal in the stomach. The corporal roared in surprise and rage, grabbing at Adam to bring him down with him as he fell, but Adam leaped free. He struggled to keep himself upright, miraculously managed it, and turned toward the gunshots. Then, against the warnings shrieking in his mind, he ran toward the growing sounds of battle, the clanking, the shouting, the screaming, the continuous blasts of gunfire, volley after volley of fiery death.

He heard Renaud pursuing him, howling oaths of rage,

and the agony of his wound felt fresh and tearing, as if he had been shot a second time. He had to lead Renaud into the battle. If he could get the corporal killed, then Lidia would be safe—she would be safe under his father's care. The trees snatched at him, ripping his shirt and breeches, whipping his face as he leaped over fallen logs and wound his way through grasping clumps of thorny blackberry bushes, the berries leaving stains of purple and red upon his clothes and skin, like a million new wounds opening. He felt as if each jolt of pain from the scratching thorns was threaded with a strange, piercing joy, for in the sensation of each scrape there came the knowledge that he was alive. He was still alive to feel the pain. If he was still alive and Renaud was still following him then there was still hope that Lidia would be all right. He redoubled his efforts, feeling the agony of every breath against the wound in his right flank, his lungs raw and bursting, his broken rib scraping against its severed end, sweat pouring down his face, his back, his chest. Still he ran onward.

Then Renaud was upon him from behind, punching at him, knocking him down. They rolled for a few moments on the ground, Adam striking out with his bound fists. Adam twisted, wriggling free of Renaud's grasp, kicking the other man in the face and lunging upward again, but Renaud caught hold of his leg and tripped him and he fell headlong, the breath forced from his lungs. He leaped up, the image of the girl bursting into his mind again, the girl that had haunted him for so long. Then he was running once more, almost before he was on his feet, and he could hear Renaud's curses, closer, louder. He wasn't putting space between himself and the corporal anymore, and was barely maintaining the little head start that he had.

Then he burst into a clearing and ahead of him was

chaos and carnage, and the fiery explosion of another volley, directed at a line of white coats before him. In an instant he saw the bulwark, the approaching men in red wool coats, kneeling intermittently to take aim and fire, and he could see the French line was breaking, and the British were advancing and men were panicking and running toward him. Far to his right, just for an instant, he thought he saw his father on horseback, riding directly toward a smaller British line that waited, half-hidden behind a barricade of bracken, and then Lignery was gone, as if some magician had performed a vanishing act, and Adam heard the squeal of a horse in pain. Then Renaud was on him again, slamming him to the ground, beating him over and over with the butt of his gun.

Adam rolled over to face the painful blows, not raising his hands to defend himself. Another resounding crack hit his head and he was stunned, and even if he had the will or the strength to keep fighting, he could not. The world spun madly around him. It felt as if all the fragments of color and the cries of men were part of his exploding mind. Then everything stilled, the voices and shots becoming far away, and it was just him, breathing slowly, heavily, gazing up at Renaud, who stood over him with the barrel of his musket pointing at Adam's face, and this was it. The last moment. The last delicious, eternal breath. The end.

Through all the chaos now dimming around him, a single shot rang out.

14
LIDIA

~

July 24, 1759
Three miles south of Fort Niagara

Adam was gone. Pushed away by a man intent on murdering him, a hateful, grotesque man that had groped her as if she was a piece of meat. Lidia had known anger, she had known anger a thousand times—a million times—but the rage boiling within her in that moment as she stood helplessly bound to a tree, unable to fight, unable to even snap at the man with her teeth, unable to do anything, was not like any feeling she had ever known before. She wanted to rip Renaud's throat out with her teeth. She wanted to dig his eyeballs from his face with her fingers. She wanted him dead, or to live into old age dismembered and mutilated, in agony, utterly ruined. She wanted to cut his penis and testicles off and feed them to him while he screamed for mercy. But she could do nothing. And then he was shoving Adam away, Adam who she had hated for so long, looking pale, but so determined and brave. Then Lidia felt not wrath, but an overwhelming sense of loss, like the day her parents had been killed, like the moment she learned that Sofie had died. A mist gathered in her eyes, blurring her vision.

She strained with all her weight against the ropes as they dug into her arms, her legs, her chest, and her abdomen. She pulled so hard she felt she would tear herself into pieces, but the ropes did not budge. She hurled herself against her bonds, screaming Adam's name through her gag as the two men disappeared into the forest ahead, following the same track that all Lignery's soldiers had taken only a little while before, toward the sound of gunshots. She began thrusting herself rapidly against the ropes, over and over again, a sob catching in her throat, cries of despair and hopeless vehemence emitted soundlessly into the dirty rag the soldiers had gagged her with. She could feel drool starting down her chin and dripping onto her chest. Still the ropes did not budge, but she kept slamming her weight against them. Within her heart there was the unmistakable, familiar tightening of irrefutable, boundless agony building; the same feeling of loss that had twisted there since her parents died, since that attack on German Flatts, when she had not been able to save her parents, and now . . . now she was just as worthless, just as ineffectual—more so even. She was helpless. At least then she had been free and had a musket, though she had still been unable to save the ones she loved. The ones she loved! She could almost hear Adam's weary voice telling her she was a hero, like her sister. Some hero. She was refuse, utter garbage, tied to a tree while men died less than a mile away.

Her sister, Adam, her parents, their faces passed like a blur before her eyes as she struggled vainly in her bonds.

Their phantom voices sounded in her ears, and in her bosom she felt the warmth that came from them being a part of her life. She yanked even harder for an instant, and then, utterly defeated and utterly wretched, Lidia slumped in her bonds, sagging against the maple's trunk, tears streaming down her cheeks, sobs shaking her shoulders, murmuring all of their names into the gag. For a moment there was a perfect stillness. All she could hear was the chittering of a squirrel in the quiet of the empty glade. She glanced up through her tears at the red animal, staring down at her, his ears piqued, scolding her for her worthlessness, for her inability to save the people she loved.

The rope gave. The line tight around her upper abdomen was loose. She had loosened it. Frantically she yanked at her arms, managing to slide them around to her front, pulling hard as the rope gave, slowly at first, but more easily with every tug. And then her hands were free, and she slid slowly down, her back scraping against the tree bark. Still dripping sweat, she twisted and strained until at last she slipped from under the coils of rope and onto the ground. She tore the cord from around her neck and spat out the gag. Then, stopping only for a second to snatch up a musket that leaned against a tree nearby, hoping that it was loaded, she began sprinting into the forest where Renaud and Adam had disappeared. If Lidia was going to keep Adam from joining the ghosts of those she loved, she had to run faster than she ever had before.

As she ran, still limping, she prayed breathlessly in German that she would not be too late, that God would grant her this one thing—she who had lost her parents, her sister, her nephew, she who had lost everything. If God would but grant her this one tiny thing, she promised Him as she ran that she would take a vow of nonviolence, become like Sofie, measured and careful in everything and slow, impossibly slow to anger. She would do whatever Christ asked; she would pore over the Scriptures, read the whole Bible, memorize the Gospel of Christ, whatever God wanted, if only He would grant her this one little favor. She heard a gunshot and felt her heart stop within her, but her legs kept moving—indeed, they redoubled in speed—and she kept praying. Then came more heart-stopping gunshots. The battle was joined. The British and French were trading volleys of death that beautiful July morning. She increased her speed still more, running faster in that moment than she ever had before, her ankle forgotten, completely mindless of the pain. She ran just the way she had with her Oneida friends as a child, wild and free, nothing holding her back, ignoring the tearing of sharp thistles and the blows of the tree branches that buffeted against her as she passed.

The gunshots were getting louder, and with them she could hear mingled screams and shouts, and the clanking of sword against sword. It brought her back, with an involuntary shudder, to that night two years ago. She could hear and feel again the same chaos, the same screams, the same smells of blood, and of burning wood and flesh. She ran faster, feeling as if she was flying, her heart beating what felt like a million times per minute. She had to reach Adam before it was too late. If it wasn't too late already.

Then, still clutching the heavy musket in her arms, she burst into the clearing and saw the French marines fleeing toward her, pursued by Haudenosaunee warriors, whooping cries of victory as they bore down upon the retreating men. She saw men being hatcheted and scalped as they fled in fear, she saw men being shot down, she saw hell opened wide before her eyes in that picturesque glade just east of the wooded shores of the broad Niagara River. Almost instantly her attention focused on one particular scene a little way ahead, and everything else faded. All she could see was the young man lying on the ground, unmoving and deathly white, his breeches and shirt covered in purple red, a big grenadier standing over him, his gun pointed down at the youth's head.

Lidia Erghamer did not breathe, did not speak, did not think. She dropped to her knees and raised the musket to her shoulder, squinted down the impossibly long barrel, the barrel that made her arms sway under its hefty weight, and she pulled the trigger. She was knocked hard backward, her ears ringing from the closeness of the awesome blast of sound. She stumbled up, dropping the gun, stunned and in despair. For a moment she still saw Renaud standing there, turning his head toward her in surprise, and then he toppled directly onto the inert form of Adam.

She raced across the battlefield, lancing pain shooting up her leg as she dodged between fleeing men, calling over and over as she ran, "Adam! Adam!" For a moment she couldn't see him at all as men in panic bumped against her and blocked her vision. The French were routed and didn't even have the sensibility in their mad flight to notice a lone, frenzied girl dashing across the glade so littered with death. They knocked into her and shoved her out of their way as she fought to make it to Adam's side, already certain that he was dead and she had been too late.

Then she was upon them and she dropped to her knees, straining to push Renaud's enormous body off Adam. The corporal's limp carcass flopped to the side, and she was looking down at the unmoving, corpselike visage of Adam. She reached down and began shaking him. She was numb and felt as if she had entered a strange, terrible nightmare.

Sofie was dead, her parents were dead, her nephew was dead, and now Adam too was dead.

"Adam! Adam! Adam, wake up! For God's sake, wake up!" she shouted, still crying, feeling as if her eyes were going to burst out of her skull. She felt like she was losing her mind—like this horror was the final straw in her sanity. Then, just as it seemed her heart would shatter within her aching chest, Adam's long dark lashes flickered, and those soft hazel eyes gazed up at her in bewilderment.

"Are you all right?" Her tone demanded an answer, rather than asking for one. She felt a flash of anger at him for his brief unconsciousness. He must have known it would make her upset, make her weep and feel such sorrow. Cruel, hateful boy. There were still shots all around them, but she had only attention for that pale face and those warm, questioning eyes, and that dull, thumping sensation of his heart beating as she placed her hand over his chest. She lifted his shirt, showing him the dark purple stains on it. "Is this blood? Are you hurt?"

"Berries," he said, his voice very faint, as he smiled a little. Then, as if not quite believing it himself, he whispered, "I'm all right." He shifted and tried to sit up, wincing, looking in bewilderment at the corporal's body lying on the ground beside him and then around at the retreating French, running in frenzied panic, and the British and Haudenosaunee bearing down upon them. "I shouldn't be, but I'm all right. My God, Lidia, they're advancing. They'll kill us both!"

"Stop saying that," she said in another fit of rage.

"What?"

"Stop saying that you should be dead. I didn't kill this corporal so you could be an ungrateful pig about it. I killed him to save you, Adam."

"Why?" he asked, still looking dazed.

"Because it's not going to make my parents come back to life if you die, Adam. It's not going to bring them back, and it's not going to heal the ache I feel for their loss every bloody day of my fucking life. It's just going to leave a new hole in my heart alongside the one that came when they died."

Adam stared at her, blinking in astonishment. Then, seeing that the British and the Haudenosaunee forces were still advancing, chasing the routed French, Lidia leaped to her feet and yanked him up beside her.

"We have to get out of here, they'll scalp us too!" she yelled, smearing the tears on her face with her dirty sleeve. She turned and began running, heading deeper into the forest, dragging Adam with his tied hands. Stumbling and panting, the two young people pushed their way into the woodlands, and in a moment the glade was lost behind them and the sounds of pursuit dulled. Lidia turned her feet left, going north, toward the British lines. It would be safer to be captured by the British now. Perhaps Will was there. He could vouch for her. Gasping for air, she continued running with her ungainly limp, her mind replaying the words she had spoken to Adam, and what they meant, how much they meant, how truly she felt the words she had spoken so passionately, so intuitively to him. She had let go of him as they wound their way through the trees, but she was sure he was still following close behind her. Then she heard a loud thump.

She spun around, her gaze flitting madly about. Adam had vanished in the trees. She saw a flashing glint of sunshine reflecting off something metal, the light of the summer sun shining on a hatchet blade. An Indian warrior, dressed for war, was kneeling over the fallen Adam, his hand on the young man's hair, yanking it up to expose the line of his scalp.

"*Sáë'he't!*" she screamed in Seneca, running back toward the Indian. "He's my friend! *Sáë'he't!* Don't harm him!" To lose Adam now was too horrible to imagine—after her desperate escape, the mad sprint, the killing of the corporal, all the things she had yet to process. The Indian froze, his hatchet held in place as she stumbled toward him. Slowly he lowered the small axe and turned to look at her. The warrior's chest heaved as he stared at Lidia, the bloodlust fading from his eyes and a strange light of recognition taking its place.

"Who are you?" he asked softly in Seneca, releasing Adam's hair.

"I . . ." She stopped, her mind racing. The faint relief she had felt when the warrior had relinquished his grip on Adam's hair was tempered by the fact he still had the young man pinned to the ground with his knee in his breast. "I am the sister of William Light," she said, with a flash of inspiration. "And that young man you have there is my friend."

"Your friend? He is French, isn't he? William Light's sister? How is it possible that one night I meet his wife and, only a few days later, his sister?"

"Sofie is alive?" asked Lidia, unable to believe the words she was saying. "She's alive? You've seen her?"

The warrior rose to his feet as he spoke. "She is alive. Or she was before the battle began."

Adam sat up, reaching with bound hands to touch his hair, as if to reassure himself that it was still there. "I don't know how long I can keep doing this, Lidia. One close call after another. What does he say?"

"He says Sofie is alive!" cried Lidia, rushing to Adam's side and trying frantically to unbind his wrists while the warrior stood over them. Then Lidia, unable to loosen the knots, reached out and grasped the warrior's arm. "Where is she? Where is Sofie? Can you take me to her? I am only Will's sister by marriage. Sofie is my sister, my sister by blood."

The warrior smiled. "I would have guessed as much. You have the same fire in your eyes and spirit as she has. Sofie is on the battlefield, with her husband. I am Kanęhsawéhte of the Tuscarora, and I can take you to her."

Lidia blushed at the comparison with her sister. Only a week ago she would have thought it a terrible insult. She felt that the smile spreading across her tear-stained face was going to split it in two. She translated excitedly while Kanęhsawéhte knelt and cut the ropes still binding Adam's wrists, and together they assisted the French youth to his feet. Then, as the sounds of fighting were beginning to die away, Lidia and Adam followed the warrior back toward the battlefield.

15

SOFIE

~

July 24, 1759
Two miles south of Fort Niagara

The light infantry had only slept for a few hours when De Lancey woke them to build up the bulwark again. He wanted it higher and better—he wanted to make his men invisible. He had prowled around in the night, inspecting their fortifications while they slept, and he told the soldiers he could see them through the gaps. After a few hours of toil—the men grunting and cursing in the darkness when their feet tangled in their own earthworks—the young captain was at last satisfied and allowed them to drift off to sleep again.

No sooner had Sofie closed her eyes, curled up with Will and their infant, than she heard the captain's footsteps moving toward them. Half-awake, Sofie could feel him watching them. She opened her eyes and there he stood in the darkness, dashing and handsome, the rich young officer from New York City, her husband had told her—a dandy, but earnest and anxious to prove himself and advance in rank. He dropped his gaze when she looked at him, and then Will startled and sat bolt upright, as much at attention as a man lying on the ground can be.

"Sir?" asked Will, his voice hoarse from sleep.

"I'm sending a detail from the Royal Americans out to fetch a six-pounder from the Montreal Point battery. I thought of sending you with them, Will. Your language skills could talk the men out of a pinch if they got into one."

Will nodded, standing and stretching. Sofie rose to join him, clutching the baby in her arms.

"I'll go, if you'll watch out for my wife here at the bulwarks, sir," said Will.

"Nonsense," Sofie interrupted. "If Mr. Light is going out there, then I am going with him."

"You said your wife was German, Mr. Light?" asked De Lancey, amusement dancing in his eyes.

"A Palatine, sir."

"Well, remind me never to marry a Palatine. They are as stubborn as goats."

"But a great deal prettier than goats, sir," replied Will.

When De Lancey turned away, Sofie saw that Will was about to scold her and protest her joining the mission. She raised her hand to stop him and spoke first. "We're just going to get one piece of artillery, how dangerous can it be? We go out, we get the weapon, we bring it back. Or we could sit here twiddling our thumbs like everyone else and going mad from the tension of waiting."

"Anything can happen in these forests, Sofie, and it usually does. It would be better if you didn't come, and if you didn't bring our son out there."

"It would be better by far if you hadn't marched off to

war a year ago, leaving me alone in our home to give birth by myself. But I didn't really get to have a say in that decision, did I?"

"I understand your point, Sofie, believe me, I understand. You don't have to keep driving it in or putting yourself in danger just to prove something to me."

Sofie clamped her mouth shut, chagrined by her husband's words. She kept pushing him because she was angry, still angry and bitter that he had left her. She didn't believe that he really understood. How could he understand those months she had spent alone in the dead of a Lake Erie winter, snowed in by impenetrable white walls, taller than he was? How could he know what it had felt like, not knowing if he was even alive? How could he imagine her pain as she had clutched her child to herself and faced the possibility that her infant might die in his first year, as so many did, and that his father would never have even known he existed? The anger simmered behind her pursed lips, but she did not speak again, instead feeding the infant, changing his urine-soaked napkin, and then packing him into the cradleboard. She lifted the frame to settle it on her raw and aching shoulders.

"Wait, wait," said Will, reaching out to stop her. "I'll carry him."

Her eyes widened in surprise, but she slid the cradleboard off and Will fixed it on his back, letting her secure it in place. For a moment her heart swelled with joy. Her husband, carrying their son. Then they set off, joining ten privates and one sergeant from the 4th Battalion of the Royal Americans near the west side of the bulwarks. They moved into the dense forest toward the landing, where they would take a bateau across the river to obtain the artillery piece De Lancey wanted.

Occasionally, as they wound their way through the woods, a clearing among the thick trunks and foliage gave them a brief vision of the beleaguered fort, dark stone walls blackened by soot, crumbled in places by the endless mortar assaults. It was like a stark, horrific monument to the ugliness of war.

Sofie stayed close beside Will, listening to him joke with the men around him, feeling the sense of camaraderie that existed with such ease among soldiers. They tried to stay quiet, but the relief of being away from the tension of the bulwarks, the endless waiting, made them all lighter and more carefree; they had a mission, a simple mission. The act of doing something seemed easier to the soldiers than doing nothing.

They came within sight of the landing and the scattered bateaux resting on the sand along the river's edge. All around them stood a dense cluster of maple, elm, and sycamore, tangled with poison ivy vines. A faint mist was gently lifting from the water in the gray light of dawn.

Whoops and shouts split the silent morning, shattering the calm. They were under attack by Indians, but Sofie could not make out what nations or clans they hailed from. The small company of Royal Americans began firing haphazardly as Sofie spun, looking for Will. He had vanished in the chaos. All around her soldiers were screaming in agony as the Indians fell upon them, deadly and unstoppable in close combat, hacking men to pieces with their hatchets, and cutting throats and eviscerating soldiers with their long knives. She tried to run but tripped over a fallen log. Before she could stand she felt a knee jammed into the small of her back and someone tossed her hat from her head, releasing the waves of radiant gold that she had spent much of the night before untangling.

The warrior pinning her to the ground let out an exultant cry at the beauty of her scalp. He jerked her hair up, yanking her head taut on her neck. She heard the whoosh of his hatchet as she struggled uselessly in his grasp. But the expected spray of blood and the terrible thunk of mortality never came. Instead, the man's grip on her hair went slack. She felt warm blood on her back but realized immediately that it was not hers.

The Indians were herding some of the Royal Americans away through the trees, taunting them with slices across their arms and legs and torsos as they raced in a wild, hopeless dash toward the river. Sofie took this in quickly as she scrambled out from beneath the fallen body of the warrior. Will was standing over her, a bloody knife in his hand. He had slit the man's throat and there was a mad, exultant look in his eyes. It was a look that Sofie had never seen on her husband's face before—a look that made her shudder.

"Come on!" he cried, sheathing the gory weapon and helping her to her feet. She glanced one more time after the few remaining Royal Americans. Then she turned and raced after Will, dodging and ducking in the foliage, staying low, trying to remain as hidden as possible in the bracken and blackberry bushes. As they ran, the baby chuckled on Will's back, unaware of the danger, only aware of the bouncing, delightful ride his father was giving him. Sofie stayed close on Will's heels, not daring to look behind again as every second the screams grew louder and more awful. The screams of men undergoing impossibly painful, torturous deaths.

They did not stop running until they reached the bulwarks, where the soldiers of De Lancey's light infantry stood on alert, eyes wide, staring back the way Sofie and Will had come. Will dashed behind the cover of the wall and cast himself down, careful not to dislodge the cradle-board or roll upon the infant. Sofie crouched beside him, gasping to catch her own breath, her chest heaving from the effort of their mad flight.

"Ambushed! We were ambushed," Will gasped out when De Lancey approached him in alarm. Everyone was looking back into the forest as the awful sounds of torture dragged on, muffled and distant, but still audible.

"The entire boat party is lost," Will continued, rising to his feet and standing at attention before his captain. "Those were French-allied Indians, Captain, Mississauga. The reinforcements are here."

De Lancey glanced about, and Sofie thought he was weighing his soldiers' fortitude with that quick sweep of his eyes. Would they be routed if they were attacked or would they remain firm? He called to a few young, fit men standing at attention nearby.

"Run to Colonel Johnson, tell him we need reinforcements here," ordered De Lancey. "Go now, we haven't much time. The rest of us will hold them for as long as we can, but we cannot hope to stand long against a thousand Frenchmen and Indians with this small of a company."

The runners bobbed their heads and took off at once. Then Kanęhsawéhte approached and stood before De Lancey, speaking in Tuscarora, which Will quickly translated.

"He says the sachems of his clan are going out to meet with the sachems of the Indians allied with the French, near the river. They think they can convince those of the Six Nations that are with the French to stay neutral today. If the Indians don't fight, it'll cut the number against us in half, easily."

"Good. Tell him to have his sachems take their time with

the negotiations. Give Johnson a little more time to send up reinforcements."

Kanęhsawéhte nodded after Will's translation and a moment later he had disappeared among the trees. The last of the distant screams faded away as De Lancey's soldiers crouched behind their bulwarks, dripping sweat and yet trembling, like men who were both hot and cold at the same time. Guns loaded, they stared intently through the gnarled branches and logs piled high before them. After catching their breath, Sofie and Will joined the soldiers in their quivering vigil. Sofie undid the infant from Will's back and held him close against her chest, wherein her heart was still beating far too rapidly. She could scarcely believe what she had witnessed only moments before. She glanced down at her waistcoat and found the dark, damp stains of the Mississauga warrior's blood.

"Is my back covered in blood?" she asked Will.

Will peered at her back, then nodded. His own hand and his sleeves were also wet and stained with scarlet. "Yes, it is . . . but . . . you're alive."

"Yes, I'm alive," she whispered, removing the bloody garment in disgust. She was alive, but at the cost of another life. But what else could Will have done besides kill? Maybe just wound the man or maim him to get him off her. But it would not have worked, not in the bloodlust that had animated that warrior. The only answer for Will had been to kill or let his wife be killed. Perhaps, she reflected, it was not the killing itself that was so evil, but the situation that forced men to murder. War and the powers that made war, that used men as if their lives meant nothing and were easily disposed of on the battlefield. She had gotten herself into a situation that had forced Will to murder. He had killed, and judging by the look on his face and the ease with which he had performed the task, it was not the first time, nor even the tenth time. Perhaps it was as much her fault as anyone else's. She shouldn't have been there. She still shouldn't be there. Simply by being present she was putting her husband not only in mortal danger, but perhaps putting his soul in danger as well. Her husband, a killer. Her husband had become what she had most feared he would become by going to war. She shuddered again, finding that she was staring at his face, at the curve of his cheeks, lost in the coarse sprigs of his red beard as he gazed out into the forest, his chest still heaving from their run and the terror that had pursued them.

"How long before they come?" she asked softly.

"I don't know. Could be any moment, could be hours. All I know, Sofie, is that they're coming," replied her husband, not taking his eyes off the wood.

"I . . ." She choked, unsure what she even wanted to say.

His gaze flitted toward her, and he smiled, a warm, loving smile.

"I'm sorry," she blurted out.

"Sorry for what, Sofie?"

"Sorry that I put you in that position out there. Sorry that you had to kill to save me."

Will shook his head, reaching out to pull her close for a delicious moment and planting a fierce kiss on her forehead. "Don't be silly. No apologies needed. It's not you that placed me in that position, Sofie. Or I suppose . . ." He trailed off, reflecting for a while before he continued speaking. "I suppose I could blame you. I wouldn't have joined the British Army if I weren't driven by that need to protect my wife against the French, after all. After what I heard happened at Fort William Henry, and then what happened to your family in German Flatts, I couldn't rest without being out here, doing my part to prevent you coming to harm, Sofie. I had to do something. I couldn't just sit there and wait for them to come to us, to dash our children's heads on rocks and cut you to pieces. I had to do whatever I could to keep what happened at William Henry and German Flatts from happening to you. But . . ."

She felt tears beginning to form in her eyes, and then the relief of those tears slipping down her cheeks, cleansing away the tension that had kept her from crying as they fled that terrible ambush in the forest. Will drew her closer against him.

"I'm just teasing you, Sof. It's not your fault. None of this is your fault. And it ain't the fault of the soldiers, whether British, Indian, American, or French. I think all of this is the fault of some monster born in a palace somewhere far away, with every good thing life has to offer laid at their feet. Someone that never faced the difficulty of surviving in the wilderness. Someone that never has, nor never will, see the beauty of these forests we're so fortunate to live in. They want to stain these lands with blood to claim them as their own—lands they've never even laid eyes on, nor never will. Can you imagine? If they had seen the falls of Niagara, the mountains of New York, the rivers of Pennsylvania, the endless white beaches of Lake Erie and Lake Ontario, these lakes that stretch on forever and ever—if they had seen those things they'd know it was sacrilege to kill men over such holy, heavenly places. As if anyone could own this! As if you could call this place yours. The wilderness don't belong to man, Sofie, it belongs to God, and always will. We're all at the mercy of the rain, the snow, the drought, whatever God wills to happen in His beautiful, living world.

Yet here we are still, fighting and killing each other over something so far beyond our understanding. I'm too simple and foolish to make sense of it, Sofie, truly. And too stupid to put what I want to say in words. But . . . what I want you to know is that, whatever happens now, it ain't your fault, it ain't my fault, it ain't the fault of De Lancey, or Massey, or Johnson, or the French commander—it's all the fault of some mighty men and women living perfect, privileged lives in palaces far, far away, with no idea what they've brought on folks living here. No idea. That's the real injustice of it all. The real stupidity of all this."

Enormous drops of salt water drizzled slowly down Sofie's cheeks when Will released his tight embrace, letting her lift her head up again. She held it proudly, looking down the line of men facing the unknown forces coming at them through the forest, with little hope of any reinforcements from Colonel Johnson making it in time. She reached up and dabbed at her cheeks with her bloody sleeve, then she unbuttoned her shirt, allowing her son to suckle her nipple greedily. "You always told me you weren't an eloquent man, Will, and I thought you told the truth, but it isn't so. You speak beautifully and you can speak that truth you know in so many languages, and that's something. I am honored to fight alongside you, William Light. I don't believe in all this killing and hate, but I will reload that carbine for you for as long as you fight. And as long as you fight I'll be right here beside you, and if you fall, I will fall beside you too. In sickness and in health, for richer, for poorer, for better, for worse, until death do us part."

Will leaned down and whispered the same words back to her, touching her face with his bloodstained hand. The Lights held that quiet renewal of their vows in the minutes before a desperate battle, hopelessly outnumbered. Then the moment ended as Sofie heard the distant sound of men marching through the forest, and she glanced about in fear. Around her soldiers crouched behind the bulwark that suddenly seemed so flimsy, made only of scrub and bracken. Sofie wondered how much could be seen of them through the trees, or if the French already knew they were there, waiting, without support, one hundred and fifty troops of light infantry.

Then Sofie heard men running, crashing through the woods, coming from the north and east. Startled, she swung about, her heart hammering loudly in her ears and her hands trembling. Could they have been flanked already?

"It's all right," whispered Will. "It's just Massey."

Through the overgrowth she could see men in red coats dashing past them. A messenger darted over, conferred frantically with De Lancey and then rushed on again to rejoin Massey's forces. She watched as they melted into the underbrush, lying down in the grass until even their bright red jackets had become all but invisible, making a line that spread across the portage road. It still seemed to her a small force compared to the thousand, likely more, that Lignery would be bringing up that road at any moment.

She packed her child into his cradleboard and attached him to her back again. As she adjusted the straps around her shoulders, she felt something cold touch her fingers and glanced at Will. He was pushing a pistol into her hand. She shook her head instantly, shoving it away, feeling the thump of her heart now matching the unmistakable sound of tromping feet, marching steadily toward them.

"I can't, Will, I can't. It's enough to load your carbine for you. Please. I can't."

"Please, Sofie. I know you're brave. I know you're stubborn. It was your stubbornness that helped you make it all the way here alive to warn us. It's that same stubbornness that makes you still fight me in everything, and still insist that I'm wrong in being here. I love your bullheadedness, I do, really, even when it galls me to my core. But please, for the love of God, for your love of me, take the pistol. I ain't asking you to use it, but I need you to have it."

She opened her mouth, but she could not refuse the earnest insistence in his eyes, and after another moment of hesitation, she took the pistol, knowing it was loaded, and stowed it in the waistband of her breeches.

Then Will breathed a sigh of relief and turned his attention back toward the advancing French. They came in a broad line with their heads held high and proud, their muskets on their shoulders, the sun glinting from their brass buckles and the hilts of their sabers and gun barrels. They were perfect, like toy soldiers on parade, but they were not toys. They were living, seasoned, and deadly marines. Either they were unaware of Massey's men lying in wait for them, or they did know and did not care, so sure were they of their superiority. At their head fluttered two checkered flags of blue, white, and red with yellow fleur-de-lis, rippling as they entered the wide clearing beyond which the ambushing forces waited, perfectly still.

Sofie's gaze shifted toward an officer on horseback advancing near the front of the line, his spirited sorrel dancing under his direction. He rode proudly, his shoulders back and his chest thrust out. She found herself wondering if he might be the Lignery that had written the note she had given to Lieutenant Colonel Massey, what now seemed so long ago.

Then the French broke into double time and they began to chant and shout as they raced toward Massey's soldiers, still lying on the ground. An unstoppable rushing wave of ferocious, roaring French troopers, a sea of white and gray and blue and green, rolled toward the hidden redcoats. Sofie glanced once more toward Massey's men, concealed in the bracken, not moving or running before the wild advance of the French. She saw Massey himself take a stand upon a stump and peer out from around an oak tree, only partially hidden, an expression of crazed exaltation on his flushed face.

The French began to fan out, spreading to form a battle line and intermittently dropping in unison to fire. The sounds of gunshots filled the air, the zing of bullets through leaves, and trees, and then through flesh, punctuated by the cries of wounded men. Massey disappeared for an instant, and then she saw him struggling up again, and, as the French drew impossibly close, she heard Massey scream for his soldiers to fire.

The explosion of noise as the British line fired nearly deafened Sofie. Dazed and bewildered, she realized with a start that her own company was also firing into the French, despite the distance. She began reloading Will's carbine as fast as she could, losing track of the chaotic maneuvers on the battlefield before her. Her hands shook as she worked the flintlock mechanism. Between reloads, while Will aimed over their bulwarks, she would glance up and try to take stock of what was happening. The French appeared to still be trying to set up a battle line, but to little effect. Then she saw the men in white wheeling about, turning and beginning to move directly toward the bulwark where she and her family waited. De Lancey's men gave another volley, and another, and French soldiers were falling like bloody snowdrops in the green clearing. Everything smelled of smoke and gunpowder and death.

She saw the officer on horseback again, leading his

troopers toward De Lancey's line. In the midst of all the horror, she was struck by the officer's face, somehow fatherly and kind, at odds with all the evil happening around him. She felt her heart soften momentarily, strangely, toward the men rushing to destroy her, her husband, her baby, and the light infantry. Were those men in white on the other side of their flimsy bulwark, so different from the men in red and blue along her own line? A command went through De Lancey's company to hold fire. For a moment no one moved, and for a strange, unearthly few seconds there was no gunfire at all. Then, when the French were almost upon them, the order came, shouted by De Lancey at the top of his lungs, his voice sounding hoarse and childish in the chaos.

"Fire, men, fire!"

Like a mighty tidal wave, the carbines crackled and Sofie saw men falling and then Will thrust his gun back into her hands and she reloaded it automatically, staring out at the French wounded as they tried to crawl away, while those still standing knelt and fired. Around her, behind the bulwark, twigs snapped, and men died under the hail of bullets, and then the light infantry discharged another volley, and then De Lancey's voice rang out again.

"Push them back! Push them back! Over the bulwarks, lads! Drive them back!"

The soldiers around her began clambering and leaping madly over their blockade as the French formation splintered before them. They were backing away slowly, not fleeing in desperation yet, still urged on by the proud officer on his sorrel horse. Sofie reloaded the gun again and reached to give it back to Will, but he was not there. He had leaped over the bulwark with his regiment and was rushing the French soldiers, his hatchet held awkwardly in his left hand. She saw the mounted French officer rallying his men and leading them toward the eastern flank of De Lancey's infantry in a desperate stampede. They followed him bravely, while so many of their own forces were already fleeing in terror, chased by British soldiers and whooping Haudenosaunee who had come tearing down onto the battlefield, seemingly from nowhere.

She stumbled from behind the bulwark and ran, crouching low as she did so, following Will, who was charging directly toward the French officer. Another crackle of muskets and carbines sounded from somewhere and Sofie dropped to the ground. All was madness. There were no more organized volleys of fire, just men against men, bayonets, hatchets, knives, and swords, musket butts to the head, thudding fists, screams and roars of rage and unspeakable agony. Over it all she could hear the faint, whimpering cries of her own son on her back.

Bewildered in the chaos, unsure who was winning, she saw the French officer wheeling his horse to face Will and spurring the animal toward her husband, swinging his sword. But, to her momentary relief, the officer's charge was blocked by bodies, living and dead, and the horse would not cooperate, maddened by the blasts of gunfire all around. The French officer lowered his sword and raised his pistol with his other hand, aiming directly at Will. For Sofie, time stopped. Smoke burst from the officer's handgun and Will fell and Sofie screamed, snatching Will's pistol from her belt and pointing it at the officer. It snapped back in her hand and she saw the spurt of blood from the French officer's thigh, saw the horse rear up as the bullet went through its master's leg and into its own flank. The horse twisted, fell back onto its haunches and then to the ground, crushing its rider before struggling to its feet and bolting, harness clanking.

Feeling as if she could not breathe, Sofie raced across the field of battle, sliding to the dirt at Will's side. He rolled over before she even touched him, a reassuring smile on his face, but there was pain there too, and she saw the blood on his waistcoat and jacket. She yanked his shirt open to reassure herself. The bullet had grazed along his rib cage, leaving him wounded and in pain, but it didn't appear to have struck anything vital.

"Are you all right?" she demanded.

He nodded his head, breathless.

Soldiers were rushing all around them, heading south into the forest. Tears began pouring down Sofie's face.

"I killed him!" she cried, stricken, her eyes wide. Then she stumbled to her feet again and ran, ran like a person running for their very life, toward the French officer in his white uniform, lying unmoving on the ground. She flew over the logs and bodies and discarded packs and weapons that blocked her path, and at last fell by the man's side, rolling him over. She could see the wound she had made in his leg, still streaming blood, but more alarming was his labored breathing and the obvious crushing injuries she could feel when she touched his shoulder and his chest. The crepitus of broken bone against broken bone. He gasped in a lungful of air, his face purpling, blood drizzling from the corner of his mouth. He stared at her in confusion.

"Lidia?" he whispered in English. "How come you to be here?"

"I'm not Lidia. I'm not Lidia!" she gasped in response, unsure why he was saying her sister's name. Her sister, the last person she expected to hear mentioned on this field of death. "Who are you?"

He started to speak, but then he stilled, and Sofie sobbed, shaking him viciously. He couldn't be dead. She couldn't have killed a man. She couldn't have done such a thing. Better if she had died than to have killed a man herself, by her own hand. He couldn't be dead. She couldn't be a murderer.

16

ADAM

~

July 24, 1759
Two miles south of Fort Niagara

It astounded Adam that he was still alive. Within less than an hour's span he had been as close to death as ever in his life, not once but twice, more than that if he included the incessant peril of the bullets ricocheting off branches and tree trunks all around him. He struggled to keep up with Lidia's sprint. Her eyes had lit up at the news that her sister might yet be living, and she was running directly onto the battlefield, paying no heed to all the death surrounding her, intent on only one thing: her sister. She was a singularly focused young lady, and someday Adam was sure it was going to get her killed. But today would not be that day, not if he could help it. No, today Lidia's singular focus was more likely to get him killed than her. Even with her limp she was fast, but he surged forward, ignoring the searing pain in his side. It felt as if his wound had opened anew, the broken rib ends scraping against each other with each lungful of air.

He overtook her and slammed her to the ground just as the British soldiers fired another volley, the bullets zinging over their heads. They weren't aiming at the girl and the young man with no justaucorps to denote which side he belonged to; they were aiming past them, at the French fleeing in panic and disarray. Indeed, the British, seeing that they followed so close behind the trusted Kanęhsawéhte, let the two young people run by with barely a glance.

Despite her limp, Lidia surged past Adam again as soon as she scrambled to her feet. He sighed with relief when she moved beyond the majority of the heavy fighting, into a place between the British advancers and the bulwarks they had built in the forest. Adam paused for a second, struggling to breathe. Then he saw it. He saw the still figure in white lying on the ground and a woman wearing men's clothes leaning over him. There was a baby in a cradleboard on the woman's back, and she had long yellow hair that cascaded down upon the fallen form. Adam let out a cry of anguish and broke into a sprint, using all the strength he had left.

He passed Lidia; he could barely hear her calling her sister's name, so intent was he on the unmoving, bloody body on the ground. He dropped to his knees beside the man, practically shoving the golden-haired woman out of the way.

"*Papa, Papa! Réveille-toi! Réveille-toi!*" He was sobbing as he spoke—enormous, gulping, horrible sobs ripped from deep within him. He continued pleading in French, shaking his father's shoulders, as Lidia drew near behind him, along with another person, a big, hulking British soldier with a red beard. They were all blurs to Adam, though; all he could see through his tears was his father's pale face. "Please," he whispered, his voice catching and breaking. "Please, you have to wake up, Papa, you have to wake up."

The older man's lashes flickered and kind hazel eyes, so familiar, so understanding, stared up at Adam dully, then comprehension spread across his face, through waves of pain. Lignery reached out his right arm, the left clearly broken, catching Adam's chin in his palm.

"My boy, my boy," he whispered faintly, every word seeming to catch in his throat.

"Papa, I'm sorry. I'm so sorry, Papa," Adam sobbed, feeling as if someone were tearing his heart out of his chest. "I didn't mean it. All those things I said, what I did to you. I didn't mean to hurt you. I was . . . I was . . ."

"You were hurting," replied Lignery, and blood bubbled up from the corner of his mouth. He coughed a few times, nearly passing out again, but his strength returned and he clasped Adam's shoulder tightly, almost desperately, as a man might if he was given his last chance to give a message to someone he loved. "You were hurting, and so you wanted to make me hurt too. And it was my fault, Adam, it was my fault you were hurting. I know you're sorry. I know you didn't mean it. I . . . I just want . . ." He trailed off, his eyes blurring, staring sightlessly at the blue sky above.

"Papa, please, please, I'm listening," Adam cried, his voice urgent and desperate, becoming shrill from an anguish far more terrible than any pain he had felt from any of his wounds. "What do you want, Papa?"

Lignery's eyes brightened again. "I just want you to live, Adam, to live and to be happy. That's all I ever wanted for you. That's all I want now. I don't care what you do with your life, as long as you live and be happy, Adam, for me. Will you do that . . . for me?"

A terrible groan burst from deep within Adam, a groan

so gut-wrenching and awful he didn't think it was his own voice, more of an animal cry than a human sound. He nodded as warm tears poured down his cheeks and dripped onto his father's face and chest. He kept nodding, and as he nodded he saw the brilliance of his father's smile, a smile of peace through the agony.

"Of course I will, Papa. But, Papa, I need you to live too. I need you to get better. Do you hear me? I . . . I need you, Father, I need you. *Je t'aime, Papa. Je t'aime!*"

"I know, I know, my dear boy," replied Lignery, and, with one last squeeze of Adam's shoulder, he faded into unconsciousness, his breathing becoming ragged and strained.

The golden-haired woman, who Adam knew must be Lidia's sister, the fabled Sofie, was binding Lignery's leg tightly with a strip of cloth ripped from her shirt, but it was too little, too late. The bullet wound was not killing Adam's father; it was the internal wounds from being crushed by his own horse that were killing him—the wounds his son couldn't see, deep within Lignery's chest, abdomen, and pelvis. Adam began undoing the straps and buttons of his father's layers of uniform, as if laying bare the devastation wrought upon him could somehow save him.

"It's too late. It's too late. My God, it's too late," Lidia was whispering, and she was crying too. Adam could see the great tears dripping down her face and into the grass as she tried to help him.

"I'm so sorry. I'm so sorry," Sofie kept repeating, as if in a trance. Then men with stretchers arrived, and they tore Lignery from the hands of his son, rolled him onto a stretcher, and carried him away. As Adam watched the motionless body on the litter disappear into the trees, he felt poignantly that it was the last he would ever see of his father.

"It wasn't your fault, Sofie. *De'saiwa'*. It was that mare's fault, more than anything else. *Das ist nicht deine Schuld*. Even if you were to blame, you took one life, by accident, but you saved a thousand. At least a thousand lives. A thousand saved lives must outweigh the cost of one . . ." Lidia kept babbling to her distraught sister, sometimes in English, sometimes in German, sometimes in the Iroquois tongues she spoke, desperate fumbling attempts to comfort the other woman.

"*Ton père, comment s'appelait-il?*" Sofie asked, her voice breathless. Lidia was embracing her and still talking, but Sofie barely looked at her younger sister, staring instead at Adam with wild eyes.

"François. François-Marie Le Marchand de Lignery," he replied, feeling like a man trapped in a nightmare.

"François, François . . . ," whispered Sofie, and then she undid the cradleboard on her back and swung it around, lifting the baby from it. She turned to the red-bearded giant standing beside her and held the child up to him. "Francis," she said. "Will, his name is Francis."

Will nodded solemnly, gathering both of the tearful women in his arms, and, for the first time, Adam noticed the man's missing hand. Then suddenly Will stiffened and murmured, "Captain De Lancey is coming."

"That boy, take him!" came a shout, and Adam looked up in bewilderment to find himself flanked by British soldiers in blue, who grabbed his arms, yanking them behind his back. He did not fight them, but Lidia did.

"Stop!" she screamed, rushing to attempt to pry Adam's arms free from the tight grips of the soldiers.

It was Captain De Lancey that had given the order. He strode forward as Lidia fought the men holding Adam.

"What are you doing, girl? I heard this boy speaking French. He is our prisoner."

"No! He's not French. Well, I mean, I guess he is French, but he's not a soldier like them."

"Oh no? I saw him speaking with their commander, passionately, sobbing over his wounded body. What, then, is he, if not one of the French troopers? And who are you to defend him?"

"I am Lidia Erghamer, the sister of Sofie Light, who is the wife of this man, William Light, and this is Adam, Adam Regnant de Montréal, and he's . . . he's my husband."

Adam stared at her, uncomprehending.

"Your husband?" asked De Lancey dubiously. "Can you prove that, Lidia Erghamer?"

Lidia glanced around wildly, the old, fierce fight back in her blazing blue eyes, the same expression she had worn the first day Adam had met her, on the battlefield of German Flatts, grasping that musket that was longer than she was tall. She let her fiery gaze linger on each person there—Sofie, Will, the soldiers holding Adam, De Lancey, Kanęh-sawéhte—and last of all she turned to Adam. Then she was on him, her arms around his neck, dragging him down toward her face and crushing her lips against his, and through all the pain and sorrow, Adam felt a burst of life so intense he thought he might faint from the exquisite joy of it.

Here was a fervor and bliss that far outweighed anything that even the strongest, headiest whiskey had ever offered him. Here was a future, here was life, here was perfect, passionate, unimaginable happiness. Here—he hardly dared to think the word—but here was love. As she kept pushing into him, her sweet tongue darting into his mouth, he saw De Lancey wave his soldiers off, and they released

Adam's arms. He immediately wrapped them around Lidia's sturdy, curved body, pulling her tighter toward him, feeling as if he was losing his very being into that ardent, heavenly kiss. There was no pain anymore; it was as if the agony of his wounds could not touch him in Lidia's all-consuming embrace.

She pulled her lips from his, bent her head and slid her mouth gently over the hideous scar on his neck from her bite two years before. Adam felt a shiver run through him, from the base of his skull to his tailbone, every hair on his body standing on end. Then Lidia drew back, tears still shining in her eyes, and turned toward the British captain, as if daring him to deny the truth of her statement. De Lancey was blushing. Sofie was blushing. Will was grinning foolishly. Kanęhsawéhte had a childish smirk on his face. Adam fancied he was probably blushing like the others, but it didn't feel like a blush. There was no shame in it, only the flush of unimaginable joy, and gratitude, and hope, and life.

"You've quite a peculiar family, Mr. Light," remarked De Lancey, his cheeks still scarlet red. "Very well, then, Miss Erghamer, you may keep your husband with you. But, Mr. Light, I will hold you personally accountable for your brother-in-law's conduct, is that understood?"

"Understood, sir," answered Will, nodding as De Lancey moved away.

Lidia wrapped an arm around Adam's side, and he felt as if he would fall if she did not hold him steady. He smiled through his tears, taking slow gulps of air as he studied the clearing in which they stood. The sun filtered gold through the tree leaves, dappling diamonds of light upon that wide-open space, where the tall grass waved in a gentle breeze off the lake. The chirping of birds, for a while hushed in the horror of the battle, had already started again, punctuated by the scolding chitters of squirrels in the oaks above, and harmonized by the faint whisper of Lake Ontario's waves in the distance.

"What is this place?" asked Adam softly.

"This meadow?" replied Will. "I think they call it La Belle Famille."

Adam glanced down at the rapidly drying bloodstains in the grass where his father had lain only moments before. He blinked back the pools of moisture still forming in his eyes, but one last tear slipped out and streaked its way down his bruised and grimey face.

"It's a good name . . . for such a place," he whispered, and squeezed Lidia even closer against him as the summer sun beamed down upon La Belle Famille.

C'EST FINI

APPENDIX: ONEIDA & SENECA PHRASES

Phrases and Words in Oneida and Seneca.

Words in Oneida/*Ukwehuwehnéke*:

- *Tehsatkahkwalísi!* - Open your eyes!
- *Tetwa'suh'tha* - Niagara Falls.
- *Teyakotele'takályat* - She is demanding/she is hard on the nerves.
- *Yako'nikulatshánit* - She is strong-willed.

Words/phrases in Seneca/*Onödonwa' ga:' gawën:ö'*:

- *De'sadögwe:ta'* - You are not well.
- *De'saiwa'* - It's not your fault.
- *Do:gës* - it's true.
- *Eodi'nigoiyo-ak* - Their minds will be at peace.
- *Ganyë'geh* - Seneca word for the Mohawk territory.
- *Ne:' waih ho'nih shöwöye:ëh.* - He resembles his father.

- *Nya:wëh* - Thank you.
- *Nya:wëh sgë:nö'*- I am thankful you are well (traditional greeting).
- *Sáë'he't*! - Stop!
- *Së̈ni:hë:h! Sö:ga:' dayögyenö:wö's!* - Stop doing that! Someone help me!
- *Së:nöh ëhsasdaëh he:awak, nö:koh i:yë's sano'ëh.* - Don't cry, my son, your mother is here.
- *Së:nöh ëhsasdaëh he:awak. Ta'sa:je:h.* - Don't cry, my son. Settle down.
- *Sešnye's onödowa'ga:' gawë:nö'* - You speak Seneca?

I am impossibly grateful for the assistance of a skilled translator of the Seneca Nation in checking and correcting these Seneca phrases obtained from the works of Wallace Chafe and Phyllis Bardeau. Oneida phrases were obtained from Karin Michelson and Mercy Doxtator's *Oneida-English/English-Oneida Dictionary.*

Yaw^ko and *Nya:wëh* to the scholars who provided this information!

A NOTE TO THE READER

Dear Reader,

Thank you for taking the time to read *La Belle Famille*. If you enjoyed the book and have a few minutes to spare, I sincerely appreciate any ratings or reviews you are able to provide on whatever retail site you used to purchase the book, or through Amazon, Goodreads, LibraryThing, or StoryGraph. Your honest ratings and reviews are incredibly helpful in reaching other readers who may enjoy this work.

I would also like to invite you to join other readers for discussion of this and my other books at the discord server for fans. The link may be found at my website: https://www.amvergara.com. You may also find information about my other works there and sign up to follow my substack, where I occasionally release musings on life, books, and updates on forthcoming works.

Again, many thanks for your time.

With gratitude and in solidarity,

Amelia Maria Vergara

ALSO BY A.M. VERGARA

FIREFAX

"I would advise you, young man, to take care around anyone with the surname Firefax. I know not if the rumors be true that they be king killers, but they are, without any doubt, a dangerous family."

Legend tells of a city of gold on a phantom island. The wealth of that city could end the American Revolution. But the only person who knows the island's location is the world's deadliest assassin. And he's not giving up that secret without a fight . . .

"Original, deftly crafted, riveting, and a fun read from start to finish." ~Midwest Book Review

Available wherever books are sold in ebook, hardcover, paperback, and audiobook!

ACKNOWLEDGMENTS

This book would not have been possible if not for the tireless support of my beloved husband, Eric, who also provided the French translations. I must also acknowledge my critique partner, PurpleEggHead, who is always a joy and an encouragement in my writing endeavors. Special thanks to Ellie, my sister, and most faithful beta reader as well as to all my other beta readers. This work would probably be unreadable without the assistance of my tireless and meticulous copyeditor, Eliza Dee of Clio Editing Services, and my careful proofreader, Martha D.

I spent countless hours researching the history of the time period and this battle from many sources, but would like to particularly acknowledge the work of Brian Dunnigan, whose book *Siege - 1759: The Campaign Against Niagara* served as one of the most important and detailed resources used in this work. Additional sources of information include, but are not limited, to the books of Allan Eckert, Stephen Brumwell, Dale Taylor, Bobbie Kalman, Timothy J. Shannon, and Andrew Gallup, whose book *La Marine: The French Colonial Soldier in Canada, 1745-1761*, helped to provide authenticity and detail to Lignery's *troupes de la marine*. I am deeply grateful to Albert Schmidt, who provided careful checking of the German translations. Wallace Chafe's compilation *English - Seneca Dictionary* is where I found many Seneca phrases along with the extensive works of Phyllis Bardeau. These phrases were then checked and corrected by a wonderful Onödowá'ga: translator through TranslationServices.com. Please do take the time to read more about this beautiful but severely endangered language and fascinating culture at: https://senecalanguage.com/. Oneida words were taken from Karen Michelson and Mercy Doxtator's *Oneida-English/English-Oneida Dictionary*.

The map at the beginning was made by the talented Teddy J., who can be found at https://www.fiverr.com/teddysj/. There were many other people who, whether they knew it or not, were an enormous encouragement and support during the process of writing this work and provided help with publishing. I am eternally grateful for the incredibly skilled photographer, Cosmo Condina, who graciously allowed me the license to use his photos in creating the cover for this book. I would highly encourage you to review his breathtaking work at his website: https://cosmocondina.com/. Thanks to Logolane for the publisher's logo. For typography on the cover, I am indebted to Casey White. For my author portrait I would like to give a huge thanks to Erika Saguran.

I would also like to thank my siblings who cheered me on through this process, my weekly library writing group (especially Natalie and Anne-Sophie), and many other friends who were unspeakably important in the process of writing this. As always, I would especially like to thank my mother who put the drive and love of reading and writing in me, and my father, who gave me my fanatical devotion to the outdoors and history, which I know shines through these pages. My father also inspired me with his genealogical explorations into our own family's Palatine ancestors, and without that, this tale would never have come about.

Thank you all for believing in me and encouraging me to tell this story.

ABOUT THE AUTHOR

(author portrait courtesy of Erika Seguran)

A.M. Vergara is a physician assistant and paramedic. When not writing and reading voraciously, she can be found working her day jobs in the hospital or on the ambulance, or out in the woods, camping, hiking, foraging for edible mushrooms, searching for reptiles and amphibians, riding her mule, or playing her banjo.